The House at the End of Hope Street

Menna van Praag

W F HOWES LTD

This large print edition published in 2016 by
W F Howes Ltd
Unit 5, St George's House, Rearsby Business Park,
Gaddesby Lane, Rearsby, Leicester LE7 4YH

1 3 5 7 9 10 8 6 4 2

First published in the United Kingdom in 2015
by Allison & Busby

A CIP catalogue record for this book is available
from the British Library

ISBN 978 1 51002 379 6

Typeset by Palimpsest Book Production Limited,
Falkirk, Stirlingshire

Printed and bound by
Printforce Nederland b.v., Alphen aan den Rijn,
The Netherlands

For my father, to whom I owe everything!

CHAPTER 1

The house has stood at the end of Hope Street for nearly two hundred years. It's larger than all the others, with turrets and chimneys rising high into the sky. The front garden grows wild, the long grasses scattered with cowslips, reaching toward the low-hanging leaves of the willow trees. At night the house looks like a Victorian orphanage housing a hundred despairing souls, but when the clouds part and it is lit by moonlight, the house appears enchanted. As if Rapunzel lives in the tower and a hundred Sleeping Beauties lie in the beds.

The house is built in red brick, the colour of rust, and of Alba Ashby's coat – a rare splash of brightness in a wardrobe of black. Alba doesn't know what she's doing, standing on the doorstep, staring at the number eleven nailed to the silver door. She's lived in Cambridge for four of her nineteen years, but has never been down this street before. And there is no reason for her to be here now, except that she has nowhere else to go.

In the silence Alba's thoughts, the ones she's been trying to escape on her midnight walks

1

through town, begin to circle, gathering, ready to whip themselves into a hurricane. *How did this happen? How could this happen to me?* She's always been so careful, never inviting any drama or disaster, living like a very sensible seventy-nine-year-old: in a tiny box with a tight lid.

And while most people wouldn't achieve much under such strict limitations, Alba achieved more than most: five A-levels at fifteen, a place at King's College, Cambridge, to read Modern History, and full PhD funding at eighteen. All this by virtue of two extraordinary traits: her intelligence and her sight. At age four and a half, as well as being able to name and date all the kings and queens of England, Alba started to realise she could see things other people couldn't: the ghost of her grandma at the breakfast table, the paw prints of long-disappeared cats in the grass, the aura of her mother moments before she entered a room. Alba could see smells drifting toward her before she smelt them and sounds vibrating in the air minutes before she heard them. So, because Alba knew things other people didn't, they never noticed she lived her life in a box.

But ever since the worst event of Alba's life, she's barely been able to see anything at all, constantly tripping over pavement edges, falling down steps, and walking into walls. She still hasn't cried because to stay in shock feels safer, it keeps a distance between her and the thing she's trying to pretend hasn't happened. The numbness surrounds her, a buffer against the outside world, through which Alba can hardly breathe or see.

Today is the first of May, just after midnight. The moon is full and bright. Vines of wisteria and jasmine twist together across the red bricks, their flowers hanging over the windows and above the door. Their scent puffs through the air and, though she's sorry she can't see their colours, the smell begins to fill Alba with a sense of calm she's never felt before. Her shoulders soften as she reaches up to touch the flowers hanging in wispy bunches above her head. Soon she'll feel strong enough to walk again. But then she remembers, she no longer has anywhere to go.

In the silence Alba hears a low hum in the air, almost indistinguishable from the breeze. Still cupping the flowers in her palm, she listens. The hum grows louder and becomes a tune, the notes drifting toward her, and suddenly Alba is captivated. She knows the words to this song:

Sleep, sleep my sweet
Sleep and dream of butterflies . . .

The next line slips away as Alba thinks of the summer her mother sang that song, when she was eight years old, just before her father left. The tune grows louder, seeping through Alba's skin, sending shivers down her spine. She knows she should be scared, but she's not; she's captivated.

Alba steps back to look up at the house, at its rows of dark windows, the panes of glass glinting. For a second Alba thinks she sees a face, a flash of white and blonde that disappears so the night is mirrored back at her. She notices a plant with flowers so purple they're almost black. Its strangeness beckons Alba to come closer, rub its leaves, smell its flowers, slide her fingers into the earth . . . The charms of the house and its garden sink deeper into Alba and, without realising what she's doing, she steps forward and rings the bell.

As Peggy Abbot scurries down the steps, pulling on her patchwork dressing gown, a picture of Alba starts to take shape in her mind: tiny and built like a boy, spiky black hair, intense blue eyes, a mouth that rarely smiles, a weight of sadness and self-doubt heavier than Peggy has ever felt before, but a sense of sight stronger even than her own. Suddenly she knows that this might be a dangerous thing indeed. The midnight glory is in bloom tonight. If Alba looks for too long she might see what makes its petals glow and, worst of all, sense what's buried beneath it.

Wishing she were forty years younger, Peggy hurries along the hallway, slipping on the wood in her woollen socks.

When the door swings open, Alba steps back in shock, staring into the face of the oldest and most beautiful woman she's ever seen.

The moment Alba steps into the house, she knows it's different from any home she's ever known. It is, quite clearly, alive. The walls breathe, gently rising and falling beside Alba as she follows the old woman down the hall. The stripped oak floorboards soften under her feet in welcome, the light bulbs and lampshades pull at the ceiling to get a closer look.

As she walks Alba gazes at the walls, weighted down by hundreds of framed photographs: black-and-white pictures of different women, in group shots and singles, wearing trouser suits and top hats, flapper dresses and flat caps, ribbons and pearls. Among the photographs are pictures, pencil drawings and silhouettes, and a few miniature oil paintings of powder-puffed female faces with curls piled high on their heads.

'Wait.' Alba almost stumbles into the wall. 'That's Florence Nightingale.'

'Oh yes,' Peggy says. 'She stayed with us for a spell before she went off to the Crimea. When my great-, great-, great-aunt Grace Abbot ran the house. A lovely girl by all accounts, Flo, though rather strong willed and a little too fond of sailors . . .' Peggy smiles.

'Gosh, really?' Alba whispers. 'That's . . . gosh.'

As Peggy ushers her into the kitchen Alba feels a flash of fear. She ought to think twice before entering the homes of complete strangers. Hidden under the folds of Peggy's patchwork dressing gown could beat the heart of an evil witch who sees Alba as a modern-day Gretel. But when Alba enters the kitchen she's enveloped in the scent of something magical: cinnamon, ginger, lavender and several spices she can't possibly name, and her fears evaporate. She feels three years old again, transported to a wished-for childhood of baking biscuits with her mother on Sunday afternoons. If Peggy is bewitching her, then the spell is complete.

A few minutes later Alba sits at one end of a long oak table, watching Peggy search for a saucepan. The old woman is bent over, clattering around in the wooden cupboards, muttering swear words as she flings unwanted pans aside. Alba begins to wonder just how old Peggy is. With her white hair and papery skin, slight stoop and frail limbs, she might be anything from seventy to a hundred and seven. But her movements are quick and light and her voice doesn't carry any quiver or depth from age.

Peggy stands, brandishing a saucepan. 'Do you like hot chocolate, dear?' she asks. 'I don't think tea will do, we need something more fortifying on such an auspicious occasion. Hot chocolate with fresh cream, that's the thing.'

Alba nods, still captivated by the kitchen's smells, still shocked by the turn her night has taken, not really registering Peggy's words. While the old woman pours a pint of milk into the saucepan, Alba glances around the kitchen. It's vast, the length of a long garden, with creamy yellow walls that reach up to meet black oak beams running across the arched ceiling. As in the hall, every inch of the kitchen is covered with rows and rows of photographs. Alba gazes at them, wondering who they are and why they are decorating the old woman's walls.

'They've all lived here, at one time or another.' Still stirring the milk at the stove, Peggy speaks without turning around. 'They came to the house, just like you, when they'd run out of hope.'

Alba frowns at the back of Peggy's patchwork dressing gown, at the wild white hair reaching down to her waist, wondering how on the old woman knew what she was thinking.

'They left to lead wonderful lives or, in some cases, afterlives.' Peggy chuckles. 'The old residents can inspire you, if you let them. One in particular, actually.'

'Oh?' Alba asks, only half listening. In a frame just above the kitchen sink she sees an oil painting of a woman with blonde hair twisted into knots at the sides of her head. Alba squints for a better look. 'But, that's—'

'Yes.' Peggy doesn't turn to look. 'She stayed here in 1859, suffering from a severe bout of writer's block. She started writing *Middlemarch* in this very kitchen.'

'No,' Alba gasps, 'really?'

'Oh yes. Half the history of England would be quite different if this house had never been built, believe me.'

And although she can't explain why, Alba does. She already feels closer to this woman than to her own family. Peggy stops stirring, steps over to the fridge, tugs open the door, sticks her head inside and takes out a china bowl. 'This cream is the real stuff,' she says, and smiles. 'I whipped it up myself. I can't countenance that synthetic crap one squirts from a bottle, can you?'

'No.' Alba agrees, amused to hear such a sweet old lady swear.

'I'm glad to hear it.' Peggy sets the bowl down on the marble counter next to the stove. 'I can't trust anyone who won't take real cream, or real sugar. Those' – Peggy searches for the word and shudders – 'sweeteners, such a *seemingly* sweet, really are beyond the pale, don't you think?'

Alba watches Peggy stirring cocoa into the milk. Suddenly she never wants to leave. She wants to sit in this kitchen, surrounded by the smell of spices, forever. Alba slips off her coat. 'Why did you invite me in?' she asks. 'It was very kind, but I don't see . . .'

'You don't?' Peggy smiles. 'Because I think you see an awful lot more than most people.' She sets two giant mugs down on the table. 'Don't you?'

'Thank you.' Alba glances at her cup. It's the first time in her life that anyone has ever guessed who she is and what she can do. 'Yes,' she admits softly, 'I suppose so, though not since . . .'

Peggy takes a sip of hot chocolate. 'Since what, my dear?'

Alba looks up. How can she possibly explain the devastating events of the last few days? Her head is so full of fury, her heart so steeped in sadness, that she can hardly make sense of anything

8

anymore. All Alba knows is that she wants to undo time, run backward through the last seven months, unravel everything and begin again: finish her MPhil, write a groundbreaking thesis, publish papers, until she's at the forefront of the next generation of great historical minds. And if she can't achieve that, something truly brilliant, then what's the point in living at all? Because in her family, being mediocre, ordinary, run-of-the-mill, simply isn't allowed.

As though Alba had just spoken her thoughts aloud, Peggy smiles sympathetically. 'You know, in my long and extensive experience, what we want isn't always what will make us happiest,' she says. 'But we'll come back to that. First, tell me what brought you to my doorstep. Start from the beginning, and don't leave anything out.' Peggy sits back in her chair, smoothing her patchwork dressing gown across her lap, hugging her mug of hot chocolate to her chest. This is her favourite part. After more than a thousand stories in sixty-one years, she never fails to get excited at the prospect of a new one.

'Well . . .' Alba stalls. 'I don't . . . I mean, I was just walking around town, not going anywhere, and then . . . and then I just found myself here.' Nervous, she scratches the back of her neck, tugging at short spikes of black hair, hoping she doesn't look as messy as usual, then realising she probably looks even worse. 'I didn't mean to knock on your door, it just sort of . . . happened.'

'Take a sip of chocolate,' Peggy suggests. 'It'll help to clear your head.'

As the warmth slips down her throat and into her belly, Alba starts to feel soft and snug, as if the kitchen has just hugged her. And, after a few minutes she isn't scared to tell the truth any more. At least a little bit of the truth. But, where should she begin? History. Love. Trust. Betrayal. Heartbreak. Alba shifts the words around in her head, wondering what to hide and what to reveal.

By the time the last of the hot chocolate has gone, Alba has told Peggy about failing her MPhil and ending her career. However, she has carefully, deliberately omitted the single most important piece of information, the thing that slots it all together.

'I can't stay in college any longer, and I can't go home,' Alba says, though she stops short of explaining why. 'So I was wandering the streets in the middle of the night.'

In the ensuing silence, the spices circle the kitchen, even stronger than before, and although Alba can't see the smells, she can hear the hum of her mother's song again in the back of her head. It rocks her like a lullaby.

'You can stay here,' Peggy says, 'for ninety-nine nights, until the seventh of August, just before midnight. And then you must go.'

'Sorry?' Alba wonders if the hot chocolate was spiked with rum because she's suddenly light-headed. 'But I couldn't possibly . . .'

'No rent, no bills. Your room will be your own, to do with as you like.' She smiles, and Alba can almost hear the old woman's papery skin crinkle. 'But take care of the house, and it'll take care of you.'

'Well, I . . .' A thousand questions crowd Alba's mind, so she asks the first one that comes to her lips. 'But why ninety-nine nights?'

'Ah, yes,' Peggy says. 'Well, because it's long enough to help you turn your life around and short enough so you can't put it off forever.'

'Oh,' Alba says, thinking it'll be impossible to pick up the pieces of her shattered life in such a tiny amount of time, let alone get everything back on track.

'Oh, it is possible,' Peggy says. 'I can promise you that. And you won't have to do it alone. That's the point of being here. The house will help you. It's all yours, except for the tower, which is only mine. And you can never go there. That's my one rule. Do you understand?'

When Alba nods, it's clear to them both that she's staying, even though she hasn't yet said yes. But how can she say no? A secret tower. How deliciously intriguing. It reminds her of another fairy tale. When Alba first saw the house she thought of Rapunzel, then Sleeping Beauty and now Bluebeard. Alba smiles. She loves fairy tales.

'If you stay I can promise you this,' Peggy says. 'This house may not give you what you want, but it will give you what you need. And the event that brought you here, the thing you think is the worst thing could have happened? When you leave, you'll realise it was the very best thing of all.'

After showing a sedated, sleepy Alba to her bedroom, Peggy shuffles along the corridor toward the tower, creaks up her own stairs and hurries into her kitchen to find a pile of glittering presents and a cake. An enormous, three-tiered extravaganza, iced with thick white chocolate cream, decorated with sugar flowers and scattered with fresh ones: red and yellow roses, wisteria, sunflowers, bluebells and buttercups. Just as Peggy knew it would be, just as it has been every year for as long as she's lived in the house. Along with the cake, the kitchen is decorated with a rainbow of balloons, streamers and a banner emblazoned with the words

HAPPY 82ND, PEG!

Still catching her breath, Peggy glances up at the clock and smiles.

'Eighty-two years, two hours and twenty-nine minutes old.' She eases herself into the little sky blue chair at the wooden table in front of her cake. After blowing out the candles and cutting herself an extremely large slice, Peggy slowly, methodically begins to devour the first tier and very soon, icing is smeared around her mouth and all over her fingers.

'Delicious.' She grins, displaying a mouthful of cake. 'Even better than my eighty-first. I must say, you outdo yourself every year.' Peggy looks up and the ceiling lights flicker in appreciation of the compliment.

Peggy's kitchen is smaller and prettier than the one downstairs. The furniture is made of beech and painted white, excepting the blue chair. Vases, pots and jam jars sit on every surface, filled with flowers that alter according to Peggy's moods but never wilt or die. The cupboards have glass doors to display a collection of crockery: bone china cups covered with tarot cards that read the future of whoever drinks from them, teapots and plates painted with characters from *Alice in Wonderland*, 'Cinderella', *Don Giovanni*, 'The Frog Prince', 'The Lady of Shalott' and 'The Flower Queen's Daughter'. The characters shift around at night, indulging in various games and love affairs. They are Peggy's own celebrity magazines and, when she shuffles in for her first cup of tea every morning, she's always curious to see who's fallen in love and who's split up overnight. Now, on the teapot, Rumpelstiltskin is slipping off Guinevere's blouse while, on her plate and almost hidden by the remains of a third slice of cake, the Mad Hatter is kissing an Ugly Sister. The Star – the tarot card that always appears on her birthday – shines from her teacup.

Peggy celebrates her birthday twice. First, just after midnight, always alone. Then in the morning, with whoever is residing in the house. Peggy never knows how many guests she'll have, sometimes as many as twelve. Today, with the arrival of Alba, she'll have just three: a rare island of calm and tranquillity in a sea of usual confusion and chaos. Though, sadly, Peggy knows the relative peace won't last. She can already sense several women whose hope is almost extinguished, who'll be turning up on her doorstep before too long.

The house always joins in the birthday festivities, creaking its beams and rattling its pipes because it's celebrating too. The house was completed, its last brick laid, on the first of May 1811, and every Abbot woman who has inherited the house since has been born on its anniversary. The house was a gift from the prince regent to his lover Grace Abbot. And when the prince moved on to his next mistress, Grace opened the house to women who needed it. Slowly they came, drawn by their own sixth sense, staying for their ninety-nine nights, and, with a few tragic exceptions, leaving with their spirits high and their hearts healed.

Peggy sips her tea. The tarot card on her cup has changed. Death looks up at her now: the card of beginnings and endings, sudden shifts and dramatic transformations. She puts down her cup.

And on the table is a note:

Congratulations on your 82nd and final birthday. You have been a beautiful land-lady. One of the very best. We thank you for your service. Now it is time to find your successor. Then you will be free from this life and can move on to the next.

Peggy has to read the note nearly a dozen times before she can believe it. She knew she couldn't live forever, but the shock has still left her a little shaken. If she were another sort of woman she might be scared, she might cry and wish for more time. She might look back on her life and be filled with regrets. But Peggy won't. She is made of stronger stuff. She's also in the rather unique position of being very well acquainted with a great many departed souls and knows that death is nothing to fear. It's merely an adjustment in living conditions. In fact, if it wasn't for Harry, she wouldn't mind at all.

Peggy holds the cup to her lips, thinking of him, and wondering just how many days of life she has left.

CHAPTER 2

When Alba wakes all she can see are books. Thousands line every inch of every wall and the ceiling, some drift through the air like birds, lifting off from one shelf and settling on another; precarious stacks are spread across the floor like skyscrapers. For a moment, Alba thinks she's dreaming.

Slowly, she slides out of the bed, stepping through the city of books to the nearest wall. She reaches up to touch the spines: *Tractarians and the Condition of England, Disraeli and the Art of Victorian Politics, The Oxford Movement* . . . Alba stops. When, a little drunk on sugar and cream, she'd stumbled into the room last night, it had been empty except for a bed. Now every historical text she's ever read is at her fingertips.

Slowly Alba steps back, slips on a pile of books and hits the floor.

'Shit!' She snatches up *The Liberal Ascendancy* and hurls it at the wall. The room watches her silently, waiting. Whispered words float through the air. Alba shakes her head, wishing she could forget. But every seductive sentence Dr Skinner ever said has seared itself onto her skin. At last Alba's tears begin to fall. She pulls her knees to her chest and sobs.

Peggy is putting off getting out of bed. It is her birthday, after all, so she deserves a little lie-in. From the corner of the room comes a plaintive *meow*. She smiles at the big fat ginger cat attempting, yet again, to dig his claws into a chair leg.

'Oh, Mog, when are you going to give that up?' Peggy pats the bed, feeling a little sorry for her pet who is forever trying and failing to mark the furniture. 'Now, come and give your mama a hug.' Lately Peggy has been missing her lover, Harry Landon, a little more than usual. She wants to be cuddled at night and kissed in the morning, though the archaic house rule of no overnight male visitors won't allow it. And, after last night's revelation, she's missing him rather more. Not that she needs comforting. She's resigned to her fate and isn't scared. But since she might not have much time left, she'd rather like to spend some of it with him.

Peggy clicks her fingers at the cat. 'Let it go, Mog, I haven't got forever any more.' The cat ambles across the carpet with a yawn. When Mog reaches the bed he stretches up to scratch his claws along the wood and Peggy just sighs, knowing he can't make a mark.

Mog has haunted the house since it was built. In life he'd belonged to Grace Abbot, but he has been loved and spoilt by her six successors, all

17

Abbot women chosen for their psychic skills, selflessness and sense of duty. But with the passing of her niece last summer, all Peggy has left now are second cousins. And they, without a flicker of foresight or a touch of telepathic thought, will never do. So, for the first time, it seems as though someone outside the family will inherit Hope Street. Perhaps, with her extraordinary sense of sight, Alba might be the one. But she would need extraordinary strength, too, and she doesn't have that. At least, not yet. The recipe for running the house on Hope Street is special indeed: four parts psychic ability, one part patience, two parts fortitude, three parts altruism, and Peggy has yet to find every ingredient in another woman.

Mog leaps onto the bed, making dips in the duvet as he pads to Peggy's outstretched hand. When he's feeling frisky Mog roams the house to startle the residents, who can feel but not see him. After he died, to his never-ending annoyance, Mog has only been able to brush his silky fur against skin and momentarily leave his paw prints on the softest surfaces, but never make satisfyingly solid scratches.

'Hello, Moggy.' Peggy settles back into a cloud of pillows to gaze up at the ceiling, while Mog pushes his nose into her armpit. A vast skylight is cut into the ceiling, so she can fall asleep studying the stars. She doesn't know their real names, preferring mysteries to facts, but loves to trace her fingers along their shapes. She wonders if she'll be lucky enough to land among them when she dies. Peggy closes her eyes and, a moment later, feels a scrap of paper land on her nose. She picks it up and reads:

I never knew a man come to greatness or eminence who lay abed late in the morning.

'I need advice about my successor, Anne Abbot.' Peggy rips the paper into tiny pieces. 'Not a critique of my sleeping habits. And no one believes you had an affair with Jonathan Swift, no matter how many times you quote him.'

Entirely oblivious, Mog stretches and yawns. Peggy strokes his head, absently scratching his ears until he purrs and starts to drool. Watching the expanding patch of wetness on her sleeve, Peggy sighs. 'You can sleep in my bed, you little minx, but I draw the line at drool.'

Mog opens a single eye and gives her a reproachful look. While they're staring at each other, another note floats from the ceiling and settles between Mog's ears. The cat shakes it off and Peggy picks it up.

Trust yourself and you shall know how to live.

Peggy hears a ripple of laughter through the walls, and sighs. 'You are all entirely useless.'

Having finally stopped crying, pulled herself off the floor, and yanked open her bedroom door,

19

Alba steps into the hallway. She has a headache, and needs fresh air. At the end of the hallway she finds a balcony and, hoping no one will mind, clicks open the French doors and walks out to lean over the railing. A low mist hangs over the front garden, floating beneath the branches of the willow trees and engulfing the cowslips. In the light Alba can see just how grand the garden is, and how far from the street. Wisteria twists over every inch of the house in a maze of branches and a blanket of flowers. Looking out across the town she can see the tops of every house and tree for miles. All of a sudden Alba is dizzy.

She turns, stumbles back into the hallway and trips over a small wooden stool. She steadies herself against the wall, perplexed because the stool wasn't there a moment ago. Another wave of dizziness comes over her, and she sits down. She's stepped into another world, one that makes no sense at all, with objects that don't have the decency to obey the proper laws of physics. *Just like me*, Alba realises. Having felt odd and out of place all her life, she's finally found somewhere she fits perfectly.

From the walls the photographs take surreptitious glances at Alba. She catches the curious eyes of two sisters: Elizabeth Garrett Anderson, the first woman to qualify as a doctor in England, and Millicent Garrett Fawcett, co-founder of Newnham College in 1871. Though, Alba remembers, women weren't actually awarded degrees until thirty-two years after that. She smiles. The idea that this house has been a temporary home to such prestigious figures sparks a tiny glow of hope inside her. Maybe, just maybe, it can help her too.

Suddenly aware that someone is coming, Alba jumps up off the stool and hurries down the corridor, away from the smell of cigarettes and sex drifting toward her. Alba is only halfway to her bedroom before a voice calls her back.

'*Espera, por favor, espera!*'

Alba can't help turning. At the top of the stairs stands a woman so striking that Alba has to steady herself while she stares. Carmen Viera is tall and voluptuous, about ten years older than Alba, wearing a dress that clings to every curve. She has thick dark curls that float over her shoulders and fall down her back. She makes Alba feel scrawny and unkempt. But as she stares, Alba starts to see something else. The woman is scared, wearing her self-confidence like perfume: a heavy, sultry scent to distract onlookers from the broken, blackened pieces of herself she wants no one else to see. Her body is bruised underneath the dress; purple shadows that linger on, her olive skin scarred with cigarette burns, her heart cracked in so many pieces it's a wonder it still beats.

'Hello,' Alba says, pleased that her sense of sight is already getting stronger.

'*Ola.*' The woman reaches out a delicate hand with long fingers. 'I am Carmen.'

Alba hurries forward to take it, noticing the

manicured nails and suddenly feeling self-conscious of her bitten-down stubs.

'*Muito prazer.*' Carmen smiles, wondering why this pretty girl is dressed so shabbily, why she hasn't bothered to brush her messy hair or put on make-up. Carmen doesn't understand why a woman would want to hide her own beauty. A gift from God should be put on display. Even though she barely believes in God any more, after all that she's been through, she still believes in this. 'Okay,' Carmen says. 'You come for breakfast now?'

'Well, um . . .' Alba stalls, not at all sure what she's doing. 'I—'

'It's a special day.' Carmen cuts her off. 'The day you come, and Peggy's birthday. She will make a cake and – *qual e a palavra?* – yes, pancakes with cherries and cream. She is crazy for this stuff. You will stay for this, celebrate with me and Greer, *nao*?'

'I'm not sure . . . I don't know,' Alba says. 'Who's Greer?'

'She lived here a few weeks already.' Carmen leans against the wall with a little sigh, apparently tired from standing for so long. 'She is an actress, tall, long red hair, green eyes. I not met her yet but Peggy say she very glamorous.'

Oh, great, Alba thinks, another beautiful one. I've stumbled into a cult of extraordinarily beautiful women and I'm their sacrificial virgin. 'Greer's a funny name.'

Carmen shrugs, swallowing a comment about

pots and kettles she recently heard but can't now quite recall. 'She is named from an actress, English with also red hair and many awards.'

'Oh.' Alba frowns. She finds films frivolous and knows nothing of actresses. 'I've never heard of her.'

Carmen regards Alba curiously, still not quite able to make sense of her. The new girl seems so timid, so *careful*, shut up tight as a clam, that Carmen longs to shake her up. She wants to take this little mouse to the bar where she works, get her drunk and see her dance on table tops. Resolving to fulfil this ambition before she leaves the house, Carmen smiles, flashing bright white teeth against olive skin. 'You will join us for this, *nao*?'

Unsettled by the directness of the question, Alba gathers herself and considers her options: she'd rather live on the streets than see her family again or, more specifically, her siblings, who will be utterly horrified by what happened. They will interfere, demand to know the truth, and she can't tell them. Her mother is a different matter. She won't throw around threats, in fact she won't say a thing, she'll just stare at her daughter until both are soaked in sadness. And that is more than Alba can bear at the moment.

'Yes,' Alba replies, 'I'll join you.'

Greer is nearly forty and has no home, no career and no fiancé. Two weeks ago the abysmal play she was struggling through finally closed. That same night she'd come home to find her fiancé with a twenty-two-year-old on the kitchen table. After throwing saucepans while he declared his love for this new girl, Greer ran out of his flat, wandering through a fog of tears until she finally found herself on Hope Street, standing in the garden of a house she'd never seen before.

After nearly two weeks Greer still isn't completely used to its strange ways, but it no longer scares her. Like every other resident who lives there – breathing its air, eating its food, drinking its water – she has become entirely enchanted by her new home. Slowly, her heart is beginning to beat in time to its gentle pulse, and her lungs fill with its soft breath.

Now she sits up in bed to see something new in her bedroom: an enormous wooden wardrobe filling the opposite wall, with its doors flung open. Greer stares at rows and rows of clothes, at every kind of theatrical costume she could possibly imagine. To the left are those from her favourite era, the screwball comedies of the 1940s: dozens of A-line dresses and flared trousers, fitted shirts and pencil skirts. To the right, costumes from the 1950s: puffball skirts, halter-style tops and sweetie swing dresses. And in the middle, a row of Jane Austen: empire gowns and summer dresses with matching coats in linen, velvet and silk. Along the floor are vintage shoes, heels and flats, and hanging above the clothes, rows of hats.

'Oh my God,' Greer gasps. Of everything she's seen so far, this is without a doubt her absolute favourite. The wardrobe beckons, enticing her out of bed. In a gap between a blue dress and a red skirt Greer can see the wardrobe is several metres deep. Tentatively she reaches out to the blue dress, hesitant to step inside behind the curtains of cotton and silk, almost expecting to see Mr Tumnus trot out from behind the veils.

A delicate pea green dress catches her eye and the memory rises up again, the one that never really leaves, that always flutters at the edges of her mind. It pushes forward now, and suddenly Greer is numb to everything except the past. Standing in front of a hundred colours, all she can see is her daughter's face, the bright green eyes blinking up at her. For, despite the doctor's saying it was impossible, that all babies are born with blue or brown eyes, Lily's were green. Bright shining green, like leaves lit by sunlight. Greer will never forget gazing into them for the first and last time. The one person she loved more than anyone in the world, she met for only a moment.

Greer bites her lip and swallows the memory, pushing it back to where it belongs, locked in her heart and held there, a private pain that is hers and hers alone. She has to focus on the present now and find something to wear. She's hardly in the mood to socialise, to shine and smile, but now it's time. After twelve days of hiding out in her bedroom with a broken heart, she must finally meet her housemates. Greer takes a deep breath. She can do this – she is an actress, after all.

Alba sits at the kitchen table, pushing the remains of a barely touched piece of birthday cake around her plate, sneaking looks at Greer, who's dressed in a green silk gown with red satin heels and matching bolero, looking as though she's attending the Oscars, except that she's hardly smiling. Alba studies the two women: where Carmen is stunning and sexy, Greer is more subtly beautiful. They both dress impeccably. Feeling self-conscious and out of place, Alba tries to think of something to say. Carmen munches her way through the bowl of cherries, Greer chats half-heartedly about a production of *Twelfth Night* at the theatre in town and Peggy licks out a bowl of cream.

'How many people live here?' Alba ventures.

'That depends on the season.' Peggy lifts her head up from the bowl, a peak of cream on the tip of her nose. 'On the weather and the amount of despair in the air. We're always the most crowded around Christmas.' She swipes off the cream with her finger. 'But right now we're virtually empty. Before you turned up last night it was just the three of us, wasn't it?'

She looks at Greer, who flashes Alba a film-star smile, and at Carmen, who nods, then accidentally swallows a cherry pip and coughs. Alba glances around the kitchen at the multicoloured helium balloons floating around the room, bobbing in midair just above their heads. How funny, Alba thinks, that they don't float up to the ceiling.

'We're very happy to have you here,' Peggy says. 'Aren't we, girls?'

'Absolutely.' Greer grins, momentarily blinding Alba, who blinks. 'The more the merrier.'

Nodding, Carmen drains her glass and coughs again. '*Sim*, I never have sisters, I always want some. I can take you drinking, we can go shopping, get makeups, go dancing.' She grins. 'We will have much fun.'

'Oh.' Alba tries not to look too horrified at the suggestion of socialising with someone so luscious and loud, someone with whom she has absolutely nothing in common, excepting the broken heart. 'Well, um, I don't really know . . .'

'Cream?' Peggy hides a smile and offers Alba the bowl.

'No, thanks—'

'Pancake?' Greer says perkily, wishing she were upstairs in bed.

'No, I'm—'

'Cherry?' Carmen drops one onto Alba's plate.

'No, but' – Alba eyes it – 'thank you.' As she pops the cherry into her mouth, Alba feels a prickle of anticipation along her spine, the same sensation she used to get as a girl the moment before seeing her grandmother's ghost. She glances up and there, sitting in the kitchen sink, is a young woman: tall, thin and entirely transparent. She's in her early twenties, very pretty, with long blond hair and blue eyes, wearing a long dress dotted with daisies. She gives a little wave, kicks her transparent legs against the kitchen counter and smiles.

She reminds Alba of hippies, flower power and feminism, of an essay she once wrote about the effects of the pill on the liberation of working-class women in 1960s Britain. The young woman waves again, and it's only then that Alba realises she is the only one who can see her.

CHAPTER 3

Alba has scarcely left her bedroom for three days. She's pulled on a pair of pyjamas and a safety blanket of books and lost herself in the dark labyrinths of Victorian history. The song she heard that first night still floats through the house every night and Alba senses that it's somehow connected to the ghost. She can't prove it, but something about the ghost's smile made her wonder. It was a knowing smile, the sort someone makes when she has a secret and wants to give a hint of it.

Alba shuts her biography of Gladstone, sits up in bed and rubs her eyes, brushing away the last traces of sleep. On the bedside table, atop a pile of books, sits a little slip of white paper. Alba thinks of Alice at the threshold of Wonderland as she picks it up and reads:

You Are Loved

She frowns. What does it mean? Is it a generic statement, or a message of hope suggesting Dr Skinner loves her after all? Both are unlikely, since her ex-supervisor was a fraud, her family barely acknowledge her existence and, being a freak genius with no social skills, she has no friends. In fact, the only person Alba can remotely claim as any sort of friend is Zoë, assistant librarian at the university library, the only human being she's shared more than three words with on a weekly basis. When they met, Alba instantly liked the short, skinny, spiky-haired girl who looked so much like her, just a little older, prettier and far more friendly. But Alba has never gone beyond small talk and the formalities of book requests, so she really can't claim to know anything about Zoë beyond her name.

Alba folds the note and tucks it into her pyjama pocket. Perhaps if she keeps it close to her heart for long enough, she'll be able to work out its message. Or, she could ask someone else. As soon as that thought floats into her head it is followed by another. All at once Alba senses that the ghost is sitting in the kitchen sink, and that she knows something, something worth knowing. Alba loves mysteries. It's one of the reasons she studied history, the chance to solve all the grand questions of the past. And now she has one on her own doorstep. It's enough to get her out of bed.

Three minutes later Alba catapults through the kitchen door, the lights flicker on and there is the girl, smiling from her spot in the sink. A little embarrassed at her eager entrance, Alba slides slowly into the nearest chair.

'Hello,' Alba ventures, wondering if the ghost can talk.

'Hello.'

They sit in silence for a few seconds when Alba, too nervous yet to ask about the note, stands and walks to the nearest wall, searching for a familiar face among the photographs to give her something to talk about. She stops at a picture of two women: one tall with curly black hair and a wide-brimmed feather hat, the other with trousers and a pageboy haircut.

'That's Vita Sackville-West and Dora Carrington.' Alba feels the ghost just behind her. 'This is where they first met, great friends by all accounts, perhaps even a little more than that . . .'

'Really?' Alba asks softly, still conscious of the ghost's being so close.

'Oh, yes, you'd be rather surprised by all that's happened here, stuff you'll never read about in your history books.'

Alba feels the ghost float away and turns to see her sitting cross-legged in the middle of the kitchen table. 'What's your name?'

'Stella.'

'Why are you here?'

'Why are *you* here?'

Ignoring the question, Alba pulls the note out of her pocket. 'Do you know what this means?' She steps forward and slips the paper onto the table. Stella leans down to read it.

'Ah,' she says. 'Yes.'

'What?'

'Someone loves you.'

Alba resists the temptation to raise her eyebrows. 'Yes, that's what it says. But I was wondering . . . Well, who?'

'Ah.' Stella smiles. 'That would be telling, now wouldn't it?'

Greer wakes to find, much to her surprise, that she's actually feeling rather happy. After two weeks of tears she no longer longs for the fiancé or even cares she lost him at all. It's possible, she's starting to realise, that she never really loved him at all. Or maybe it's that the house is the most comforting, strangely healing place she's ever been.

She slips out of bed, steps carefully over the piles of clothes strewn across the floor and walks out onto the balcony, her very favourite place in the house. She stands and looks out at the garden. Wind blows a mist of drizzle through the air, dusting Greer with drops, but she doesn't care: the air is warm, and the water on her face isn't tears. She can close her eyes without seeing the philandering fiancé. She will sleep without dreaming of him. She will wake without thinking of him. It's over and done.

An unfamiliar urge nudges Greer and, wiping the misty rain from her face, she turns back to her bedroom and, reaching the bedside table, stops. Next to the red velvet-shaded lamp is a note.

First of all, find a job

Greer sits on her bed with a little sigh. Truthfully, she's exhausted with her career, if you can call it that. She still adores the thrill of the theatre, but her passion for acting is becoming bloody and bruised from the severe beating it's taken over a lifetime. Acting has always been everything to Greer. At age six, after being a donkey in the school play, she had wanted only to act every day for the rest of her life. But now, after nearly twenty years of countless failed auditions, innumerable rejections and lacklustre roles, Greer is almost ready to give up. The problem is, having focused on it for so long and having tried so hard, she can't quite bear to let it go. Anyway she has absolutely no idea what else she could do.

Greer falls back into her pillows, burying her face in them. She wants to keep hiding, to wrap herself up in a ball in the dark. But she can't. She'll be out of the house by August and needs gainful employment before then. On the positive side, she thinks, looking for a job will enable her to debut her new dresses. So far, excepting the morning with her housemates, she hasn't shown them to anyone, which is a shame. Beautiful things are supposed to be worn in public, not hidden away in a wardrobe. It's not fair to the clothes not to show them off.

Greer has always loved dressing up to go onstage, delighting in the transformation of slipping on a costume. She always preferred glamorous roles to dowdy ones, but even the thrill of pretending to be someone entirely new is something she'll never tire of. If only the journey from her heart to the stage was an easier one, less fraught with disappointment and heartache. If only she'd fallen in love with a profession that wasn't so damn difficult to sustain. She could have been a doctor, a lawyer, an architect, earning oodles of cash and enjoying a life of security and success instead of struggle.

With a theatrical sigh, Greer pulls her head out from the pillows and is surprised to see something else. Close to the balcony windows stands a purple dressing table, every inch crowded with bottles: polish, lipsticks, blushers, pencils, eye shadows – all in a dozen different colours. The mirror is huge and edged with light bulbs.

Greer stares at it, speechless. Not taking her eyes off the lights, she untangles herself from the sheets, steps out of bed and tiptoes to the table, as though approaching the last living bird of paradise about to take flight. She reaches the velvet purple chair, presses her palms on its upholstered back, then sits. She picks up a bottle of perfume, sprays a few puffs into the air and lets out a happy sigh. She sweeps her hand over the nail polishes and picks one. In an hour, with nails as red as her hair and a dress to match, Greer will be ready for her next role.

Peggy stands in front of the door to the forbidden room. She's been knocking for nearly thirty minutes and has had no answer. She's being ignored. Which is very odd. Ever since she received the note she's been trying to get into the room, seeking a little advice about what to do next. She needs some help. But, for some reason she's quite unable to make sense of, the powers that be aren't giving her any. Peggy's frustration mounts and she sighs. Then she clenches her fists and gives the door a swift kick. She waits for some sign of life, a sound from the other side. But there is nothing. Just silence.

'You can't lock me out forever,' Peggy snaps. 'I'll bash down that bloody door if I have to.'

Carmen is dreaming. She's three years old, standing at the bottom of her childhood garden, hiding behind her favourite tree. She gazes up at the apple blossoms scattered along the branches: a thousand tiny moons against the evening sky. Her throat is tight and dry and Carmen realises she hasn't yet spoken a single word aloud. She leans one pudgy hand against the tree trunk, kicks off her shoes and plucks at the grass with her toes, waiting.

A moment later she takes a deep breath and starts to sing. The notes are soft and sweet, their echoes dancing through her tiny body long after they've disappeared into the night air. Everything is silent. Carmen looks up at the blossoms, then opens her mouth to sing another note. It sweeps out of her and, caught by a breeze, floats gently through the air. Carmen watches it drift upward, wishing with all her heart she could follow it, gliding above the garden, past the chimney tops and into the clouds. Instead she stands perfectly still, utterly captivated by the sound that has come from within her but seemed to come from somewhere else altogether. It's so surprising, so beautiful, she laughs. Then, behind the tree, she sees a shadow. Someone else has stepped into her dream. And the sight of him so scares Carmen that it wakes her up.

When Alba opens her eyes she can already feel her sense of sight getting stronger. The hurricane in her head has stilled. She's stopped shaking. The parts of herself that have been breaking off and scattering into the air are, piece by piece, coming back and beginning to settle. She can see sounds and smells again, just as before, long before she hears or sniffs them. And very gradually, as though looking through an out-of-focus telescope, she's starting to get a picture of what's buried under the midnight glory.

Alba knows her senses are stronger now because of the healing powers of the house, and because of Stella. That the ghost appears only to her at least makes Alba feel rather special. They now meet every night, just after midnight.

Alba isn't intrigued by Stella because she's a ghost, she's seen ghosts before, but because she's a complete mystery. Stella talks about everything but nothing personal, she asks questions but never answers them. So far all Alba really knows is her name; everything else is guesswork. Alba's fascination with Stella has achieved what, so far, no living person has done: tempt her away from books. In the last few days she's read only two biographies and three novels: *Great Expectations*, *The Mandarins* and *Far from the Madding Crowd*. Considering her average is usually thirty textbooks a week this is a significant slow-down. And she's visited the library only once. Now, except for the hours when she reads, Alba talks to Stella all night and sleeps all day.

They talk about everything: literature, history, philosophy, politics, science, art . . . But most of all, they talk about books. Stella, it seems, has spent her death working through every great work of fiction ever written.

'What are your top ten books of all time?' Alba asks. Talking about her greatest passion doesn't exactly heal Alba's heart, or solve the problem of what she's going to do next – but it certainly lifts her spirits.

'That's an impossible question.' Stella laughs. 'What are yours?'

'*Rebecca. Middlemarch. Mrs Dalloway.* Those are my top three, after that I'm not sure,' Alba admits. 'Okay then, which books have changed you?'

'*The Golden Notebook*,' Stella says, 'probably more than any other.'

'I haven't read it,' Alba admits reluctantly.

'Oh dear,' Stella smiles, 'Doris Lessing wouldn't be too impressed to hear that. She actually stayed here while she wrote it, a few years before I arrived. She now resides on the living room wall. You should visit her, she's an inspiration to any writer.'

'I'm not a writer.' Alba frowns. 'I'm a historian. At least I . . .' She doesn't quite have the stomach to finish the sentence. Could it be that she's lost forever her single chance at success, stability and security? Of doing the only thing she has ever wanted to do. Or at least, the only thing that made any sense. Alba can remember an old, secret wish for herself but it was ridiculously unrealistic and she'd let go of it long ago. 'Anyway, what do you mean, visit her? It's only a photograph.'

'Not at all,' Stella says. 'Don't you hear them whispering to each other at night? Any of them would be delighted to talk to you, you only have to ask.'

'Really?' Alba brightens. 'Gosh. How exciting.' She's not sure if she has the courage to approach figures such as Doris Lessing or Florence Nightingale and simply strike up a conversation, but the thought of it sends tingles of excitement along her fingertips.

'How many books have you read?' Stella asks. As of last night, when Stella completed the final volume of *À la recherche du temps perdu*, her total is three hundred and forty-one thousand, nine hundred and two.

'I don't know. A lot.' Alba shrugs. 'You?'

'A few.' Stella smiles. 'Not when I was alive

though, I never bothered with books then. But being dead doesn't give you much else to do. Not that it's boring. It's rather blissful, really.'

Alba sits forward, delighted that Stella is at last saying something about herself.

'And time isn't the same,' Stella continues, wistful. 'It doesn't go forward or back. It's vertical. Eternity sits inside you. So you can spend ten thousand years in one spot and it feels no different than an hour, you see?'

'No,' Alba says, 'not really.'

'Well, I suppose you can't yet,' Stella admits. 'Not until you do.'

'How long have you been here?' Alba ventures.

Stella smiles at Alba's hopeful look and decides to give her a little gift. 'Forty-two years, eight months and seven days.'

'Why, why so long?'

'I've been waiting.'

'For what?'

'For you.'

For the past four years Alba, eschewing the cold austerity of online book-ordering for the comfort of paper and pen, has gone to the university library three times a week, every week, without fail. Now she hasn't shown up since last Wednesday. This morning, Zoë was finally so worried she looked up Alba's details and almost called King's College, but the head librarian stopped her. Now Zoë leans against the library counter, doodling lightning bolts in a notebook. She'd promised herself that today she'd finally start the novel, the story that's been floating around in her head for four years while she's been procrastinating with endless amounts of research. Although it hasn't all been a waste of time, because that was how she found out about Alba.

Zoë noticed Alba immediately, a scared, silent fifteen-year-old who, though five years younger than Zoë, could have been her twin. In fact, with the exception of Zoë's striped blue hair and Alba's bright blue eyes, it was like looking in a mirror. It had taken months before they exchanged their first words, and several years until they had anything approaching a conversation: about Sir Robert Peel and the Poor Law of 1844 – an exchange that had lasted less than three minutes.

And then, while doing research for her non-existent novel, Zoë accidentally stumbled upon the Ashby family, and a scandal: the disappearance of Lord Ashby eleven years ago. Zoë read everything she could find about the case. Charles and Elizabeth Ashby had been second cousins. It had been a loveless marriage by all accounts, producing three children before Lord Ashby took a flat in London and thereafter was often caught in discreet locations with indiscreet socialites. And then, nearly a decade after that, to everyone's surprise, another child was born. It seemed that Alba's arrival had triggered a change of heart in her father, who surrendered his bachelor pad and returned to the family home. There he remained, until his disappearance eight years later.

As the single product of a stable suburban relationship, Zoë was desperately intrigued by it all. She longed to ask Alba for more details, but there was no easy way to bring such delicate matters into casual conversation. So Zoë has been biding her time, waiting for an opportune moment to take her acquaintance with Alba to the next level. Though she has to admit her methods are perhaps over-cautious, at this rate they won't progress to afternoon tea for another twenty years. Zoë glances down at the lightning bolts scattered across her page and tells herself she won't wait any longer. Next time Alba comes into the library she'll invite her out. Zoë writes this in big, bold capital letters:

NEXT TIME.

So big and bold are the words that, this time, she almost believes she'll actually do it.

CHAPTER 4

Carmen hasn't slept again. She stares up at the ceiling, at the shards of early morning light slipping through the curtains, and tries to will herself into unconsciousness. But she knows there is no point.

When she first moved in, the only thing that settled Carmen's anxiety was being in her bedroom. With its sponge-painted blue walls, bright yellow floorboards and inexplicable view of the ocean, it's an exact replica of her cousin's childhood bedroom in Bragança, the place Carmen used to run to when her father came home drunk and started trying to pull her onto his lap. Carmen would pretend her cousin's home was her own and that they were sisters as they lay together listening to records, lulled by the music and smells of her aunt's cooking rising up from the kitchen below. Her own childhood bedroom had been entirely different, the size of a cupboard and without a lock. But it is not her father's face she sees in the darkness any more, it's her husband's. He is the one who haunts her now.

Tiago Viera was the most handsome man Carmen

had ever met. She was nineteen, working at the only bar in Santo Estêvão, and one night he came with his band. With the first note, the first word out of his mouth, Carmen was hooked. Sipping lemonade, she stared at him throughout the set, ignoring all her customers, watching Tiago weave his spell over every woman in the bar. She'd never felt much for men until then, never responded to their advances. Instead she liked to dress provocatively, to cast the illusion that she was available, then tell them to go to hell, just as she had never been able to do when she was a little girl.

But Tiago was different. He was the first one Carmen ever wanted to say yes to, the first one she ever flirted with, the first one she ever pursued. It was the music that bound them. When he played, every thought left her head and her heart went still in her chest. Tiago taught Carmen about the great composers, played her every sonata and concerto he knew until she learnt every note. Soon she was in love, though whether with the music or the musician, she couldn't quite tell. The night she arrived at Hope Street, Peggy had read her a poem by William Butler Yeats, which had summed up Carmen's feelings about Tiago perfectly: 'O body swayed to music, O brightening glance, How can we know the dancer from the dance?'

Carmen sits up in bed and sniffs the air. The scent of the midnight glory lingers in her room. She can't get rid of it. No matter if she shuts and locks all her windows, sprays the room with rose

43

water, burns incense or smokes cigarettes, the smell always sneaks back. Carmen hoped burying it would mean she'd be free, but it's not letting her forget. She knows she should dig up the flower and move what's buried beneath it, in case the smell gets any stronger. Unfortunately she simply doesn't have the courage and can't imagine she ever will.

The toast pops up and Alba picks out the crispy slices, burning her fingertips before dropping the toast onto a plate. She can just see faint spirals of scent, the colour of soot, swirl into the air. She walks back to the table where *Tractarians and the Condition of England* lies open at chapter two. Although reading this book brings painful associations, Alba can't help herself, it's like scratching at a scab even though she knows it will leave a scar. She's an academic, it's the only thing she's sure of. And even though it's all been snatched away (Dr Skinner's lies having no doubt already spread like wildfire through the history professors of England, ensuring she'll never find another supervisor anywhere else), she can't let it go. It's in her blood. It's what her brain was made to do.

Her obsession with history drives her current hobby: searching the photographs for famous women. The house joins in, rattling its pipes as if telling her where to look, shaking and whistling as she gets closer to someone, as if they were playing a game of 'hot and cold.' Last night she found Sylvia Plath and Dorothy Parker in a bathroom, their photographs sitting above the loo. Alba guesses the poet came to the house in 1955 while studying at Newnham College, just before she met and married Ted Hughes. Given that hers was an unhappy ending, Plath must have been one of the tragic residents Peggy mentioned. Alba hasn't managed to find the courage yet to strike up a conversation with any of them, though she's working on it.

Now, munching toast, Alba glances at the book, turns the page and slips inside the cocoon of words. She could quite happily spend the remaining eighty-three days at Hope Street without engaging in real life at all, hiding the shards of her shattered heart. She isn't yet worried about what she's going to do after she has to leave – August feels so far away – but knows she should start thinking about it soon.

Before she's finished reading the page Alba sees the rich scent of roasting coffee circling around her. She glances at the stove, upon which sits a pot of coffee and, on the counter next to it, Stella: the reason Alba's favourite reading place is now the kitchen.

'I thought you might be in the mood for a little caffeine,' Stella says.

'Thank you, I am.' Alba stands, walks to the stove and lifts the whistling coffee pot off the gas. 'Do you want one?'

'Shut up.'

'Sorry.' Alba smiles and spoons a considerable amount of sugar into her cup. She feels the pinch in her cheeks, an unfamiliar sensation, and realises it's the closest she's come to laughing in quite some time.

'Now you're just tormenting me,' Stella says, gazing at the sugar.

'Oh, sorry, I forgot about your sweet tooth,' Alba says. 'So, how about ginger biscuits? Any of those floating around?'

'Oh, ha, ha.' Stella raises her eyebrows. 'You are so cruel, and so unfunny.' In truth, she doesn't mind not eating at all, hasn't cared a fig for food since she died. But Stella loves to see Alba smile.

Alba turns back to the table to see – a plate of ginger biscuits. She picks one off the plate, dunks it in her coffee and bites off the soggy half. Since she first tried the biscuits three days ago, they went straight to the top of the very short list of foods she actually likes to eat.

'Best biscuits I've ever had.' Alba takes another bite. 'Promise me, if you ever decide to disappear, you'll leave me the recipe. Not that I'll ever make them, of course.'

'There's as much chance of me leaving this kitchen,' Stella says, 'as you putting down a book.'

Alba picks up another biscuit. She's not sure whether it's the caffeine, the sugar or Stella, but in the last few minutes her spirits have lifted considerably. 'I don't understand why you can't leave.'

'You and me both,' Stella says, 'though it doesn't

matter now I have you to keep me company, to come and bother me for biscuits. I'm a ghost, I've got nothing better to do. But do you really want to spend your life like this, as if you're locked in a library?'

'Of course.' Alba grins. 'I can't think of anything better.'

'Then you have a more limited imagination than I thought.' Stella smiles.

Stuck for a retort, Alba returns to her book. She wants to know everything about Stella. How she lived, how she died, if she sleeps or dreams, how she can walk through things yet sit on them as well. Scientifically speaking, it doesn't make much sense. But then there's nothing very scientific about spirits. 'What's that you're reading now?'

Alba shrugs, embarrassed. She shouldn't still be reading Dr Skinner's book. She should burn the book, scatter the ashes under the midnight glory and let the soil erase her memories. Perhaps that's how the residents at Hope Street deal with their secrets.

'Tell me what happened.' Stella hops off the counter. Her dress puffs out above her feet but they don't make a sound as she lands on the floor.

Alba looks at Stella and, for a moment, considers telling her everything. Then the kitchen door swings open and Carmen strides in, wearing a short red skirt and a blue T-shirt that clings to her breasts. Stella evaporates and Alba frowns at Carmen, annoyed.

Oblivious, Carmen smiles at her. 'Good morning,' she trills, reaching into the fridge, removing a half-eaten chocolate bar off the top shelf and snapping off a chunk. 'I wish I do not love sweets so much, but I can't help it. When I not have a man to kiss I must find something else delicious for my lips. Do you find this true?'

Alba shrugs, unwilling to discuss such intimate subjects with a virtual stranger.

Leaning against the fridge, Carmen sizes Alba up. She finds herself drawn to the diminutive young woman in a rather maternal way, wanting to take care of her, wanting to liberate her. But how? And then it comes to her. Music will do it, of this she is certain. Music will quiet her mind. Music will touch her heart. Music will set her soul free. More than anything else, Carmen understands the power of music. She knows exactly how it can transform a mood, a moment, a life.

Sensing an imminent social invitation in the offing, Alba stands. 'Well, I think I better . . .'

'You must come to The Archer, the bar where I work,' Carmen says, confirming Alba's suspicion. 'Tomorrow a singer does a show there, you will love to see her, I am sure.'

Alba picks *Tractarians* up off the table. 'I don't really like music.' She steps toward the door. 'Or singing. Anyway, better go, you know . . .' And she hurries out of the kitchen, leaving a bemused Carmen behind.

'Not like music?' She frowns. 'Who does not like music?'

Greer sits at the kitchen table munching an apple and flicking through the classifieds, having found a copy of the *Cambridge Evening News* outside her bedroom door. She's wearing her Katharine Hepburn costume: flared tweed trousers, matching waistcoat and crisp cotton shirt. The clothes imbue her with a strength she really needs right now. Every day she searches the Internet for auditions and opportunities, on a computer that materialised in her bedroom a week ago, but has so far failed to find anything promising. It's all adverts or amateur dramatics, and frankly she'd almost rather be a waitress than do am-dram or adverts. Such efforts were fine in her twenties while she was just starting out, and okay in her thirties, but would be a bit bloody embarrassing in her forties. As a young, aspiring actress she'd always felt sorry for old, and still aspiring, actors who'd dress up as a carrot or a pantomime dame just to remain onstage.

As she reads, Greer considers how lucky she is to have found this house. Without it she'd be sleeping at the YMCA or in the spare room of her mother's flat in Bristol. She shudders at the thought and wonders if she can persuade Peggy to let her stay longer in exchange for extensive cooking and cleaning duties. Greer turns the page to read each career offering. Cleaner. Night porter. Postman. Waiter. Checkout assistant. Au pair. She isn't quite sure what she's supposed to be looking for. Is it any job at all, just to get started, or one she actually wants? In which case, she has no idea what that might be.

On the stove a pot of blueberry porridge bubbles, and the smell of coffee still lingers. Every now and then Greer senses something moving behind her, but when she turns, all she sees is the stove, the cupboards, the walls lined with photographs of unknown women. If she didn't know better, Greer would swear someone is stirring her porridge, because every time she gets up to check, it hasn't stuck to the bottom of the pan.

The kitchen door bangs open and Greer glances up from the newspaper to see Carmen. '*Bom dia.*' She walks to the stove. 'You looking very gorgeous.' She lifts the lid off Greer's porridge, sniffs it, then continues to the fridge and rummages around inside before extracting another chocolate bar. She munches enthusiastically while Greer watches.

'So.' Carmen licks her lips. 'Peggy tell me you want a job.'

'Yes, I need something if I want to keep eating, and all that,' Greer admits. 'I'm not sure what yet, but I'm checking . . .'

'What you like?' Carmen sits at the table. 'What you want to do?'

'I don't know.' Greer twirls the apple core between her fingers. Lady Macbeth, she thinks. Juliet, Ophelia, Titania, Viola, Beatrice. That last female, the heroine of *Much Ado About Nothing*, is her absolute favourite and she'd give anything to play her. But, apart from five nights at university as Viola in *Twelfth Night* she's never had the opportunity to step into the shoes of any of these women. However Greer isn't about to confess her hopes and disappointments to Carmen. Nobody, not even her mother, sees this side of Greer. One of the perks of being an actress is that she can hide behind masks, concealing the parts of herself she wants no one else to know. So instead she says, 'I think anything will do for now.'

'I know something is free at the wine bar I working at.' Carmen finishes her chocolate. 'Maybe you come tonight? I introduce you to my boss. If he like you, you have a job.'

Greer considers this. She could play that role. It might be fun for a little while, and a much-needed rest for her spirit from all the recent rejection. 'Yes, that'd be great.' She smiles. 'Thank you.'

'*Nao problema*.' Carmen studies her. 'I like very much your clothes. Like a movie star.'

'I just like beautiful things.' Greer shrugs off the compliment. 'Hey, but if you want to borrow any from the collection in my bedroom, you're very—'

'Yes, please.' Carmen sits up straight. An offer of this nature is exactly what she was hoping for. 'I would love this. Can we do it right now?'

'Okay.' Greer laughs. 'Right now.'

Alba lies across her bed in her pyjamas reading *Rebecca*. She found it last night in her personal library slipped between biographies of Queen Victoria and Gladstone: a flower of fiction in a field of facts. And after opening the first page and reading the first line for the fifteenth time, she hasn't been able to stop. It is the one novel that, no matter how well she knows the story, still shocks and surprises her. She is always scared by Mrs Danvers, fooled by Maxim and utterly mesmerised by Manderley. The mansion reminds her of home and Alba finds the spookiness cathartic somehow, knowing that she wasn't the only one who'd felt abandoned in a decadence of bricks and mortar and an absence of warmth and words.

As a child Alba read *Rebecca* under the sheets with a flashlight, pausing every now and then, when fear got the better of her, to hold imaginary conversations with the unnamed heroine (whom she called Lucy) about life, loneliness and homicidal housekeepers. The novel and its protagonist were companions Alba reserved for after midnight, when Ashby Hall was at its coldest and darkest. During the day she had other playmates, ones who could stem the longing for real friends, but not so absolutely necessary to her survival as Lucy and Rebecca.

The book brings her comfort still, now soothing different pains, a literary safety blanket Alba can wrap around her fingers and hold until she forgets all the things she wants to forget. Few other novels have been able to offer similar protection against poisoned memories, excepting *Middlemarch* and *Mrs Dalloway*. History textbooks have never had any such effect; they've always stimulated rather than soothed. Which is fine since, as her father had always said, too much mollycoddling creates weakness of character. Which was, he also said, exactly what had gone wrong with her mother's mind.

'Okay, Harry, time's up, I've got things to do.' Peggy sits up. Much as she'd like to spend the day in bed with Harry, he can't be here when she makes another attempt to get into the forbidden room. The door wouldn't open yesterday. Not when she begged, pleaded and threatened. She doesn't understand what's going on. Why is the house being so obtuse? Why the note with no further explanation? She'd like a little clarification and extra details on the fact of her imminent demise. Is that too much to ask? She has questions. Not least of which, now that she knows she's going to die, why isn't she being given any help to find a successor? She can feel herself starting to fade; she can hear the slow tick-tock of the clock.

'Aw, Peg, please, just another cuddle.'

'You think I was born yesterday?' Peggy smiles. 'I know full well what your cuddles lead to. Now bugger off.' She gently pushes Harry, who doesn't budge.

'I've taken two little blue pills today,' he says. 'If you give me twenty minutes, we can try again.'

'You're a hedonist, Harry.' Peggy laughs. 'Labouring under the illusion that you are forty-eight instead of seventy-eight.'

'You're lovely, Peg,' he says, 'you're still the most beautiful woman I've ever seen.'

'Don't be silly, I'm ancient.'

'You're gorgeous. You glow. You're lit from within.'

Peggy brushes a wisp of white hair out of her eyes. 'Does that illuminate all my wrinkles?'

Harry nods. 'So I can see every smile you've ever had, I can hear the echoes of every giggle.'

And although she's too modest to admit it, Peggy knows he's telling the truth, that she's marked with the particular beauty that every Abbot woman has: magical and ethereal, as though their features have been sprinkled with fairy dust until they sparkle.

With a cheeky smile that Peggy can rarely resist, Harry slips his hand under the sheets, running his fingers in little circles toward her belly. In twenty years, Peggy has always surrendered to this particular move. For a moment it seems as though she will again.

'No,' she says softly, 'not now. I've got something important to do.'

'Oh, Peg, don't be so heartless, I've missed you.'

She can't tell him that she's missed him, too, that she wishes he could stay all day and all night, every night. Because then he'll only propose again and she can't say yes, certainly not now that she has less than a year to live. Harry slides closer, gazing up at her with watery blue eyes. 'And it'll

54

be another week before I see you again. Give me a little something to remember you by.' He pats his short white hair and, despite herself, Peggy smiles; she's always liked a man with hair.

'Harold Landon,' she laughs, 'if you've already forgotten what we just did, then you need to see your doctor.'

Suddenly, Harry's serious. 'Peg. We've got to talk about us, I need to say . . .'

'Please.' She squeezes his hand. 'Not now.'

'You can't keep putting this off,' he says, 'I won't let you. Not any more.'

'Okay,' she says, 'but not *now*.' And with that, she lets go of his hand and slides out of bed. Peggy wishes she could tell Harry everything, but she isn't allowed. And the house is very careful never to be magical when Harry's around. Its walls stop breathing, its pipes stop rattling, the cast of characters on the china stop chasing each other around. So, even if she tried, he probably wouldn't believe her.

Harry watches Peggy shuffle across the room, pausing at a chair to pick up her dressing gown, and, with a barely audible sigh, puts his hand to his chest and rests it there.

The house is silent and dark, except for the kitchen, where Alba and Stella talk endlessly into the night about books, long-dead authors, anything and everything except themselves. Despite this, Alba won't give up trying to pry information out

55

of her tight-lipped friend. 'Why will you never tell me anything about yourself?' Alba waves her hand to disperse the orange vapour filling the kitchen from a fresh batch of ginger biscuits.

'Because I can't.' Stella sits in the sink, her knees folded over the ceramic edge. 'I don't have any memories. That's how it is. You don't remember your life after you die. So why don't *you* tell *me* something? Anything.'

'Well . . .' Alba considers that perhaps a quid pro quo of information might be in order. 'How about when my sister Charlotte got caught hiding cards in biology class?'

Stella puts her chin on her knees. 'Go on.'

'They were revision cards she'd made for her history test. The biology teacher gave her detention. Charlotte wrote a letter of complaint to the headmaster. Aged seven. Lotte always was an obsequious little swot, even then. Just like the rest of my siblings.' She sighs. 'They'd disown me if they knew.'

'Knew what?'

Alba shrugs and tells Stella what she told Peggy: carefully phrased half-truths scattered with a few facts about getting kicked out of King's College, about losing the life she worked so hard for. 'So I'm not telling them—'

'But haven't they been asking?'

'We don't talk much.' Alba shrugs. 'They're too busy being rich and successful. The only one who won't mind is Edward, and Mum. But she's not 'very' – Alba searches for a nonspecific word – 'very strong.'

'Oh,' Stella says. She wants to say more, but knows she'll have to wait. The subject of Lady Ashby is one that must be approached with sensitivity and care. 'So, what will you do, when you have to leave here? Teach history in school?' Stella has only seventy-eight more days with Alba. And if the ghost is to help the girl believe in herself and her dreams, then she's got to make more progress.

'And spend the rest of my days trying to ram facts down the throats of hideously behaved children? I think I'd rather die,' Alba says, before realising her insensitive choice of words. 'Oh, I'm sorry, I didn't mean—'

But Stella just giggles, louder and louder until she hides her face in her knees to muffle the noise. The sound is so ticklish that Alba begins to smile. Soon they're both shaking with laughter, along with the ceiling and the kitchen walls. Hundreds of faces in hundreds of photographs regard them curiously. 'I don't see what's so funny about being dead.' Vita turns to her friend. 'Indeed,' Dora agrees, 'it rather puts a cramp in one's ambitions.'

All of a sudden, a sharp ringing, insistent and shrill, sounds through the silent house. Alba glances up at the clock. It's half past two. The noise will wake everyone. Alba leaps up from the table, dashes to the end of the hallway and picks up the phone.

'Hello?' she hisses into the receiver, 'hello?'

'Is that you, Alba?' a voice echoes down the line. 'Al, it's me.'

Alba almost drops the phone. 'Lotte?'

Successive waves of panic sweep along Alba's spine, her hands start to shake. In the few seconds of silence that follow, fear-soaked questions flood Alba's mind: How does her sister know? Will she tell the whole family? What will everyone say? How can she face them? Will they even want to see her again? And then she wonders how the hell Charlotte knew where to find her, how she got this number, a number even Alba didn't know? But in the next second, all those questions are forgotten.

'Alba, listen,' Charlotte says. 'Mother is dead.'

CHAPTER 5

'My m-m-um.' Alba stumbles over the word, hardly getting it out. 'My mum, I don't, I can't . . . I have to go home.' This awful fact falls on top of the unbearable one, crushing Alba's chest until she's taking little gasps of air, barely able to breathe.

'Oh, love.' Stella looks at Alba, broken again so quickly, her whole world crashing down upon her. But with a gift of foresight such as only the dead and clairvoyant possess, Stella knows Alba must be allowed to feel her grief, must dive headlong into despair, before she can emerge again, her spirit deeper and richer than before. She knows that if she lifts Alba's pain now, it'll only postpone her healing. So she can do nothing, except stay so Alba is not alone.

'She's dead,' Alba says softly. 'She killed herself. She finally did it.' She sits in the kitchen doorway and leans her head against the wall. It softens in response, gently holding her.

Stella knows there are no words to say. Nothing will do, or fit, or make anything better at all. The only thing to be done is something she can't do.

She wishes with every fibre of her non-beating heart, that she could hold Alba in her arms now. 'Will you come with me?'

Alba looks up at Stella, who gently shakes her head. 'I can't.'

'Why, why not?'

'I'm sorry, I can't leave the house, the kitchen . . .'

'Yes, but, are you sure?' Alba feels tears stinging her eyes. 'Have you tried?'

Stella nods. 'I'm sorry.'

'I can't go alone,' Alba chokes, 'I just can't . . .'

'I know you're scared,' Stella says softly, 'I understand and I'm sorry.'

'No, you don't.' Alba's voice is sharp now. 'You don't have any idea, any idea at all. They're awful. They hate me. They've always hated me.'

Quietly Alba begins to cry. Not for the loss of her mother, which hasn't sunk in yet, but for the fact that she has to face them. And that the one friend she wishes could hold her, can't.

Alba catches the earliest morning train to London, makes the connection to Aldershot and waits outside the station for her sister. Biting her fingernails and rubbing her red eyes, Alba absently observes the chattering commuters swirling around her, their conversations a rainbow of colours. When Charlotte finally screeches along the road Alba sees flashes of silver lightning snapping from her tyres just before the car turns the corner.

'Ouch!' Alba glances down at her raw thumb she just bit and tastes blood on her lip.

When Charlotte gets out of the car, they don't hug. For a tiny, fleeting moment Alba thinks they might, but instead her sister just reaches out a delicate bejewelled and manicured hand to take the small bag Alba grips in hers.

'Is this all you have?' Charlotte is carelessly dressed with the utmost care. Every piece of her outfit has been meticulously put together, precisely planned for maximum effect. And all of it, from the ivory silk shirt to the sky blue jeans and scuffed brown suede boots, cost more than Alba's entire wardrobe, indeed probably more than all her worldly possessions. This was true even when they were children. As a teenager Charlotte would have her black hair trimmed in the London salons and pick her couture from the Mayfair boutiques. Ten years after her, Alba cut her own hair and wore boy's clothes found in the village charity shops.

'I didn't . . .' Alba shrugs. 'I didn't know how long I'd be staying.'

'It's always wiser to over-prepare,' Charlotte says, throwing the bag into the boot of her BMW, 'or you risk being caught short.'

Alba nods, wondering if her perfectly prepared sister has ever actually been caught short or unprepared for anything. She doubts it. As they drive Alba closes her eyes and pretends to sleep. At last, when she hears the car's tyres crunching on gravel, she turns her head to look out of the window.

They speed down the long drive-way, passing through fields of flowers and sheep, and Alba feels her chest tighten, squeezing all the blood out of her heart. A moment later the family home comes into view, an overblown Victorian doll's house with forty windows, eight chimneys (one for each wing) and a wide flight of stone steps leading up to a double oak door flanked with pillars.

Alba misses Hope Street so sharply it hurts. It is the home she dreamt of as a little girl. Somewhere soft and loving, where the walls breathe, the garden hides your secrets, the inhabitants lift your spirits and the kitchen soothes your soul. Not a draughty mansion with dozens of sparsely furnished, freezing rooms and windswept corridors that never end. As a child Alba wished for a house the size of a shoebox, with everyone always within reach, so that when she cried or called out somebody would come to comfort her. But since she never had it, she learnt to live without, to pretend she preferred to be alone. And Alba's been doing it for so long now, she nearly always believes it to be true.

As they drive Alba remembers the last time she baked biscuits with her mother. She was six years old and it was three o'clock in the morning. Elizabeth Ashby, dressed for dinner in a silk gown, woke Alba, carried her to the kitchen and sat her on the table amid a mess of flour, eggs and sugar.

'What are we doing, Mummy?' Alba rubbed her eyes.

'We're making your favourite, sweetie, ginger-bread men.'

'But it's night-time. I have school in the morning.'

'We're having a midnight snack. You love them, remember?' Great puffs of flour filled the air as Elizabeth frantically stirred the ingredients. 'We'll eat them together, won't that be fun?'

'Yes, Mummy.' Alba had nodded. 'It'll be fun.'

Charlotte brakes to a halt at the stone steps, spitting gravel at the feet of Alba's oldest brother, Charles. He glances down at his shoes then looks up, flicking his hand in a half-wave, while walking around to the back of the car.

'Hello girls.' Charles opens the boot and lifts out Alba's bag. 'Pleasant trip, I trust, under the circumstances?'

Alba holds her breath, begging herself not to cry, then pushes open her door. Charles waits at the steps until Alba reaches him, patting her shoulder so quickly Alba wonders if he touched her at all.

'Did Edward bring Tilly?' Alba asks, thinking that her niece's soft little cheek pressed against hers might be the only thing to get her through this agony. 'I miss—'

'Left her in London with the nanny, thank God.' Charles walks toward the stone steps.

'Bloody dreadful traffic on the M11.' Charlotte slams her door and the sports car shudders. 'Can't stand queuing for hours for no discernible reason.'

'Cook isn't happy she's had to hold dinner,' Charles calls out, taking the steps two by two, 'though she's only clanging pots, not throwing them. Out of respect for Mother, I believe.'

And sure enough, Alba can see flashes of electricity striking the air around the kitchen in the east wing: long, spiky snakes that crack up into the clouds. The colours are so bright, so vibrant it surprises her. She thought the sadness of her mother's death would have clouded her sight again, but it now seems brighter than ever before.

'Oh, hell,' Charlotte sighs, 'I suppose we'd better get a move on.'

As her sister strides after Charles, Alba follows, taking each step as slowly as she possibly can. She knows that even the family tragedy won't stop the interrogation about her career. Her heartless siblings, with the exception of her brother Edward, softened by fatherhood and the loss of his wife a year ago, won't be shedding tears that might dampen their curiosity. So Alba will eventually have to tell them what happened, though she won't tell them why. Because, apart from anything else, they'll never believe her.

That afternoon Greer sits on the floor of her wardrobe, surrounded by discarded dresses. Carmen stands in front of the mirror, trying on a blue silk trouser suit while Peggy perches on the bed in a cream linen shirt and skirt emblazoned with bright purple orchids.

'This is so fun,' Peggy giggles. 'I've never felt so fancy, like I should be out courting with a man on each arm.'

'Try this.' Greer holds out a dark red poodle skirt to Carmen. 'Tight tops set off by big belts and flouncy skirts, that's your thing. Perfect for your figure.'

Carmen discards her trousers, slips on the skirt and smiles. '*Perfecto.*'

'So, my dear.' Peggy turns to Greer. 'Apart from playing dress-up, have you given any thought to what you want to do with your life?'

Greer gives a nonchalant shrug, not in the mood to delve into her angst about acting and her seemingly bleak future in general. 'I've an interview with Carmen's boss on Saturday.'

'Well.' Peggy smoothes her skirt. 'That might do for now, but I think, since you're here, the house probably has bigger plans for you than that.'

'Oh?' Greer says. 'And will you tell me what they are?'

'No, my dear.' Peggy smiles. 'I'm afraid it doesn't quite work like that.'

Alba shuffles through the east wing of Ashby Hall, shivering. She can't sleep and she's starving – not that she wants to eat, her stomach is too full of sorrow. She refused dinner with Charlotte and Charles, pleading a migraine, knowing they wouldn't settle for the simple reason of grief. For an Ashby mustn't be buckled or broken by emotion, an Ashby must be strong. She imagines them downstairs, ploughing through Cook's four courses, drinking until they can't feel anything anymore.

As Alba turns a corner along the corridor the clouds part and her way is lit by moonlight. She sees the door, exactly as she remembers it, painted blue: the shade of a muted spring sky, her mother's favourite colour. It stands out against all the ancient oak that lines the walls and shapes the ceilings, the only painted door in the whole of Ashby Hall, a gift to Alba's mother from a grateful husband on the birth of their first child: Charles Ashby IV.

Alba places her palm on the wood, her pale fingers made marble by the moonlight, and stares at the door as though trying to see through it. She wonders if it's been opened since her mother's death and if, indeed, this was where she died. The siblings haven't explained the circumstances yet, and she hasn't asked, hardly sure whether or not she really wants to know.

A cloud drifts across the moon. Alba's hand disappears and the corridor is dark again. In the blackness she feels herself starting to fray at the edges, her molecules drifting off, evaporating, dissolving . . . She could be eight years old again, standing outside her mother's bedroom door, pleading with her to stop crying and come out and play. Then Alba hears that song again, the one she heard the first night at Hope Street. Alba presses her ear to the door, but then the tune changes to another she knows, one about all the colours of the rainbow. Another memory rises up. She's lying on the grass in a field, under an oak. Her mother lies next to her, singing that song. Alba can hear her own voice, young and bright. 'Look.' Her tiny hand points up at the tree. 'It's breathing, Mummy, bright yellow like buttercups.'

'The colour of inspiration,' her mother says, 'and youth.'

'Yes,' Alba laughs. 'Yes!'

'What other colours can you see, my darling?'

Alba sits up, glancing around the field. 'That bird is singing dark green,' she says. 'The tiny one in black, he's complaining.'

'Maybe someone stole his worm.'

'I can't understand what he's singing, Mummy.' Alba frowns. 'That's what Dr Doolittle does.'

'Quite right,' her mother smiles, 'so what else do you see?'

But just as Alba is about to answer, the memory lets go and leaves Alba standing alone in the silence. A slip of light now shines from underneath the door and slowly she pushes it open. The room is exactly as she remembers: sparse and bare, with sky blue walls, wooden bed, wardrobe and rocking chair by the single long window. On the chair, Alba thinks she can see her mother, rocking back and forth, twisting her hands in her lap, muttering the same sentence to herself over and over again.

The words are too soft for Alba to hear and the light too dim for her to see their letters, so she creeps a little closer, stepping across the wooden floorboards with great care so they won't squeak. When she's only a few feet away Alba stops, seeing what her mother says before she can hear her. The words are royal blue, the colour of sorrow.

'*Where are you? Why did you leave me? I need you. Please, Ella, please come back, I need you, I need you now.*'

Alba frowns. Who on earth is Ella?

CHAPTER 6

Alba is curled up on the bed in her childhood bedroom. She's always hated it: the dark mahogany-panelled walls, four-hundred-year-old furniture, ancient oak bed facing an enormous wardrobe and everything draped in the dust of long-dead Ashby ancestors.

Hot white sparks flash in the air around her. From far off she hears the high-pitched shriek of her sister's laugh as the siblings set the table for dinner. During the few instances of family tragedy to date – their father's disappearance and their mother's madness – Charlotte has always tended toward slightly maniacal laughter instead of tears. Her brothers, on the other hand, just shut down their emotions completely and say nothing.

After getting out of dinner last night, Alba knows they won't let her off the hook again and she's dreading it, wondering how long she'll be able to fend off their interrogation. She wishes she could stay locked up in her bedroom until the funeral. She still can't believe her mother is actually gone, after half a dozen suicide attempts in the last decade. Alba had long since stopped believing her mother even wanted to die. It was a bid for attention, the doctors had said, the act of a broken mind, though Alba had never entirely understood that rationale. If Elizabeth Ashby wanted attention, then why didn't she speak to anyone? Why did she lock herself away and refuse to see her children? A psychotic breakdown, the doctors explained. An already unstable person pushed over the edge by the desertion and disappearance of her husband.

Alba can feel tears running down her cheeks. After a lifetime of shutting down, she's now overwhelmed by emotions. Loss. Love. Longing. Grief. Fear. Relief. Relief is the one she really can't bear. It makes her feel selfish and guilty.

Alba shuts her eyes and switches off her heart and wills herself not to think of her mother. But memories of seeing her in so many hospital beds rise up, memories of Elizabeth staring out of windows, rocking back and forth, of finding her in the garden in the middle of winter in her nightie. When Alba was very little she loved the manic times until she learnt to be scared of those, too, because she knew what followed. Once, when Alba was five her mother turned up at school in pyjamas, telling the teachers it was a family emergency and she had to take Alba home. Instead they had gone to the zoo.

'Let's go and see the monkeys, Mummy, they have the best laughs.'

'The chimps blow blue bubbles,' Elizabeth, said, smiling. 'The baboons' bubbles are yellow.'

'Yes,' Alba giggled, happy to be with the one person who shared her strange secret. She gripped her mother's hand as they walked to the monkey cage. It had been a wonderful afternoon until at last they reached the hippos and Elizabeth started to cry. She couldn't explain why but sat by the enclosure sobbing until a zoo attendant finally ushered them both away. Alba had sat in a cold white waiting room, her cheeks stained with ice cream and tears, until her father had come to collect them.

Of all her childhood memories, most are of her mother or of nannies, very few of her father or siblings. Alba saw her brothers and sister only when they returned from their respective boarding schools during the summer. All extreme extroverts, they refused to play with their strange and painfully shy sister. Occasionally, while having picnics with cream teas and jugs of Pimm's, Charlotte would permit Alba to sit on the same lawn and read while her giggly teenager friends squealed about boys and other things Alba didn't understand. These experiences rarely ended well for Alba but, suffering with a manic-depressive mother and an uninterested father, she continued to covet Charlotte's picnics anyway.

One summer afternoon, a month after her seventh birthday, Alba lay on the grass with her feet in the air, reading an Agatha Christie mystery. She loved solving the murders in advance, and always did. She never tried talking to the teenagers, just liked hearing their giggles close by, seeing the coloured bubbles of their laughter floating above their heads. But although Alba always kept a careful distance from the group, invariably one of them couldn't resist teasing her.

'What you reading?' a voice asked.

Pulling away from Poirot and his 'little grey cells,' Alba looked up to see Katherine, Charlotte's best friend of five years, gazing at her.

'*The Murder of Roger Ackroyd.*' Alba held the book up to prove it, then returned to reading it. But Katherine wasn't done with her yet. 'Aren't you going to Chelt in Sep?'

Alba looked up again to see the girl's words hanging in the air: pitch black and blood red. She shivered slightly and nodded.

'So, shouldn't you be reading more sophisticated stuff? I thought you were supposed to be a super brain-box, or something. I thought you read Shakespeare in your sleep.'

'No.' Alba frowned. 'Only when I'm awake.'

At this the giggling girls burst into raucous laughter and Charlotte glared at her sister as though she wished she'd spontaneously combust.

'Well, aren't you the teacher's pet,' Katherine sneered. 'I bet you'll go straight to the top of the class.'

'Really?' Alba smiled. 'I hope so.'

72

With that the girls burst into another bout of cackles. Alba stared at them, completely confused.

Katherine turned to Charlotte and said, 'With the exception of your gorgeous brother Charlie, you really do have the most ridiculous family. You have my deepest sympathies.'

'She's your sister?' a new girl piped up. 'But she's so plain, and her clothes are beyond tragic. Have your folks fallen on hard times, or something?'

Charlotte looked at Alba with fury. 'It's not my fault she's like that. Anyway she's not my sister, she's an orphaned cousin who stays with us during the summers.'

'Oh,' the girl said, 'poor you.'

'Yeah.' Charlotte continued to glare at Alba. 'Exactly.'

Afterward, even though Alba locked herself in her bedroom for two whole days, Charlotte refused to apologise. Her brothers didn't want to get involved. It was only the cook who eventually coaxed her out with a strawberry blancmange made from real fruit. As a child Alba had adored red foods – strawberries, peppers, chillies, tomatoes – for the bright flaming colours they emitted. She ate them all the time, though her siblings neither knew nor cared why.

Greer stands in front of Carmen's boss, Blake, trying to focus on what he's saying and formulate words in response. But the impact of his presence makes it difficult. He's tall, with thick blond hair, green eyes and a smile that is almost too bright. His thick southern U.S. accent speaks of swamps and alligators, colonial houses and cotton fields, sweat and heat. As though he's stepped out of *A Streetcar Named Desire* and into a small Cambridge bar, purely for his own pleasure.

It's the green eyes that are her undoing. She just wants to kiss him, press her lips against his perfect mouth until they are both naked and sweating.

Carmen nudges Greer with an elbow in the ribs. With a blink she returns to reality to see Blake looking at her with a slight frown.

'So then,' he says, 'what do you say? Yea or nay?'

'I'm sorry.' Greer flushes. 'Could you repeat the question?'

'Sure.' Blake laughs. 'I asked if you were gonna take the job?'

And although Greer hasn't been hearing a single thing that the job actually entails, she just grins. 'Oh yes, I will. Absolutely.'

For Harry Landon, it was love at first sight. A clichéd phrase and one he never believed in before. It was the day he met Peggy, in the cinema at a matinee of an obscure French film. Until that day he'd been perfectly content with life as it was. A confirmed bachelor, a nearly retired milkman who spent his afternoons, and some of his evenings, watching films. Harry loved the cinema. Ever since his father took him to a Saturday matinee showing of *Gone With the Wind* in 1939, the year it took eight Oscars, stole the hearts of millions of women worldwide and broke every box office record to date, and the year Harry senior went to war and was never seen again.

Little Harry had hated the film but fell in love with everything about movies: the soft seats, the enormous flickering pictures, the darkness, the sweet smells of popcorn, sugar and Earl Grey tea served during the intervals. During the war he'd delivered papers, shined shoes, stolen milk bottles – anything to get the fourpence necessary for admission every Saturday. And when he snuggled down deep into his red velvet seat, his feet dangling off the edge, when the lights went off and the picture came on, he forgot – for two glorious hours – that his father was gone. His first favourite film was *Ninotchka*, when he fell in love with Greta Garbo, a crush he loyally stoked for seven years, until his fourteenth birthday and Rita Hayworth appeared in *Gilda*. Two months after that, with the revelation of Lana Turner in *The Postman Always Rings Twice*, he was never monogamous again, at least not where celluloid was concerned.

As a man Harry had a few affairs in real life, but none that touched the heights of his film-star fantasies, so he never bothered with them for long. Women always looked at Harry, even after his hair turned white and his wrinkles multiplied. He rather resembled Paul Newman, with a strong jaw, high cheekbones and bright blue eyes, and had aged just as well. Sometimes they waited for him when he delivered their milk, and sometimes he went inside when they invited him in.

Harry heard Peggy Abbot before he saw her. The cinema was almost empty, no more than a dozen other people cluttering the seats, just how Harry liked it. She sat three rows in front, her wild white hair slightly obscuring his view, so he disliked her at first, until he heard her laugh. There was something about Peggy's laugh: a magical mixture of sunshine and champagne that floated through the air and lifted him out of his seat. He'd never heard anything so beautiful, so inviting, and, despite the fact that the giggling mess of white hair was ruining his film, he knew he had to meet her.

When the credits rolled, Harry hurried down the aisle and back along her row before sitting in the seat right next to her. Peggy turned to him and smiled. 'Hello.'

Harry opened his mouth, but his mind was blank. She was in her early sixties and the most beautiful woman he'd ever seen, either in real life or in film.

'And you are?' Peggy prompted him.

'H-Harry,' he said at last.

'Well, hello, Harry.' Peggy smiled again and he felt his heart thump against his chest. 'What can I do for you?' She waited, gazing at him.

'Did you like it?' he finally asked.

'What?' she asked, giving him a look that sent a

sharp shiver of excitement through his body and made his heart beat faster still.

'The film,' he said.

'It was funny.'

'It wasn't supposed to be.'

'Isn't all that just a matter of perspective?'

That was the moment Harry knew he was hooked. 'Do you come here often?' he asked, regretting the cliché before the last word was out.

'No.' Peggy laughed. 'I really came in just to get out of the rain. Not that I don't love the cinema, but I just wasn't in the mood today, you know?'

Harry had never met a woman quite so unpredictable, whose words knocked him off balance and whose way of being – her stillness and total lack of self-consciousness – made him forget where and who he was.

'Anyway.' She picked her bag up off the floor and stood, letting the seat flip back into place. 'I'd better be off, now the rain's stopped.'

'Has it?' Harry asked. He didn't mind that it was a strange thing to say, or care how she knew; he just didn't want her to leave. She waited, pulling on her gloves, while he gazed up at her. He opened his mouth again, desperately trying to think up something witty or charming to say, but nothing came out.

'Okay.' Peggy slipped her hat on. 'Since you're clearly a little lost for words, would you like to come for tea on Sunday morning? You could practise some conversational subjects before then, give yourself a head start.'

'What?' he said, torn between shock and sheer delight. 'I—'

'I believe that's yes, then.' She smiled, then pulled a card out of her bag and handed it to him. 'Ten o'clock is fine, but don't be early. I like to sleep in.'

And that was how Harry's love story began.

The four Ashby siblings sit around a long mahogany table. It's ancient, dark and gleaming. Alba stares at her plate while her two brothers and sister consume vast quantities of wine. Every humiliating childhood memory settles around the table, materialising in the empty chairs, ghosts anchoring Alba to her past. Until somewhere between the pea soup and the pheasant she can't remember who she is any more. All she knows is how much she hates Ashby Hall with all its heavy, oppressive Tudor trappings.

'You're playing your cards close to the chest this evening, Al,' Edward says softly.

'Yes, indeed,' Charles declares. 'Tell us how life in academia is progressing. I'm guessing your MPhil is going swimmingly, you little swot.'

'It's fine,' Alba says, still staring at her plate.

'Is it Dr Skinner supervising you?' Charlotte asks. 'I can't recall.'

'I must drop in next time I'm down.' Charles takes another gulp of wine. 'Skinner helped get me a first in finals. And I promised the old beaut a bottle of Bolly for it.'

Alba holds her breath. She has to say something now, or she'll never find the courage. She'll tell them the bare minimum, nothing more. And if she's very, very lucky, they'll leave it at that.

'Oh, I've been meaning to mention this friend of mine,' Charlotte says. 'He's written a brilliant paper you must read, especially—'

'N-no,' Alba stutters, not knowing what she's going to say, only that she has to say it now. 'No, I, well, that is, I mean . . .'

'What are you blathering about?' Charles says. 'Speak in sentences.'

'Charlie,' Edward says softly, 'go easy.'

'Yes, well,' Alba stumbles on. 'I, um . . .'

'What is it?' Charlotte asks. 'Spit it out.'

'I wasn't doing well enough,' Alba finally blurts out. 'Dr Skinner dropped me. My studies, my PhD, I don't . . .'

She trails off, her words drying up under the combined force of her three siblings staring at her. For one long, agonising moment, nobody speaks. Then, suddenly, they all sober up.

'But, but you only needed a high pass,' Charles says, breaking the silence. 'How could you mess that up? It's virtually impossible.'

'I don't understand,' Charlotte says, 'I simply don't understand. Are you a complete idiot?'

'Oh dear, Al,' Edward whispers, looking at his little sister, his eyes full of pity. 'I don't believe it.'

'What the hell happened?' Charles brandishes his knife at Alba.

'I don't know,' Alba lies. 'I just couldn't—'

'Well, I can't say I'm surprised, really,' Charlotte snaps, 'since you're not—'

'No, Lotte, don't,' Edward says. 'Not now.'

'Look, I'm sorry, all right?' Alba says. 'I'd give anything, anything to be starting my PhD in October. I have no idea what I'm going to do.'

'You'll have to appeal,' Edward says. 'That's all. It's okay, not unheard of.'

'Oh God, how perfectly humiliating.' Charlotte tips the last of a bottle of wine into her glass. 'I'm so glad Father didn't have to witness this, that Mother isn't here to see what—'

'Don't!' Alba bites back tears. 'Don't, please.'

'Oh, calm down,' Charles sighs. 'It's clearly a mistake, a mess of some kind. I'll call Dr Skinner first thing, we'll sort this out.'

'No, no.' Alba wants to scream. 'You can't. You can't.'

'Why?' Edward gazes gently at his little sister. 'Why can't we help?'

But Alba just shakes her head. She can't tell him. She can't tell anyone. Suddenly Alba feels as though she's drowning, her lungs filling faster than she can breathe. She wants to relive the last year, to undo what she's done. Although now she's starting to remember more clearly what that life was really like at King's: every day running a race she could never win. Something has begun to unfold inside her, a seed that Stella has planted, so Alba is no longer quite sure she wants that life back any more.

'What's the point?' Alba says softly. 'What is the point?'

'Sorry?' Edward asks.

'Well, what's the point of it all?' Alba repeats loudly, looking up. 'No matter what I do, if I got five PhDs, I'll still never get your approval. Will I? You've always hated me, haven't you? Always treated me like an interloper: your unwanted, unexpected little sister. So it doesn't matter what I do, does it? You're never going to love me, you're never going to approve of me—'

This sudden and rare burst of truth has the unusual effect of shocking the Ashby siblings into silence. Charlotte and Charles stare at her coldly. But Edward has tears in his eyes.

'Forgive me,' Charles says, 'but your question is entirely irrelevant. The *point* is to push you to greatness. If you got our approval before achieving anything, we'd be doing you a huge disservice.'

He glances at Charlotte, who half-nods and half-shrugs, as though she doesn't care either way, and then at Edward, who just looks pained.

'And what about unconditional love,' Alba snaps. 'Isn't that what families are for?' She waits, but Charles is stone-faced. Charlotte slowly drains her glass. Edward just looks on, speechless, regret tugging at his fingers. He twists them in his lap, locking his thumbs together.

81

Alba sighs. 'Okay. Right. Well, I shouldn't be surprised since the only member of this family who ever loved me like that was Mum, and—'

'And she was mad.' Charlotte sets down her glass. 'So I really wouldn't put much stock in that.'

Alba stares at her sister, unable to believe what she's just said. Stunned, clipped words flap through her mind, but before they can reach her mouth, Alba pushes her chair away from the table and runs out of the room.

Peggy is a great lover of sleep; she luxuriates in it for long, lazy hours in the morning and looks forward to embracing it again every night. But as soon as the clocks go forward in spring, she wakes early and goes to the garden to see her flowers opening their petals to the sun. The back garden is Peggy's domain, the one place, excepting the tower, that is hers alone. And in the sixty-one years she's presided over the house, not a single resident has ever stepped into it. Every time another woman turns up, Peggy holds her breath a little, waiting. But no one has yet looked beyond the back of the house and Peggy knows why: the power of her possessive desire is so strong it renders the garden invisible to everyone else. She guards it as her place to be alone, her reward for a lifetime of giving. And so far, at least, the house has acquiesced to her silent request, allowing her solitary Eden to remain hidden, while its windows reflect a false view of fields and trees. Only Alba has seen beyond the mirage, but luckily she doesn't seem interested.

In return for keeping itself secret, Peggy adores and nurtures the garden as if it's her favourite lover. The scent of the honeysuckle soothes her, the breeze strokes her skin and the grass infuses her feet with a warmth that fills her whole body, like sips of ancient, expensive whisky she sometimes treats herself to before bedtime. And just as she attends to Harry's every need (except the one to marry and live together), so she tends to the garden, taking care of each and every plant. Peggy thinks of Harry more often now, knowing that she won't have long left with him. She treasures their time together more than usual. And, though Peggy has never been a woman with regrets, she has noticed them starting to sneak up on her lately when she's not paying attention.

Scattered through the long grasses of the lawn are old stone birdbaths, feeders hanging from the branches of every tree. In the late spring and early summer, hundreds of multicoloured butterflies dip in and out: holly blues, cardinals, monarchs, small skippers, swallowtails . . . Today a tiny pair of lemon yellow butterflies follow each other on a figure-eights tour of the garden, each settling on Peggy's shoulder before they leave.

'Mog.' Peggy catches sight of the flick of a ginger tail from behind a patch of tall white daisies. 'Get out of the flower bed. When will you give up chasing butterflies? They're just toying with your emotions.'

Mog replies with a haughty meow and stalks off in the direction of the lawn, his tail held high. Peggy kneels at the edge of the grass, plucking at weeds surrounding a cluster of black roses she created herself, cross-pollinating the darkest flowers she could find for years before finally getting lucky. She's extremely proud of the results.

The roses remind Peggy of the midnight glory in the front garden. It's growing too fast and starting to shine so brightly at night, it'll begin to attract attention. At the moment the house is visible only to those who need it, but if the plant keeps growing it'll be seen by everyone, and the house will be overrun by tourists, scientists, journalists who will expose it and tear the house apart trying to make sense of its magic. It won't survive for long after that.

Last night Peggy looked out of the tower window to see the tendrils of the midnight glory wrapping around drainpipes and slithering up the walls, its dark purple flowers glistening just under the second-storey balcony, the moonlight illuminating their glow. She knows there's no point cutting it down, she has to remove what's feeding it, to dig up what is buried beneath it. But only Carmen can do that.

Carmen kneels on the floor, scraping chewing gum off the bottom of a black leather chair. Blake asked her to do the morning cleaning shift and, unattractive as the job is, Carmen finds she can't say no to him. Luckily she loves being in the bar when it's empty. No one else there, just the polished oak floors, walls of exposed red brick, bottles of expensive wines on display in alcoves, a raised stage for singers with a microphone and a baby grand piano. There was nothing like it in Bragança. It's quite the opposite of the shady little bar where she met Tiago, and Carmen adores every brick, seat and floorboard.

This morning she has a plan. Every few minutes she stops scratching the seat and looks up at the stage. Last night Carmen saw the singer she'd invited Alba to see. The woman sang Bessie Smith, Nina Simone and Ella Fitzgerald, and Carmen was utterly captivated. Echoes of the notes play in stereo now, bouncing around her brain, knocking out every other thought. Last night she actually slept, lulled to sleep by all that wonderful music. Everything fell away, leaving only white space and sound. And now Carmen can't think about anything else. Which is exactly the way she wants it.

When she's scraped the chair clean, she stands and stretches. Then, instead of returning to cleaning, as she should, Carmen hurries across the wooden floor and steps onto the stage. A dust-sheet covers the baby grand piano. She pulls it off and sits on the wooden stool.

She hasn't played in over a year, not since Tiago first taught her. She shakes her head to unlock the memories, places her fingers on the ivories, and slowly begins testing the notes, seeing what will come. But as she tries to remember the songs she most loved, Carmen realises it's impossible. They're locked away in some distant place she can't reach, trapped deep in her mind, along with all the other things Carmen never wants to remember. And so, just as Tiago gave her the music, now he has taken it away.

CHAPTER 7

'I'm not saying you *should* get back together with him, sweetie, I'm only saying you should think about it.'

'Mum, I couldn't, even if I wanted to,' Greer says, having only just confessed to her engagement ending. 'He's with the twenty-two-year-old and he's welcome to her.'

'Stop feigning flippancy,' Celia says, 'you're too old for it. If you were the twenty-two-year-old, then perhaps, but you're nearly forty.'

'In eleven months, Mum, not tomorrow.' Greer sits on the bottom step of the stairs, wearing 1950s men's silk pyjamas, the phone cord wrapped around her wrist. This is the topic she always dreads and the one her mother always brings up. Greer stares at the photographs lining the walls. She can picture Celia now: perched on the edge of the kitchen counter, legs crossed, phone in one hand, cigarette in the other. Greer's grandmother named her daughter after Celia Johnson when she went into labour while watching *Brief Encounter*, and her mother in turn named her own after Greer Garson, star of her favourite film, *Mrs Miniver*.

They'd both been trying to live up to their names ever since. Sadly, neither of them has proved any good at either being brilliant actresses or managing to get married.

'You're no spring chicken,' Celia says. 'And if you leave it too late you'll end up regretting it, I promise you. If I hadn't had you I'd have nothing now, would I?'

'No, Mum.' Greer sighs. 'I suppose not.' Her mother is the only one Greer can't act with, the only one who isn't fooled by the smile, the laugh, the pretending that everything is wonderful when it isn't. No, Celia knows her daughter too well for that. The only thing she doesn't know is the secret Greer's been keeping since she was nineteen years old. Greer sighs again.

'I heard that,' Celia snaps.

'Sorry, Mum, it's not you,' Greer lies. 'I'm just knackered, that's all. I had to do a double shift last night. Blake asked if—'

'Blake?' Celia perks up and Greer inwardly curses. 'He's my boss, Mum.'

'Is he . . .?'

'No, and we're not.'

'Oh.' Celia blows out a puff of smoke. 'Shame. He sounds nice.'

Greer laughs. 'I only told you his name.'

'Well, it's a good one,' her mother insists. 'It holds promise. I'll bet he has strong sperm.'

'Mum!'

'Listen, love, you can't count on a man to stick

around, but your kids will always love you. And you can't wait much longer. I know it's unfair, but that's how it is for women, we . . .'

Greer squeezes her eyes shut and stops listening. All she can see now is Lily: big green eyes, bump of a nose, little bow mouth, dusting of dark red hair and tiny fingers that wrapped themselves tightly around hers and held on as long as they could. Celia knew nothing of the pregnancy and never suspected. Greer hardly showed until the sixth month, and by then she was at university. When she went into labour early, she didn't call anyone. She met, loved and lost Lily in a single day, all by herself.

'Mum,' Greer says softly, 'I'm doing the best I can, okay?' She can feel her voice crack and has the sudden urge to confess everything. To admit that sometimes she wakes from dreams so vivid she can still feel Lily's head on her breast, the tuft of soft red hair brushing her skin. She wants to tell her mother the truth: that complications during the birth left her unable to have another child. But then they'd both be without hope.

'I know, love, I just worry about you, that's all.' Celia sighs. 'And why are you wasting your time in a bar? You should be onstage, that's where you belong. I can—'

Greer mumbles something incoherent. She won't get drawn in. This is one conversation she is determined to avoid today. Her insubstantial acting career has always been an explosive subject between them, almost as much as Greer's child-lessness. Celia, having failed to achieve the stardom she dreamt of, has always invested an intrusive level of interest in Greer's own career. If Greer admits that she's all but given up on the idea that she'll ever be an actress of any significance, she knows she'll never hear the end of it. Celia will hound her until she promises never to give up. Because if Greer lets her dreams of stardom die, her mother's dreams die with them.

The other thing she certainly won't tell her mother is that, last night, the charming American asked her out and she said no. At the end of their shift he'd offered her a cigarette, then suggested dinner, and had seemed extremely surprised when she turned him down. But she knows Blake is only interested in a fling. Of course, Celia would be furious that she'd passed up a prospect of any kind, no matter how improbable. For it is her mother's firm belief that a man can always be changed, given incentive enough. Greer does not share this illusion and since she's reluctant to subject herself to artistic or romantic rejection, she's rather starting to suspect that she is destined to die a ninety-year-old waitress, single and surrounded by cats.

Alba sits on the floor of her childhood playroom, leaning against the piano. It's far from her favourite room – the piano holds particularly painful memories – but it's also the last place her siblings

90

will look for her. And for that, she's prepared to endure echoes of sorrow. The playroom has never contained toys because Alba's father didn't believe in them. Everything was educational: science kits, maps, globes, an abacus with wooden beads, diagrams of the Pythagorean theorem, exact replicas of major historical battles . . . Alba spent hours here as a child, before her father disappeared and she was sent to Cheltenham Ladies' College.

And, if growing up alone in a cold, silent mansion was bad, then being sent away to boarding school turned out to be even worse. At last, Alba thought, she'd have friends, companions to confide in and share secrets with. But when Alba told the other girls that she could see sounds and smells, they didn't respond as enthusiastically as she thought they would. Even though Alba promised she couldn't see their thoughts, the girls in her class were still scared she'd discover their secrets, their hopes and fears, that she'd know when they wet their beds, cried for their mummies, or stole cookies from the kitchen. So they shunned and teased her and called her a liar. When the tormenting spread to the rest of the school, Alba stopped trying to make friends and instead sought refuge in the library. It was there she discovered worlds far more wonderful than hers, populated by characters so captivating and lives so sensational that it was quite easy, after a few pages, to forget about her own life.

By the time she reached university, Alba had given up trying to befriend anyone with a beating heart and pretended she was only truly interested in fiction and in historical fact, learning about lives that would reward her with excellent examination marks. So, when she met Dr Skinner, the first person who seemed to see behind her pretences and into her heart, it didn't take Alba long to fall in love.

At first it didn't matter that her feelings were unrequited. But as they spent more time together, Alba began trying to win the love she wanted so much. She stole library books so she could stay up all night, uncovering obscure research, creating brilliant and complex theories to convince Dr Skinner she was someone worth loving. After nearly a year of unfulfilled longing, Alba would do anything for a kind word or suggestive smile. When Dr Skinner agreed to be her MPhil supervisor, there was nothing she wouldn't have done in return. So, when her esteemed and beloved supervisor asked for help in writing a paper on marriage in Victorian England, Alba didn't hesitate to say yes.

Zoë doodles hearts around the edges of her page. Hearts are so much more clichéd than lightning bolts, but she doesn't care. Love is a common, unoriginal emotion that turns people into simpering idiots who resort to the same terms of affection, gifts, silly iconography and the same tears when it all goes wrong.

Zoë has seen the love affairs and mating rituals of hundreds of students, like an anthropologist dedicated to the study of a cliché: how they circle each other, sneaking secret kisses behind the stacks, giggling with an optimistic, all-embracing *joie de vivre*, gazing out of windows for hours on end with smiles plastered across their faces, unable to focus. She sees how love breaks them when it leaves, splitting them open like pea pods, their hearts exposed, their eyes red, their souls much darker than before.

Zoë also sees the worst type of love, the sort that never illuminates those it afflicts but renders them perpetually raw: love of the unrequited kind. This is the one she knows best of all. She can identify it at five hundred paces, across a crowded room, behind closed doors. She can see the signs in anyone: the dazed gaze, the hollow eyes, the sallow complexion, the look of resigned despair tinged with the tiniest spark of hope. For it is the love she's infected with, and fellow sufferers can always recognise one another.

Zoë has often thought she ought to try to do something useful with her pain, like channelling it into a bestseller. But whenever she tries, she can't get past page one. Because when she writes it down, it's the same tale shared by a hundred thousand others, not worth the waste of paper or ink. So instead she absently fills the little hearts with A's.

Admiring her handiwork, Zoë thinks of another

'A' in her life, her colleague Andy, with whom she had a rather strange encounter last summer, one that momentarily knocked Zoë out of the monotonous ache of her own unrequited love. It began when Andy accidentally brushed against Zoë's breasts in the rare-book room while reaching for a first edition of *Salome*. He apologised, laughing, expecting Zoë to slap him. But she didn't. Instead she shocked herself by kissing him. Bemused by it, but never one to reject a pretty girl, Andy shrugged and kissed her back. It was an interaction they repeated once or twice a week for three months, until the students returned at the end of the summer and the library was too crowded to risk such encounters. After which they never touched or spoke about it again.

Zoë can't say she actually enjoyed it. It was an experiment, a foray to the other side. And even the shock of sexual experimentation didn't stop Zoë from thinking about the one she loved. For, even while she had allowed another 'A' to touch her lips, Alba Ashby remained firmly lodged in her heart.

The desire to run the hundred and fifty miles back to Hope Street wraps its fingers around Alba's heart and squeezes hard. She shivers with that fever all night, and the next day she doesn't go down to breakfast, lunch or dinner. Whiffs of colour float up to her room but she blows them away. She hears Charlotte, Edward and Charles arguing over funeral arrangements – their words black and spiked as they drift past her window. Alba wonders what her mother would have wanted.

Since visiting Elizabeth's bedroom, Alba hasn't slept well. She wonders who Ella was, why her father left and why her mother went mad. She stares at memories on the ceiling: random pictures passing like a reel of film haphazardly spliced together. In an odd way she feels closer to her mother now than she did when Elizabeth was alive. Hardly surprising, perhaps, since Lady Ashby spent the last decade of her life lost inside the mazes of her own mind, a labyrinth she could navigate only alone. So, even with her special sight, Alba couldn't see the directions to find her again.

Now, in the dark, Alba picks and chooses what she wants to remember – the moments Elizabeth wasn't manic or depressed. Reading bedtime stories together, holding hands while they walked around the garden, lying in the fields, skipping along the sand, searching rock pools for limpets and crabs . . . Alba's siblings rarely step into these memories, so she can enjoy her mother alone.

The day her father left was the start of losing her mother for good. But now she's finding her again, conjuring up Elizabeth's smile, her frown, the way she could look at ordinary things as if it was the first time she'd ever seen them. As milky moonlight seeps through the curtains, Alba's heart is so full of her mother it's as though she can not only see her but reach out and touch her. It's not until Elizabeth speaks that Alba realises she's really there, sitting at the end of the bed.

Quite the opposite of her daughter, Elizabeth is tall and willowy, with long curly blond hair the colour of sunlight. She wears a fitted white dress splashed with poppies that reminds Alba of Stella.

'I've got something to tell you,' Elizabeth says softly, 'but first you must stop hiding out here.'

Sleep-deprived, Alba thinks that perhaps she's dreaming, or having a particularly vivid memory. Either way, she has no idea what to say. A decade's worth of words swell inside her and slowly subside.

'Please, my love.' Elizabeth pats Alba's feet beneath the bed sheets.

Alba nods, tears spilling down her cheeks. Now she knows why the colours were so dazzlingly bright when she first came to Ashby Hall, because they've been infused with her mother's spirit, her faith, by the one person who cared about what Alba could see.

'Oh, Mum,' she whispers at last, 'I've missed you so much.'

CHAPTER 8

Because Alba and her siblings were the only guests at the funeral, the village church was quite empty; the vicar's words bounced off the walls and there was nowhere to look but at the coffin covered with calla lilies. Charlotte had been in charge of the floral arrangements, so everything was extremely tasteful, though Alba managed to sneak in a yellow tulip, Elizabeth's favourite, at the last minute.

Alba watched Edward cry, silent sobs that floated into the air in grey clouds. She knew he must be thinking of his wife's funeral a year earlier, and wished she could find the courage to hug him now as she hadn't been able to then. Charles and Charlotte were the same as always, cold and withdrawn, treating her like an unstable mental patient since her outburst. It probably seemed strange to them, then, that Alba didn't shed a single tear. But she couldn't, even for appearance's sake, because she was so happy at seeing her mother again, and would have felt quite odd crying for a woman who spent the funeral sitting next to her in the pew singing along to every hymn.

It was only when they buried her, when the last clod of earth dropped over the coffin, that Elizabeth Ashby's ghost disappeared. But she has returned to Alba in dreams so vivid she might as well be awake. And most wonderful of all, her mother is talkative, happy and sane. They walk through the grounds of Ashby Hall, Elizabeth in her poppy-splashed dress, her words shining gold, glistening in the light, every day brighter and closer to the colour of Stella's conversations.

'I've always loved these gardens,' Elizabeth says. 'It's where I came to be alone, before you, when I had three young children, when it all got to be too much. Nature is always so peaceful, so perfect.'

'I can't imagine you five years older than me with three kids,' Alba says. 'I can still barely look after myself. I don't think I'll ever be able to look after anyone else.'

'Well, perhaps one day you'll feel differently.' Her mother smiles. 'When you fall in love you might want children of your own.'

Alba frowns. She wonders if her mother knows more than she's letting on. They sit in silence, Alba plucking daisies in the grass, then discarding them. She still hasn't told her mother about Dr Skinner, about the betrayal and heartbreak, failing her MPhil, losing her scholarship and, of course, her biggest secret of all. She wonders if Elizabeth already knows and she's just waiting to be told, the way she used to wait for Alba to confess to things as a little girl.

But it's Elizabeth who speaks first. 'You couldn't have saved me. You do know that, don't you? I was always hovering on the edge. And when Charles left there were . . . complications that just tipped me over it.'

What? Alba wants to ask. *What happened?* But she waits. 'I'm sorry, I'm sorry you were so sad.'

'I know, love,' Elizabeth says, 'me too. But more than anything I'm sorry I wasn't a better mother to you.' She sighs and, for a moment, she seems about to say something else, but instead she stands and together they walk on in silence, over hills and through woods, stopping to look at flowers: wild roses, honeysuckle and hollyhocks. They follow the tracks of foxes until they disappear, and listen to birdcalls: doves, magpies, sparrows and the distant bleats of sheep.

Alba longs to hold her mother's hand and squeeze it tight. Instead she turns and looks at Elizabeth, at her blue eyes and blond hair, at her smile and her white dress splashed with poppies, staring until the memory is imprinted forever.

Peggy has never been a reader. She can't focus on words floating in front of her on a page, and prefers films. Her knowledge of these, thanks to Harry, is great indeed. Sometimes they watch them in bed on Sunday afternoons, and on special occasions they return to the cinema. Her favourite film to date is *Kind Hearts and Coronets* and she'll never forget the day she met Joan Greenwood, who played Sibella.

The actress visited on the occasion of Peggy's fifty-fourth birthday. She was rehearsing a new play, she said, and wanted to see the house again, to remind herself of details she'd forgotten from her stay nearly twenty years earlier. The house rule permitted residents to return only if they hadn't stayed for their full ninety-nine days the first time. And since Joan had spent only a month when she was thirty-one, Peggy could allow her back. They sat in the kitchen upstairs, eating slices of birthday cake. At least Joan did, while Peggy just poked at hers with a fork.

'Would you care to talk about it?' Joan asked in her famous drawl, sending a little shiver of excitement through Peggy. How could she unburden herself to a film star? But she spent so much time taking care of strangers that sometimes she just wanted to blurt out everything to passersby in the street.

'It's just,' Peggy mused, 'I've been thinking, about things, choices . . .'

Joan waited, sipping her tea.

'I've never been in love,' Peggy said. 'I've never let myself. Because, if I'm not allowed to marry, then what's the point?' As soon as she said it, Peggy realised how strange it sounded. She waited for the questions about why she wasn't allowed to marry, or let a man live at Hope Street, but Joan said nothing. Peggy gave a little sigh of relief, knowing that she'd picked the right person to unburden herself to.

'Sometimes I wonder if I'm missing out,' Peggy

continued. 'But then I never want to leave the house. And, if that's the price I have to pay, I suppose it's all right.'

'We all have to make choices,' Joan said. 'Since we can't have two lives, only one. But, most of those choices we make fresh every day, not just once. So, if you regret something, if you want to change your mind, you usually can.'

'Yes, I suppose so,' Peggy said. 'The only problem is when you don't know what you want.'

Alba is bumping along in the back seat of Edward's brand-new Beetle, gripping the door handle in an effort to squeeze against Tilly's empty car seat and avoid accidentally knocking into her sister. Charlotte stares stolidly ahead, in a huff because they haven't taken her Mercedes. She hasn't travelled at a speed of less than a hundred miles an hour since the day she passed her test, and claims Edward drives more slowly than their dead grandmother.

'Why are we taking this little thing?' Charlotte sniffs, 'you've got an Audi.'

'It's in the garage,' Edward says through clenched teeth, 'as I told you this morning. Twice.' He glances in the mirror, trying to catch his little sister's eye, to check he's not upsetting her.

Drifting away from her siblings' fighting, Alba closes her eyes and sees Dr Skinner's face. She tries to block it out, but can't. Her defences are down. Thoughts mill around her mind with a force of their own, pushing into her personal space like unwanted guests at a dinner party. So Alba surrenders to the dark brown hair and brown eyes, the smile that fools you into thinking its owner is pure and true, not a conniving, cunning snake who'd steal your thoughts as soon as look at you. Alba opens her eyes again, staring into the bright sunshine until the image floats away.

'Stop worrying,' Charles says from the front seat. 'We'll make it and, if we don't, Stone will wait for us.'

'Unless he's due in court,' Charlotte says.

'Oh, do shut up,' Edward sighs.

And so it goes for the next hour, until they reach London. It's the first time Alba has ever had occasion to visit their solicitors, the most prestigious firm in the city, but she knows the Ashby family have been clients of Stone & Stone for well over a hundred years, they pioneered one of the first divorce cases in Britain when the seventh Lord Ashby claimed, fraudulently as it turned out, that his wife had been unfaithful with his brother.

As they park and hurry along the streets, Alba lags behind a little, unable to suppress a niggling sense that something is wrong, that she shouldn't be going with them. When they reach the solicitors' offices she stops on the pavement with an overwhelming feeling of dread.

'It's a bloody miracle we're not three days late.' Charlotte sweeps past the rest of them, striding through the sliding glass doors of Stone & Stone.

'At least we made it here in one piece,' Edward retorts, 'instead of ending up in a twenty-car pileup on the M4.'

'Shut up, both of you,' Charles snaps. He reaches the front desk and aims a smile at the pretty redheaded receptionist. 'We're here to see Mr Stone.' His voice is soft and smooth as golden syrup. 'We have an appointment at noon.'

Tiago is still visiting Carmen's dreams, refusing to let her forget him. Sometimes she dreams of the good, sometimes the bad, but it always leaves her shivering in a cold sweat. Tonight she dreams of their first duet. Six months after they met, Carmen had woken early to find him sitting at his piano. She had stood in the doorway watching him, completely and utterly captivated. It seemed to her that he wasn't sitting at the piano but floating a few feet above it, carried on the waves of his music.

She walked across the room and sat down at the piano beside him. Tiago began to play her favourite piece, Mozart's sixth quartet, and she played along with him. He shifted to the first of Vivaldi's *Four Seasons* and still she followed, despite the fact she'd been learning for only a few months. Then Tiago stopped. He began to play a piece of his own. As the notes floated through the air Carmen felt as though Tiago were tying ropes of silk around her waist, tethering her so she'd never be able to leave. That was the night he asked her to marry him, and when Carmen said yes, it was the happiest moment of her life.

A few hours later Carmen sits at the kitchen table, red-eyed and yawning, nibbling her way through a packet of chocolate biscuits, gulping down black coffee. The house is silent and still, so quiet in fact that she's a little unnerved. Pots and pans sit in the sink, waiting to be cleaned. Carmen glances at the copper frying pan balanced on top, about to topple. With a shiver, she thinks of Tiago, of blood and bones and beatings, worrying about how safe she really is.

Just then the door bumps open and Peggy shuffles in, wrapped in her patchwork dressing gown, her wild white hair even messier than usual.

'Morning,' she mumbles, passing by the table, focusing on the floor.

'*Ola*.' Carmen looks up, surprised. 'Why you up so early?'

Peggy shuffles to the fridge. 'I need cream. And coffee.'

'I make it.' Carmen stands.

'Oh, you're a dear.' Peggy slides into the nearest chair. 'Four sugars, please.'

'So, why you up so early?' Carmen flicks the kettle on.

'Give me a moment to join the living,' Peggy says, 'and I'll tell you.'

They sit in silence as the coffee boils, until Carmen hands Peggy a hot mugful. Grateful for the absence of a tarot card, she gulps mouthfuls and then, with a happy sigh, wipes her lips. 'Perfect, thank you, pet. Now,' she says brightly, all traces of tiredness gone, 'I have a favour to ask. I've a chum who runs a choir, an amateur thing. They've got some sort of performance coming up, probably just in a village hall full of deaf pensioners. Well, she needs another voice and I told her I know just the one.'

Carmen stares at Peggy with wide, disbelieving eyes. '*A serio?*'

'Oh yes, entirely.' Peggy grins, taking another gulp of coffee. 'Do you think I'd get out of bed before six, just for a joke?'

'But . . . I don't sing with other people to watch,' Carmen says. 'Not yet, no.'

'Oh, I think you can.'

'Your friend, who is she?'

'Well, yes, I suppose "friend" might be stretching it a little,' Peggy admits. 'It might've taken me a while to find her, but she's real enough.'

Carmen thinks of that fateful duet with Tiago, scared that if she sings in public again, somehow he'll hear. Peggy digs into the pockets of her dressing gown and hands Carmen a note. She takes it and slowly reads aloud:

Courage is mastery of fear – not absence
of fear.
– Mark Twain.

'It came to me this morning,' Peggy says, 'but I believe it was meant for you.'

105

'Who is Mark Twain?' Carmen asks, unconvinced.

'He was a great American writer and lover of my great-great aunt Anne, or so she'd have us believe. She had an affair with him and with Faulkner. Allegedly.'

'Oh, *sim*,' Carmen nods, though she doesn't understand at all. She fingers the note.

'It's vaguely possible, I suppose. Anyway, she loves to quote them every chance she gets, just to remind us all. You know, dear,' Peggy says, 'courageous acts can be a good way of exorcising demons.'

Carmen, hearing the change in her tone, glances up, alert.

'I know you're running away,' Peggy says, 'but you can't run forever. You have to dig up what you buried. Its spirit is too strong for the house to suppress. I'm afraid you're going to have to deal with it yourself. And quickly, before it's too late.'

Carmen looks at the old lady as though she's seen a ghost. She shouldn't be surprised that Peggy knows. She doesn't want to ask, *Too late for what?* But since those are the only words in her mouth, she can't speak. It's a long, dark moment before she finally nods.

Greer has caved. She's said yes to the charming American. He has finally worn her down. Not that it took very much, she has to admit. Now she sits inside her wardrobe, swamped by dresses: silk, satin, velvet, cotton and lace. Plain, colourful, short, long, casual, chic: every conceivable look for every conceivable occasion. And Greer has to pick one. She lies down, closes her eyes, sticks her hand in the air and points. Then she opens her eyes and follows her finger.

The first thing Greer sees is a long, delicate shift dress of green silk. She stands, lifts it carefully from the hanger, walks out of the wardrobe and slips it on. The dress is cut low down her back, exposing her white skin even below the drop of her long red curls. The front is a single column of colour that matches and lights up her eyes. Now she needs footwear. She scans the field of scattered shoes that is her bedroom floor and spots a perfect pair of silver slippers. Now she has ten minutes for make-up.

Half an hour later they're sitting in a black leather booth at the back of Blake's favourite restaurant. As the waiter pours from a bottle of rather expensive merlot, Blake grins, and Greer feels as though she's blinking into a light bulb.

'Well, well, Red,' Blake says, 'what a knockout you are.'

'My dad used to call my mum Red.' Greer smiles. 'Before he knocked her up. *The Philadelphia Story* is her favourite film. We both worship Katharine Hepburn. And Cary Grant, too, of course.'

'Of course.' Blake grins. 'And what did he call her after?'

'After what? Oh, yes, I see. Nothing. He left. I never met him.'

'Sure.' Blake nods as though he wouldn't have

expected anything else. 'My mama left us when I was six.'

'Oh?' Greer asks. She's touched that they have this in common, together with a love of Katharine Hepburn films. 'I'm sorry to—'

'Hey.' Blake shrugs as if to suggest it's a tragedy he's long since put behind him, as if he never wakes in the middle of the night, alone and scared and feeling six years old again, as if he doesn't like to keep his bed populated to avoid this very occurrence. 'I haven't seen her in near about twenty years, I can't even remember her.' He reaches for his glass and takes a gulp of merlot, swallowing down this careless lie. For although he can't recall her face, and must rely on photographs, he remembers the smell of her, Lily of the Valley face cream and perfume, and how she felt when he clasped her close, burying his face in her breasts. It is a scent that returned to him when Greer stepped into his life and it nearly stopped his heart. It's the reason he hired her, the reason he asked her out.

Blake puts down his glass and gazes thoughtfully at Greer, his veneer momentarily rattled. 'You remind me of her some,' he admits – a half-truth. 'So well fixed up all the time. I never seen someone so well dressed come to work in a bar.'

Greer would have been touched by the compliment – had she heard it. But all she can think is that he's twenty-six. Thirteen years younger than her. Greer reaches for her own glass and drinks, tipping her head back, until it's empty, then wipes her mouth. 'I'm an actress,' she blurts out – as though he'd asked, as though this explains every-thing. She regrets it the second she says it and waits for the critique of her lifestyle she knows is coming. After all, why would a successful actress work in a bar?

But Blake surprises her. 'That's cool,' he says, once again reminding her how young he is. 'I'm a writer. Hey,' he smiles, 'maybe I can write something for you to star in.'

'Really? Well.' She puts on a southern accent, a joke to hide her delight. 'My, my, that would be simply marvellous.'

Blake laughs. 'So, what d'ya wanna eat? I'm figuring on bangers, mash and beer. I think that sounds pretty darn delicious.' He draws out every syllable of the last word, sucking all the juice from the letters, and Greer stares at his lips. She nods, now thinking only of what it might be like to kiss him.

'I don't understand.' Alba sits in the solicitors' office, a shoebox of letters on her lap. 'Why would she leave these to me?'

'Elizabeth didn't inform us of the reasons why,' Mr Stone explains. 'She only requested we retain them, and pass them to you upon her death.'

'But why me?' Alba asks. 'They aren't mine.' She lifts a letter out of the box. It's addressed to her mother in a tiny black scrawl. The postmark is dated 1989. Nearly a decade before the divorce of Prince Charles and Lady Di. Three years before her birth. Suddenly she's afraid to ask any more questions.

'As I say, she didn't leave us any further instructions,' says Mr Stone, 'so perhaps, if you'll permit me, I'll continue with the will.'

Charlotte sighs. Edward shoots her a look. Alba frowns, her welling sense of dread now threatening to overflow. The black smoke of deceit circles the room, as if Mr Stone had lit a fire under his desk and everything was burning.

Charlotte says, 'I think it's about time we—'

'Don't, Lottie,' Edward warns. 'Not yet.'

'Why not? You can't keep it from her now, can you? I'm glad she'll finally know.' Charlotte crosses her legs. 'And then we can all drop this ridiculous charade.'

'Know what?' Alba's lungs are filling with the smoke. The crisp leather chairs and cream carpets are shifting. She's losing her grip on the box. 'What?'

Surprisingly, Charlotte keeps her mouth shut. Edward glares at Charles, who shrugs and says nothing, while Mr Stone continues reading the will as though nothing was wrong. But all Alba can think about are the letters sitting in her lap, weighing down their paper box until her legs are numb, her fingers white and drained of blood. When it's time to leave, Alba can't get up. She stares at Edward helplessly. While Charlotte and

Charles wait impatiently in the foyer, Edward persuades Mr Stone to let Alba stay in his office to read the letters, while they take him out for an expensive lunch.

'Do you know what these are?' Alba asks Edward as he is about to close the door. 'Do you know what they say?'

'No,' Edward says softly, 'not exactly.'

His words mix together in green and black, the colour of truth and lies. His aura is still as grey as it was when his wife died. 'But you know something, don't you?' Alba says. 'Why won't you tell me?'

'It's probably best this way.' Edward falters, hoping that's true. 'It seems this is how Mother wanted it.'

Alba looks down at the box and forgets to look up again. After a minute of watching her, of wishing he could undo years of lies, Edward gently closes the door behind him.

Several hours later, after a long and liquid lunch, the siblings return to Stone & Stone to find Alba gone. Charles questions the pretty receptionist, who says Alba left an hour ago.

'Oh, for God's sake.' Charlotte sighs. 'What are we supposed to do now?'

'Go home,' Charles says. 'She'll be there. She probably couldn't stand another endless bickering trip up the M4, and took a train.'

'Good point,' Charlotte says. 'I should do the same.'

'Shut up,' Edward snaps, 'and have a little sensitivity. How the hell must she be feeling now, knowing every minute of her life was a lie?'

'Oh, don't be so bloody dramatic,' his brother says. 'She'll be fine. Let's go. By the time she gets home, she'll be fine.'

'She'll be better than I will,' Charlotte says, 'after another three hours in your car.'

'Well, then,' Edward says, ignoring her, 'let's get a bloody move on.'

He doesn't want to leave Alba alone for long, just in case she's not okay at all. He wants to invite her to stay with him and Tilly in London for a while, to answer some of the hundreds of questions she'll have. But he won't be able to, because Alba isn't going home, at least not to Ashby Hall. While Edward is unlocking his car, Alba is sitting on the train back to Cambridge, clutching a shoebox to her chest.

CHAPTER 9

Alba sits on her bedroom floor with the shoebox in her lap.

She's read every letter, every poem, is familiar with every endearment, turn of phrase, every sentence steeped in love and longing. Reading them took a while; the words were blurred by Alba's tears. But it all makes sense now. This is why her father left, why her siblings hated her. She'd always thought she was just the new baby who stole their thunder. But she was so much worse. She was their half sister, the constant reminder of her mother's betrayal. When did they find out? she wonders. How long have they known?

Alba leans against her bookshelves and shuts her eyes. A soft wind whistles through the pipes in the wall, a low, sorrowful tone matching her mood exactly. She thinks of her father. Or rather, the man she believed to be her father. When did he discover that she wasn't really his daughter? And does this mean he's still alive? Memories of Lord Ashby are scarce but Alba dredges the depths of her blank, black mind for something.

The first picture she sees is the piano in the playroom at Ashby Hall. Her mother bought it, a miniature version of the Steinway grand that furnished the foyer, for Alba's seventh birthday. A tutor came every Wednesday afternoon at four o'clock, until it became clear that musicality was not one of Alba's talents, and the piano was left to look pretty and collect dust.

Then one night, Alba couldn't sleep, so she crept downstairs to her playroom to find a favourite doll she'd forgotten was there. Moonlight streamed in through the windows, falling in silver stripes across the piano's shiny black surface, and suddenly it seemed magical, as spooky as a coffin, as enticing as a forbidden room.

Alba crept over to the piano and slid onto the stool. She pushed at a soft pedal with her bare foot and slowly pressed the keys. Muffled notes slipped into the air and Alba listened. What had sounded dull and simple during the day, at night became exciting and eerie. Intrigued, Alba explored every ivory key. The notes were still a jumbled racket, but in the darkness she started to hear words floating into her head. They looped around, linking together, sliding and colliding in rhythms and rhymes. Alba jumped off the stool, ran across the room, found a notebook and a crayon and started scribbling her words on the page so she wouldn't forget the little songs. After that Alba crept downstairs every night to hit random notes and write down the words that came with them. Then, one evening, her father walked past the playroom. He stopped and frowned.

'Alba.'

'Hello, Papa.' Alba quickly sat on her hands and chewed at her lip.

'It would be a shame,' he said at last, 'to waste your time believing you have talent for something when you have none. Don't you agree?'

Alba nodded slowly, her wet eyes glued to his face. 'The world is filled with fools. You wouldn't want to be another one, would you?'

Alba shook her head.

'Good.' And with that, he turned and walked away.

Alba sits very still as the smoky remnants of her memory evaporate. Then, with a little sigh, she stands, shuffles across the room, opens the door and peeks into the corridor. Just before reaching the bathroom Alba stops at a photograph of a young woman with big eyes and a sleek bob, wearing strings of pearls and a collar of silk. Alba knows she's seen her before, but can't for the moment place her. And then she realises she's staring at the author of one of her very favourite novels.

'*Rebecca*,' Alba whispers. 'I mean, Miss du Maurier, sorry. Oh my goodness. I didn't see you before, I . . .'

'Well, well.' Daphne smiles. 'At last she speaks.'

Alba flushes, suddenly self-conscious. 'I adore

your books,' she says softly. '*Last night I dreamt I went to Manderley again. It seemed to me . . .*'

'No, no.' Daphne holds up a delicate hand. 'Please don't.'

'Gosh, I'm sorry,' Alba says again, 'you must get that all the time.'

'Less and less as the years pass,' Daphne admits, 'but, flattering though it is, I'd still rather have a real conversation with you.'

'Yes, of course.' But Alba has no words worthy of this grand dame of English literature, so she simply stands in silence and smiles, utterly star struck.

'Well, all right then, if you've nothing to say to me, then I've got something to say to you. So listen up,' Daphne declares with a flourish. 'There is no going back in life. No return. No second chance. When you waste your days, they are wasted forever. So be honest about the things you really want, and do them, no matter how fearful you might be.'

Alba frowns, a little taken aback. 'Gosh, well, I . . . The thing is, I'm not really sure what I want any more. I thought I wanted something, but now I'm not—'

Daphne looks up, her gaze so sharp it unnerves Alba. 'Stop lying to yourself,' she says. 'You know exactly what you want, you're just too scared to admit it.'

Peggy sits in her kitchen with Mog on her lap. She understands now, after so many thwarted attempts, that there is clearly no point asking the damn door to open any more. In sixty-one years she's never had a problem getting into the room, whenever she needed help or advice, she always got it. But she's now being denied entry and, though Peggy can't understand why, she thinks there must be some strange sense to it. Indeed, she's starting to wonder whether or not the house actually wants her to find a successor. Perhaps it's had enough, like her, it's too old and exhausted to want anything else but peace and quiet. Perhaps it simply wants to retire. In which case, it might very well get its way. So perhaps she should simply abandon the house to its fate and live out the remainder of her life with Harry, a prospect that is becoming more and more tempting as the days go by and death starts tapping on her shoulder.

Peggy tickles Mog behind his ears. He gives her a quick pitiful look before jumping off her lap and padding across the room with his tail in the air. She sips her tea, tasting sweeter memories of the days when the Abbot family was fertile and full of candidates wanting to inherit the house. When Peggy was a little girl, and her great-aunt Esme inhabited the tower, all her sisters, cousins and distant relatives aspired to the position. Though none more than Peggy.

She wasn't born with the gift, at least her mother didn't think so. She was the last of seven sisters, unexpected though not unwanted. And by the time she arrived, everyone already thought her oldest sister, Julia, would inherit the house. But Peggy was determined and, like a marathon runner in training for the Olympics, she prepared. While her sisters chased boys and stole their mother's make-up, Peggy meditated on her goals and practised her gifts, until the tiny sparks finally caught fire and burnt within her so strongly that no one could overlook her any more.

Peggy remembers the day she was chosen more clearly than any other day of her life. It was her thirteenth birthday. Esme invited her to tea, fed her slices of the three-tiered chocolate cake, explained all the rules, introduced her to Mog (then called Ginger) and took her into the forbidden room. This was the most anticipated moment, for every Abbot girl had grown up with the legend, spending innumerable hours in speculation, desperate to discover the truth.

The room's contents certainly surpassed all of Peggy's expectations and she longed to tell her jealous sisters, each of whom was born on the first of May, all about it. But it was a secret she'd have to keep forever, along with everything else she learnt that day.

From her kitchen window Peggy watches the sun setting behind her willow trees, feeling as though the same energy is draining from her, too, as if her light is gently going out. As the sky darkens Peggy notices the violet glow from the midnight glory has crept around to the back garden. It won't be long now before it exposes everything and the house will be visible to everyone. Peggy surveys the garden. She knows that, even if she might want to desert her post for a little late-in-life hedonism, she'll never do it. However much she might love Harry, she owes the house more.

Greer has stepped onto a film set, and everything is illuminated and in Technicolor. She sees him every day, and nearly every night. Now she knows how Katharine Hepburn felt, sharing all those films with Spencer Tracy. In the few days since their first date, their first kiss, since the greatest sex of her life, she hasn't even bothered looking for acting jobs. She's stopped worrying, she's stopped feeling like a failure.

Greer knew she shouldn't sleep with Blake on their first date, but when he invited her back to his flat, she simply hadn't been able to say no. It was past midnight and they'd both crept upstairs like thieves. When the bedroom door closed they fell against each other frantically, kissing and grasping, pulling and tugging at clothes. Crashing onto the bed, Greer pulled away for a moment. 'Oh my God,' she gasped, 'this is crazy.'

Blake said nothing, just slid his hand up her leg, green silk sliding over his fingers. The moon escaped the clouds and cast a pale light across the bed, illuminating them both as he smiled and began, ever so softly, to kiss her skin.

'Oh, damn it,' Greer sighed, her breath catching

in her throat as his fingers reached the tops of her thighs. He kissed her belly, reached for her breasts and lingered there before moving on to her neck, her ears, her hair . . . When Blake at last returned to her thighs, Greer's breath quickened until she couldn't hear anything except the rush of blood in her ears. 'Yes, don't stop,' she begged, 'please . . . Yes, that's it, yes, yes . . .'

It's midnight now, on a Monday night, and Greer hurries along the street toward The Archer. Blake invited her to meet him at the end of his shift and she's late. At the door she stops to catch her breath and fluff her hair. Inside, someone is playing the piano. The music is soft and gentle. The notes drift out to Greer, who swallows them like raindrops. Then, while she surrenders to the sounds (just as she surrendered to Blake), the music shifts, suddenly high-pitched and sharp. Before Greer can close her mouth she's swallowed something else, bitter and sharp, and she wonders if it might be a warning of what's to come.

Alba sits at the kitchen table, staring into a cup of cold, black coffee, half-listening to the photographs chattering away to each other. Since speaking to Daphne du Maurier, Alba now hears the photographs all the time, winking and whispering as she walks past. Last night they woke her with some sort of strange chorus, the colours filling her room like fireworks. For a moment she was scared, but then her fear evaporated. For something has taken hold of Alba now, a fire of her own, and suddenly she's no longer the scared little girl she once was. She had spent her whole life trying to get the love and approval of everyone else, only to find out most people are liars and frauds. She's not going to do that any more. The deception of Dr Skinner no longer stings so sharply, is now tainted not with sadness and longing but with hatred and anger. Though that betrayal seems almost nothing compared with the one orchestrated by her own family.

She stares into the cauldron of coffee, thinking of the three witches in *Macbeth* and how her life seems to be spiralling out of control as quickly as his did. The last few days have torn Alba's history apart, splintering her memories, fracturing her sense of self. Half her genes were provided by a man named Albert. She is a cuckoo, a cliché, the product of illicit love and lies, of her mother's affair with some penniless poet, kindled over their shared love of *A Room with a View*.

At least now she understands why she loves books so much, why she's always dreamt of being a writer. But how could she not have known? How could she not have sensed it? How could she see sounds and smells, ghosts and auras, and not see herself? And how did anything else matter when she couldn't see where she came from, when she couldn't see the truth of who she really was?

When Stella appears in the sink Alba looks up

from her coffee and tells the ghost the details of every letter, every poem, every moment and line of her mother's love affair. Stella sits silently and listens to it all. She feels the fury in Alba's heart as though it's in her own chest, but it doesn't worry her. Not being blessed with breath or life, the ghost is also relieved of some of its more irksome qualities: fear, guilt, loneliness, the need to stop those you love from feeling any pain. She knows that Alba needs to feel it before she can move on.

The only thing that balances Alba's shock and sadness at the discovery of her paternity is her happiness at the rediscovery of her mother. Since Alba fled Ashby Hall, Elizabeth has visited her daughter every evening in her dreams. They talk and hold hands and walk across the world, sometimes spending the night at the Sydney Opera House or outside the Shaolin Temple or at the bottom of the Grand Canyon. But most of the time they sit on the roof of the King's College chapel, watching Cambridge while it sleeps. Alba had feared that leaving Ashby Hall would mean leaving Elizabeth behind, so the first night she appeared, Alba was so surprised and delighted to see her mother that she woke herself up. But she is so used to the nocturnal visits now that she closes her eyes expecting them. In the morning Alba can never remember what they talked about, but she always wakes feeling lighter and brighter than when she went to bed. That feeling lasts until she opens her eyes and stretches and remembers the fact of her absent father again.

All of a sudden, a warning whistles through the pipes and the kitchen door bumps open. Stella disappears and Alba looks up to see Carmen walk in. She doesn't sashay this time, and her clothes are tight but not bright, her hair is pulled back into a bun, every curl contained. She stands behind a chair, her hands resting on the curve of the wood. 'It's okay if I sit?'

No, Alba wants to say, *I'd rather you leave me and Stella alone.* But the ingrained politeness of a private education overrides her impulses, and she slips into good manners and nods.

'I am very sorry for your mother,' Carmen says softly. 'I think not to bother you, I know you like to be alone, but . . .'

Alba looks up, surprised.

'But I hope still maybe we can be friends.'

Alba looks more closely at Carmen. Purple bruises still linger under her dress, seeping into the air and staining her aura. Alba has no idea what's happened to her housemate but the dark shadows hovering over her heart are unnerving. Uneasy under the intense stare, Carmen breaks the silence.

'I hope you will come to my bar,' she says. 'I know you do not love the music, but I just want you to see . . .'

Alba feels a twinge of guilt, remembering her lie. Carmen's eyes are so vulnerable that, for a moment, Alba wants to help her. She nods.

'Really?' Carmen asks, delighted that she can finally put her plan to release the passions buried deep within Alba into action. 'When will you come? Tonight, tomorrow?'

'Okay,' Alba says, knowing she'll regret it. 'Tomorrow.'

'*Brilliante.* Come to my room before evening, Greer will help you' – she makes a sweep of Alba's person – 'with all this. You will look beautiful. You will have wonderful time. Maybe . . .' Carmen winks. 'Maybe we even find a boy for you.'

After Carmen leaves, Alba waits for Stella to reappear. She thinks of the letters, of the clues. She thinks of her mother, who scatters little secrets about Albert in her daughter's dreams, urging her to look for him and to contact Edward, who has secrets of his own to share and who, having been lost in widowerhood for too long, now wants to connect with his sister. Alba sighs.

'Okay, enough sighing.' Stella materialises in the sink. 'What are you going to do now?'

'I'm thinking about it.'

'Enough thinking. You think too much,' Stella says. 'It's time to take action. '

'I'm not ready.'

'If you wait until you're ready, you'll be dead,' Stella says. 'And, as a life strategy, I don't really recommend it.'

Despite herself Alba smiles.

'What do you want to do?' Stella asks. 'That's the only question that really matters.'

124

The ghost looks at Alba then with such a pure and truthful gaze, unencumbered by exception or judgment, that Alba feels suddenly free. Her fear evaporates, leaving only her desire.

'I want to find my father.'

Stella smiles.

CHAPTER 10

What's it like to have a daughter who doesn't know you exist? For Albert Mackay, it's as though he's only half alive. Because, if Alba can't see him, can't touch him, then how does he know he's really here, a living, breathing man and not simply a fictional character?

When Elizabeth Ashby told him she couldn't abandon her other children, that she had to try and make her marriage work, to bring Alba up as Charles's daughter, she asked Albert to move away. She said it was too painful knowing he was nearby, close enough but impossible to touch. And so he did, for both their sakes. He knew that walking down the same streets they'd walked together, fearful of bumping into his lover and their giggling baby would be too painful to bear. Albert moved as far as he could while remaining in the same country, so he'd know he was breathing the same air and seeing the same sunset as the daughter who would never know him.

When he moved to Inverie, the most remote village in Scotland (at the time not connected to the mainland by road, with Glasgow a boat trip and five-hour train ride away), Albert thought he could pretend the rest of the world didn't exist, that there wasn't another man out there raising his daughter and sharing a bed with the love of his life. Unfortunately, Albert soon found it wasn't any easier to bear the pain of this from a distance of four hundred and ninety-one miles than it was from three.

Albert got a job in the local primary school, but being with the ten children all day, teaching them to spell and make sense of Shakespeare, pushed him over the edge. And, when he fell, it was into broken glass. Every night he finished a bottle of wine and five inches of brandy. At midnight, he smashed the empty bottles against the stone wall at the bottom of his garden so that over the years the soil was covered with layers and layers of multi-coloured glass. Every year on Alba's birthday he drank a bottle of champagne and an unspecified amount of vodka until he passed out.

And then, on her seventh birthday, he stopped. He had a dream the night before, the most vivid experience of his life. In it his daughter was crying, begging him to come and save her from something. When he woke, her terror and need for him was just as visceral as it had been in the middle of the night. It felt like a prophecy. That day he stopped drinking. Just in case. Just in case his daughter ever needed him. As the weeks went by Albert imagined that somehow, over distance and logic, if Alba ever needed him he would know, he would feel her. And, if and when that miraculous day ever came, he wanted to be sober for it.

Greer can feel herself starting to fall. She's forgetting about food, clothes and all the minor practicalities of life and instead thinks only of him. Blake has bitten her, entered her bloodstream and left her drugged. She walks around in a fog of desire, feeling him watching and waiting to pounce. It's a troubling development, since she had planned on keeping things casual, on allowing it to go only so far – an experience in light entertainment, not a full-blown epic. This isn't because she couldn't fall in love with him but because she deeply suspects he couldn't fall in love with her. Blake doesn't strike her as the type to mess around in the muckiness of deep emotions.

Greer suspects it's the sex that's done it. Her mother always warns her that sex complicates things, that it's harder to remain aloof, to hold on to your own heart, once you've been marked by a man. Women, Celia always says, no matter how savvy and self-possessed, are always affected by sex. Even casual sex, she insists, has a way of tightening the strings. Greer and Blake have had sex every night since the first night: in the wine cellar, the alleyway behind The Archer, on a table after closing time . . . And every time, it's the very best sex of her life.

Of course Greer is no fool. She knows that most

men are repelled by needy women. She can sense these men, can smell them at a hundred feet. And Blake is one such man. So Greer pretends. She pretends she doesn't feel a thing, that she couldn't care a jot. And fortunately Greer's a good enough actress that she can pull off such a deception. She knows how to laugh, how to look, how to hold herself, as though he's not affecting her at all. All those drama lessons are now paying for themselves. Greer may not yet have had the chance to play Lady Macbeth but she can play the role of nonchalant female to a T.

Now she stands at the bar polishing glasses by candlelight, humming to herself, feigning disinterest in Blake while he counts the takings. She chats to the other employees, about customers and tips and where they're going on their summer holidays. It's nearly two o'clock in the morning before everyone else has gone home, before the place is deserted, empty and still.

'Right then, Red.' Blake steps behind the bar where Greer stands, and slips one hand up her back. A single shiver ripples down her spine. 'Let's go.'

For his part, Blake is rather surprised by how much he feels for Greer. Indeed he's surprised he feels anything at all, since it's not his habit to care for the women he sleeps with. But there is an ease about Greer, a carefree, footloose, happy-go-luckiness that feels freeing. It's also entirely refreshing – not a quality he very often encounters in his bedfellows. She doesn't seem to want to trap or contain him, she doesn't ask more from him than he wants to give and so Blake finds he wants to give more. He finds himself buying little presents, seeing things he knows she'll like and being moved to acquire them for her. He finds himself asking to see her every night. He catches himself thinking of her far too often. He notices himself absently gazing at her while she works. It is quite unlike him.

Blake wonders if he is maturing, following the rest of the human race toward monogamy and matrimony. Is his heart, for the first time, starting to win influence over his head? Might he be moved to break his vow never to let a woman weasel her way into his affections? But he can't. He mustn't allow it. The twenty-year-old crack in his heart has never really healed. Blake can declare that he doesn't care that his mother left him, but he knows it's a lie. He can tell himself he's made of stone, that he's superhuman, that nothing will ever hurt him, but he knows love could. And being left is something Blake refuses to endure again.

Carmen paces along the path outside the Clare College chapel. She glances up at the carved stone spires marking the four corners of the courtyard, reaching into the nearly dark sky. Three rows of windows, interrupted by staircases and the main entrance, run along each wall and vines of honeysuckle reach up from the flower beds to the roofs, framing everything. Lemony light from several windows shines out into the dusk, giant lanterns illuminate the courtyard.

The door to the chapel is open and the soft notes of a piano spill out into the air . . . but Carmen's still not ready to step inside.

She breathes deeply, trying to relax. Tonight she's wearing the conservative clothes befitting a college choir: a black sweater with a high neck and a long blue skirt that reaches her ankles. Admittedly both are tight but, having compromised with length, she drew the line at baggy. At last, Carmen takes another deep breath and walks through the open door. Like all good Catholic girls she went to church every Sunday, sitting between her father, who slipped a hand onto her thigh at the start of every service, and her mother, who pretended not to notice. But there was no church this beautiful in Bragança.

Carmen walks carefully down the aisle, glancing up at the delicate patterns engraved in the arches. She's never seen stained-glass windows so vast, so intricate, so colourful. Final glints of sunlight fall through them, illuminating the saints' feet, shining slices of red, green and gold across the wooden pews.

As she nears the pulpit Carmen sees two women, both very short and very fat, standing side by side like two barrels of beer in the cellar of The Archer.

'I'm Nora.' The first one grins and reaches out her hand. 'And this is Sue.'

'Or, rather, I'm Sue.' The other one steps forward and reaches out her hand. 'And this is Nora. I think that's the way it should be.' She looks at Carmen. 'Don't you agree?'

'I'm sure I don't.' Nora folds her arms. 'I introduced us perfectly well, without your embellishments.'

Carmen suppresses a smile. Now the two women don't remind her of beer barrels but Tweedledum and Tweedledee. This relaxes her a little.

'Are you Meg's friend?' Sue asks. 'She called last week, to ask if you could join us. Of course we said we'd be delighted. Can't have too many bats in the belfry I always say.'

'Yes,' Nora sighs, 'and I do wish you wouldn't.'

'Peg,' Carmen corrects Sue, 'Peggy.' She might have known this was a set-up. But now she's here, she can't very well run away. And, if she did, she has the feeling that these two would chase her.

'Yes, Peg, exactly,' Sue says, 'that's what I said. Anyway, enough talking, it's time to release the Kraken, it's time to sing!'

'But,' Carmen stalls, 'Peggy tell me this not serious choir, because I am not ready for—'

'Oh, don't worry about little old us,' Nora giggles, 'we're very casual, from our knickers to our socks, you'll fit right in. We only sing because we like to be loud.'

'Speak for yourself,' Sue huffs. 'Right, enough chitter-chatter, let's get on with it.'

She starts to hum. Nora joins in and soon the chapel is filled with song. The notes dance around Carmen, across the pews, soaring past the stained-glass windows, past the stone arches of the ceiling, before disappearing through the bricks and mortar and up into the sky. Carmen is enchanted, filled with a sense of serenity she's never felt before. And then, without a single thought in her head, she begins to sing.

This time her voice isn't soft and low but high, bright and strong. For a second it soars at perfect pitch above every other sound, then dips and sinks back to meet the other voices, twirling and twisting between them, collecting their scattered and solitary notes like a strong September wind that whips through a pile of autumn leaves and brings them, for one eternal moment, into a perfect and elegant dance. And then, all of a sudden Carmen realises something is wrong: the other two women have fallen quiet, hers is the only voice in the air. She shuts her mouth to see Nora and Sue staring, their own mouths hanging open.

'What?' Carmen asks. 'What is wrong?'

'Your voice,' Sue says, 'I've never heard anything like it. You're not a bat, you're an angel.'

'Quite, quite,' Nora exclaims. 'It's exquisite, simply exquisite! Don't you know it?'

Carmen bites her lip and thinks of Tiago. 'I not really sing very often.'

'Why on God's green earth do you not?' Nora cries. 'Your voice is so full of spirit, it bursts my

133

heart right open. Blooming heck, if I could sing like that I'd never talk again.'

Sue raises an eyebrow. 'Hardly.'

'Oh, shush,' Nora says, 'we're in the presence of greatness.' She reaches out and clasps Carmen's hands. 'Your voice, my dear, is divine.'

Carmen frowns, a little startled at the enthusiasm of Nora's embrace. 'Really? You think so?'

When both women nod so vigorously it seems that their heads are on springs, for a moment Carmen forgets Tiago. She forgets about the midnight glory, about being found out and every other fear that haunts her. Then she smiles, gazing at her two friends, until she has tears in her eyes.

When Alba made the biggest discovery of her career, she couldn't wait to tell her teacher. She ran all the way from the university library to King's College. She slipped along the cobbled paving stones in the rain, falling once in Burrell's Walk, but didn't stop for a second. Dashing across the quad, darting over the grass, she arrived at Dr Skinner's rooms nearly fainting and ready to throw up. Taking a few seconds to catch her breath, she knocked – far more vigorously and insistently than she usually dared.

'Yes?' Her supervisor's voice was impatient.

Alba poked her head around the door before stepping inside. Dr Skinner sat behind an enormous wooden desk in the corner. A twitchy student sat on the sofa across the room.

'Sorry,' Alba said quickly, 'sorry to interrupt, it's just I've found something, something incredible, and it changes everything.'

'Is this about the paper?'

Alba nodded.

'All right then, bugger off, Henry,' Dr Skinner snapped at the student. 'Come back next week when you've got something decent to show me.'

As the student scampered out, Alba walked slowly across the room, eager to tell everything but wanting to prolong the glory a moment longer.

'So.' Dr Skinner leant across the desk, eyes shining. 'What have you got?'

Alba looked into the deep brown eyes, pretending for a second they were shining with delight at seeing her. 'Five hundred letters to the *Daily Telegraph* in 1888, from people all over Britain, in answer to a question posed by Mona Caird: "Is Marriage Dead?"'

'But—'

'No, no one's written about them yet, I searched every database. Nothing. And it gets better.' Alba grinned. 'Only five hundred letters were published, but twenty-seven thousand people wrote in. The population stood at twenty-eight point one million in 1891, so—'

'One percent of the whole population.'

'Almost exactly, yes.'

'Well, that's bloody incredible. It's the best source material for our paper so far.' Dr Skinner gave her a rare and brilliant smile and, reaching across the desk, squeezed Alba's hand. For a second of unrestrained joy, Alba thought she might be about to have her first kiss. But then the smile shifted. 'How are we going to sift through all this in time? We need to submit at the end of next month to stand a chance of summer publication. I've got that Harvard conference to prepare for, you've got your MPhil research—'

'It's okay, I can do it,' Alba said quickly. 'My research can wait. We can't risk anyone else getting this.'

'Wonderful.' Dr Skinner smiled. 'And when I'm done with all this, then I'll help you with the write-up.'

Alba glanced down at their fingers entwined on the desk. 'Don't worry. You don't need to. I'll finish in time. You can look it over when you're back and we can publish it together.'

'My dear,' Dr Skinner said, kissing her hand, 'you are amazing, in every way.'

And it took every ounce of willpower Alba had not to faint on the spot.

Shaking free of the memory, Alba brings herself back to the task in hand: finding her father. She is sitting on her bed writing a list: Find out if he still lives on Inverie. Go to Inverie. His surname?

Call every family on the island, try to find him. Ask Ed if he knows anything, i.e. where/who he is. Check my birth certificate. Hire a private detective? If all else fails, go to Inverie.

Every now and then she stops, bites the tip of

her pen and glances up at the bookshelves, at the infinite and ever-expanding rows of books. She wonders which ones her biological father has read. Does he like the same books as she does? What else might they have in common? Alba wants to fall asleep, so she can see her mother and quiz her about Albert. But she knows it'd be no good – she never remembers their conversations. Still, the comfort of holding Elizabeth's hand, even in dreams, would be better than nothing.

In addition to writing the list, Alba's been re-reading the same letter over and over again for the last three hours, tracing her finger along the curves of the inky letters. It was the last letter, dated nearly eleven years after the first. She folds it up again and speaks the sentences softly, by heart . . .

Dove Cottage, Inverie,
Sunday, 31st October, 1999

My dearest Liz,
I love you. There, I've said it again. I hope you'll forgive me. I know I promised never to write. But I had a dream last night – I wont explain, in case this letter is found, but you see the date, so you'll guess – and I needed you to be able to contact me, just in case. I need you to know where I am. If you want to find me, I'm here. I'll wait for you. I won't leave. And don't worry about me wasting my life

waiting. I love you, there is nothing else for me to do.

I hope it all worked out, I like to imagine you happy. And I'm happy here, whenever I think of you. I look up at the stars at night, when you might be doing the same, or the sunset – I remember how you always loved all those colours – and I imagine you next to me. I talk to you. We have wonderful conversations and hardly ever argue. On your birthday I read our favourite book aloud, from beginning to end. Perhaps you hear me. If not, I hope he reads to you, I remember how much you love to be read to.

I know you won't write back to me. Don't worry, I don't expect it. But I do hope you'll keep the letter, hide it somewhere safe for one day, a maybe day, a just-in-case day . . . And if that day comes, I will be here, waiting for you.

Forever, Albert

He must *have known about her*, Alba thinks. The date, her seventh birthday, is surely too much of a coincidence? But perhaps it was something else: their anniversary, the day they met, kissed, or made love for the first time. How can she know for certain, unless she goes to Scotland to find him? But what if he doesn't want to see her? Could she stand the rejection? After the betrayal of the unmentionable one, would her heart finally

138

snap in half and never beat properly again? It's possible.

Alba's thoughts are interrupted by a rapid staccato knocking on her bedroom door. She sits up. No one has knocked since she moved in, nearly six weeks ago. Then, with a sigh, she remembers. It's tonight, the promised trip to The Archer. Now it's too late to come up with excuses. Alba swears under her breath, jumps off the bed and dashes to the door, finding Carmen and Greer on the other side.

'Oh,' Alba says, her heart sinking even lower, 'is this a group outing?'

'No.' Carmen smiles. 'Greer's just here to make you beautiful and dress you up.'

Alba grimaces at the thought of what this might entail. 'Is this really necessary?'

'Don't worry.' Greer takes her hand. 'Wait until you see my wardrobe. By the time we're done you'll be a showstopper.'

Alba suppresses a tiny scream. She can't imagine anything worse.

Two hours later Alba and Carmen are clattering across the cobble-stones in their heels. 'We will be late,' Carmen says. 'We must go faster.'

'It's okay, it's only ten to eight.' Alba wobbles, feeling her left ankle nearly give way, wondering what the hell she's doing. She's never worn high heels before in her life and feels tall and exposed. For the first time, too, she's wearing make-up:

black mascara with heavily kohled eyes which, even Alba was surprised to see, give her a striking, sparkling blue stare. Her lips are highlighted in dark red, her skin powder-white with a little blush on her cheeks. A sapphire silk dress matches Alba's eyes. Finished off with blue velvet shoes, the effect, much to Alba's shock and embarrassment, is quite breathtaking.

'Here we are.' Carmen slides to a stop on the pavement. A few moments later, Alba, heart beating fast, arrives at her side. She glances at the door, painted the colour of her lips, before Carmen pushes it open and steps into the darkness.

Alba is grateful for the candlelight. She can hardly see the faces of the people darting around her, flitting in and out of view like butterflies, and they can hardly see her. When they reach the bar Carmen turns to Alba. 'What you want first? I will pay.'

'Just a glass of water, please.'

Carmen frowns.

Alba shrugs. 'I'm hot.'

'What about wine?'

'I don't drink,' Alba admits, feeling like a child. 'I don't really like the taste.'

'Okay.' Carmen turns to the tall barman with big green eyes. 'Red wine, please, Blake, and one water for my beautiful friend.'

'My pleasure.' He flashes Alba a smile. 'Anything else I can get you?'

Alba shakes her head, unable, for a moment, to form words.

'Well, I'm here all night, at your beck and call.' Blake puts down the drink, the glass slipping soundlessly across the marble counter-top. Then, with a wink, he turns to serve another customer.

Carmen swallows a mouthful of wine and smiles. 'That's my boss. He's very cute, right?' she whispers into Alba's ear. Alba shivers slightly at the rush of Carmen's warm, boozy breath on her skin. Suddenly the room feels like a sauna. Her palms are slippery with sweat and she feels beads of condensation on her upper lip.

'The singer must be out soon,' Carmen says, 'she's late but not long now.'

Alba follows Carmen's gaze, preparing words to explain she's not ready for adventures involving bars and men who look like film stars. She is unwilling and unprepared. It is then that she sees them, at a table near the far end of the stage, their faces barely visible in the flickering candle-light. Dr Skinner and a beautiful young student lean together, deep in conversation. A punch of pain winds Alba, she clutches the edge of the marble counter to stop herself from falling off the stool.

Carmen follows Alba's gaze. 'Are you okay?'

Alba shakes her head. She opens her mouth but no words come out.

Carmen turns to her, now rather worried. 'What's wrong?'

Alba shakes her head again. When Carmen reaches out and rests her long, delicate fingers

141

gently on her new friend's arm, Alba starts as violently as if Carmen's bright red nails had just electrocuted her.

'You are sick?' Carmen asks, quickly withdrawing the offending hand.

'I—' Alba finds her voice in a whisper. 'I'm sorry. I've got to go, I'm sorry.'

'But why? What's happening, what's wrong?'

'I've got to go.'

'No, you must not . . .' But while the rest of the sentence is still in Carmen's throat, Alba slips off her stool, throws one last withering glance in the direction of Dr Skinner and the student and hurries, with as much dignity and finesse as she can muster, toward the exit.

Outside, Alba can't catch her breath. At the end of the street she stops running and leans against a wall, gasping until she thinks she'll faint. A few people stare as they walk past and one asks if she needs help. Her lungs on the edge of explosion and her heart beating sixty times a second, Alba shakes her head and stumbles away, utterly mortified. As she makes her way back to Hope Street, she curses the fact that she let Carmen drag her along to the bar. She was just starting to recover from the whole Dr Skinner debacle, her memories were fading, the sharpness of her pain softening. And now she has to start forgetting all over again.

Now alone with her wine, Carmen glances around the bar, wondering why Alba ran away. Between sips, she sneaks glances at Blake. If she hadn't entirely sworn off men she'd gratefully succumb to his advances. But she has to be strong, no matter how stunning and seductive he is. Swivelling around on her stool, she looks at the empty stage, biting her lip. Carmen takes another sip of wine. It mixes with the taste of blood in her mouth.

CHAPTER 11

Back at Hope Street, Alba still can't believe it. The first time she allows herself to be taken out, to go somewhere public, other than a library, something horrible has to happen. A dreadful coincidence, a frightful shock that she doesn't deserve. *This,* she thinks, *is why it's best to stay indoors.* There they were, in that silly posh bar – Dr Skinner with another girl, another student. The former object of her adoration with her replacement: next year's Alba, who has already got farther than *she* ever did: being taken to a public place, a social event. A month ago this was the holy grail to Alba, more important even than a kiss. She hadn't rated physical intimacy high on the list of what she'd wanted with Dr Skinner, having no experience of it; the practicalities scared her a little.

Only once did Alba step outside King's College with her teacher. Dr Skinner had invited her to attend a two-day conference in London. They would go up on the train in the morning, stay overnight in a hotel, then return the following evening. Dr Skinner would be presenting a paper on the first day and Alba would act as a sounding board and general assistant.

They set out for London very early, sitting side by side on the train, and all Alba could think about was the closeness. She couldn't focus on a single word of the speech Dr Skinner was reading aloud, though the colours exploded around them like a fireworks display. When they finally reached the hotel, every inch of Alba's skin was alive with electricity. She felt ready for anything.

But as she stared at the door of room 236, Alba was suddenly petrified she might be faced with a double bed. She wasn't ready. She couldn't cope with it. She was suddenly and absolutely sure that, were Dr Skinner to touch her, she'd dissolve into a pile of dust on the floor. When the door opened to reveal twin beds, Alba had let out a tiny, silent sigh of relief. Then the pesky itch of disappointment started to scratch at her heart. For the next forty-eight hours she watched every move her teacher made – waiting for a sign, for a purposeful touch on her thigh. All the while torn between wanting it and fearing it.

Albert finally left Inverie in 2008, a few years after the local pub linked up to the Internet and he began spending hours on it, monitoring the Ashby family, every morning typing in Alba's name. He longed, more than anything in the world, just to see what she looked like. Sometimes the longing took him back to the edge, though he never again fell over it.

It was during one of his first searches that he learnt about Lord Ashby's disappearance, only a year after he'd written that letter. It took every ounce of willpower, loyalty and love not to jump in the next boat, then take a taxi straight to Ashby Hall. Liz was free, alone and available. But she hadn't written to him. She hadn't called him back. And so Albert had to accept that, for one reason or another, she didn't want him any more.

Lord Ashby's disappearance meant Albert no longer had to stay in Inverie, but he stayed anyway, out of habit. However, when he finally saw it – the picture of a frowning fifteen-year-old over an article announcing Alba Ashby as the youngest entrant ever to King's College – he at last left Scotland and moved to Cambridge, skipping Hampshire and the heartbreak of seeing Elizabeth on the way.

He found a flat, a teaching job and a weekend position in a little bookshop opposite Alba's college. Nearly two months passed before he finally saw her, and it was all Albert could do not to cry out and run to her. But he'd made a promise to Elizabeth and he would keep it. So he watched Alba hurry across the street, half a dozen books clutched to her chest, a tatty black scarf flapping out behind her. And he stared down the street long after she'd gone out of sight.

Over the next four years he came to know her schedule and, fortunately for Albert, his daughter was a person of habit. Every day she went to the library at the same time. Every day she bought her lunch from the same cafe and ordered the same thing. At the weekends she ate in hall. He always hoped that one weekend she'd wander into the bookshop. And then one Wednesday, a dark day of heavy rain, she finally did. Alba walked through the door, shaking her short hair free of water, and Albert looked up to smile at the new customer. He stared, gripping the counter with white knuckles, while Alba glanced around the shop, breathing it in. After that Albert ignored all the other customers, watching her walk to the section on historical fiction and slip a book about the English Civil War off the shelf. Albert prayed to all the gods he'd ever known that she'd come to the counter and buy the book. Someone smiled down on him, and she did.

'It's very good,' he said.

'Sorry?' Alba asked, and Albert realised he was whispering.

'The book.' He slid it into a paper bag. 'I hear it's very good.'

'Oh.' Alba handed him a ten-pound note. 'Okay.' Albert took the money, opened the till and gave his daughter her change.

'Thank you.' Alba dropped the coins into her coat pocket and picked the bag up off the counter. 'Have you read it?'

Albert shook his head as though this oversight was the biggest regret of his life. 'No, sadly not, but I will, tonight, as soon as I finish work.'

'Oh, okay.' Alba looked puzzled.

Albert smiled. He realised he hadn't stopped smiling since she looked at him. 'Have you read *A Room with a View*?'

'Once.' Alba frowned. 'A while ago. Why?'

'Because it's wonderful, that's all.' He tried not to stare, he tried to seem normal, nonchalant, but he couldn't manage it. 'Didn't you think so?'

'Yeah, sure.' Alba edged toward the door. 'Bye, then.'

'Bye.' Albert turned to the window to watch her cross the street and disappear through the King's College gates. While he replayed every word of their conversation, every look on his daughter's face, Alba walked to her room, wondering why she always felt drawn to that little bookshop and why on earth she'd just bought a book at random on a topic she wasn't even studying, when she could get anything and everything she wanted from the university library.

Two weeks after that, Alba seemed to disappear. She stopped coming into college, going to the library or eating in the cafe. Albert waited for her every day but, by the end of May, he realised she wasn't coming back.

Carmen sits at the piano in the empty bar. It's past midnight, everyone else has gone home and she promised Blake she'd lock up. But first, she wants to play something, even if in her excitement her fingers won't relax. She can't wait for next Friday night: three days, six hours and twenty-four minutes. She can't think of anything else. Choir practise hovers on the horizon of her week like a beacon of light calling her home. Now she stumbles around in the happy haze of someone who's finally found IT: the one thing in the world that makes her feel more alive than anything else.

She should be worried. Tonight is the tenth of June and she can stay at Hope Street only another six weeks or so, until July 31. The idea of where she'll go and how she'll stay safe after that is a troubling one. But now that she's started singing again she can't seem to get worried about anything at all. As she rests her fingers on the keys, Carmen remembers the singer last night and the fiery beauty of her songs. Then she thinks of Alba. The plan to shake Alba up, to see her get drunk and dance on tabletops, might have failed the first time, but she *will* succeed in seducing Alba's spirit with music, Carmen decides, no matter what it takes. She will free this clueless young woman, shut up tight as a clam, so that Alba can know joy and passion and love. And if Carmen is lucky, this good deed will undo the very bad deed she has done. Invigorated by the thought, she starts to play: something sensual and sexual, notes that bounce off the walls and shiver through the air. Then she starts to sing.

Sleeping in the office with his feet on the desk, Blake wakes with a start. He loses his balance, slips off the chair and falls to the floor. Then he hears the music. Slowly he gets up, opens the door, creeps down the corridor and steps into the bar

When she sees him standing in the doorway, Carmen stops.

'Please.' He tries to swallow the longing creeping up his throat. 'Don't stop.'

For several moments they are both silent and still; the air around them is heavy with the echoes of music. And then Blake walks slowly up to the stage. This woman that he never paid much mind to before, except to admire her rather splendid curves, has suddenly activated his radar. Blake can sense a familiar feeling beginning to stir. He's never been able to resist a woman who's sexy *and* talented. He gazes at Carmen as if he wants to run his fingers over every inch of her body. Here is his antidote to Greer.

'You are a knockout.' Blake draws out every syllable. 'An absolute knockout.'

Carmen stares back into his bright green eyes without blinking. She's a little surprised by how direct he is. After six weeks in England she's become used to the bumbling, stumbling seductions of British men. It's unnerving to be confronted by this confident American, so completely sure of himself. Of course, she sees how Blake can afford to be so bold. He is, even including Tiago, the best-looking man she's ever seen.

'I reckon I never heard singing like that before.' Blake smiles. It's a smile of pure seduction, fixed on her as if she were the only woman in the world. Hypnotic. Dangerous. Designed to make Carmen lose her heart as well as her head. 'Never in my life. Let's have a drink.'

It isn't a question. Carmen feels a little light-headed. Cautionary tales about dating in the workplace, along with memories of Tiago, swim around the back of her mind. She isn't sure if she really wants to do this, have a drink and whatever might follow. If she was thinking straight, Carmen really ought to decline the offer, she really ought to say no. But then, to a man like this, how can she?

Alba has now memorised every line of every letter. She can piece together the scenes, the places her parents met and what passed between them. Elizabeth met Albert by chance in a coffee shop. They were sitting on opposite sides of the small room, each reading the same book. It was Elizabeth who noticed the coincidence. She examined him – rather sweet and friendly looking, if a bit short and scruffy – before commenting.

'Are you enjoying it?' She spoke a little louder than usual and, because there was no one in the cafe besides them and the waitress, he looked up at her.

'Yes.' He smiled. 'I always do.'

'Always?'

'I read it every year, on my birthday.' She noticed the way his bright blue eyes lit up his face. 'I know it by heart now. I could probably quote long passages to you and bore you silly.'

'Oh, I'm sure you wouldn't. But I always thought it was a girly book,' she said, teasing him. 'I've not met a man before who loves this book as I do.'

'Well, I suppose I'm in touch with my feminine side.' He smiled.

Elizabeth laughed, shocked and delighted. That was the moment she fell in love with this stranger. She couldn't imagine her husband saying something like that, not if his life depended on it. It was Charles Ashby's complete lack of humour that had disappointed Elizabeth most of all, even more than his philandering, quick temper and aversion to physical affection. He was a wonderful dancer and he'd once swept her off her feet, many years ago, but that was about the best that could be said about her husband.

'Would you like to share a slice of apple cake?' she asked. 'I can never eat a whole slice.'

'Well, in that case, how can I refuse?' he said. 'I'm Albert.'

And, because she suddenly wanted to be a different woman, a carefree, single woman without

152

a husband and three children, she said: 'Liz.' A name no one had ever called her before but now he always would.

They talked about literature, writing novels and poetry (him), raising children and managing mental illness (her), watching films in the morning, going for walks in the woods, reading Shakespeare aloud in empty parks (both of them). They gazed at each other but never let their hands touch, though their fingers were only ever a few inches apart. At the end of the afternoon, they exchanged an apparently casual agreement to meet again, in the same place, the next day.

Of all the scenes from her mother's letters, this is Alba's favourite. *Thank God,* she thinks, *for letter writers.* But some of her questions are still unanswered. Her father doesn't write about everything. He never reveals his surname, for a start. And her mother won't tell her that, or very much more during Alba's dreams. Unless, of course, she does and Alba simply doesn't remember when she wakes up. Snippets return to her sometimes, bubbles float up into her day and surface at odd moments. But the information is always a smattering of silly random facts, like the colour of Albert's socks the day they met, or what dress she wore on their first date or the smell of his hair. But Alba wants information of more significance. She wants to know if her real father has the slightly mystical gifts she has? If they share similar likes and dislikes. Does he look like her? And most important of all: if she ever finds him, will he want to know her?

Elizabeth replied to Albert's last letter the day her husband left, a year and a month after she'd received it. A long letter of love telling him she was sorry, that she'd regretted her choice every day, she hoped he'd forgive her and, if he had waited as he promised, would he come back to her now?

For another year Elizabeth waited for a reply. She wrote him a letter every week: the same words on the same paper, posted on the same day from the same post box, the envelope kissed before letting it go. Her magic ritual.

Every morning of that first month, Elizabeth ran to pick up the post the moment she heard letters hit the mat; and for the whole year she kept hoping. At first she didn't think of going to find him herself. Then, as events triggered by her husband's disappearance overtook her, she wasn't allowed to travel. Finally, faced with the fact of no letters in fifty-two weeks, Elizabeth could no longer bear it. She retreated into a place where she couldn't feel the pain anymore, where nothing could touch her, a world she could no longer leave and no one else could enter. Of course, Elizabeth never knew that Albert still loved and longed for her, that none of her letters ever reached him.

* * *

Alba hurries toward the library, safe in the knowledge that she won't bump into anyone she'd rather not see, since Dr Skinner never visits the library, always sending research assistants instead. It's been at least a decade since she read *A Room with a View* and, since it was the reason her parents met, she's curious now to study it closely. Also, she hasn't been to the library in nearly a month and she's starting to get withdrawal symptoms. It's not just the books Alba craves, it's standing inside a place that houses millions of them. Libraries are Alba's churches, and the university library, containing one edition of every book ever published in England, is her cathedral.

Alba approaches the counter, where Zoë sits behind a computer, absorbed in her work.

'Hello,' Alba ventures.

Zoë glances up. 'Oh! Hi.'

'Hey!' Alba smiles shyly. 'How are you?'

'Where have you been?' Zoë asks, forgetting herself.

'I had to go away for a . . . my mother died.'

'Oh no,' Zoë's face falls. 'I'm so sorry.'

'It's okay,' Alba says, and she realises it really is. Instead of Death taking her mother away, He's actually given her back. 'Hey, do you have *Room with a View* available?'

'Gosh, I adore that book.' Zoë grins. 'I'm in love with old Mr Emerson. When he tells Lucy Honeychurch *"You can transmute love, ignore it, muddle it, but you can never pull it out of you"* –

isn't that wonderful? I think that's how you know if it's true love or not. It is if it stays with you for the rest of your life.'

Alba looks carefully at Zoë, at her words still lingering in the air: as bright as fire, glowing brightly for a few seconds before extinguishing in little puffs of smoke. Their brief heat warms Alba and colours her cheeks.

'You might like *Howards End*, too,' Zoë says. 'It's beautiful, though it doesn't end happily. "*Only connect! Live in fragments no longer. And human love will be seen at its height.*" I'm paraphrasing, of course, but that's the gist. Isn't it gorgeous? Do you know it?'

Alba shakes her head, a little embarrassed she doesn't. 'I'll take them both.'

'Okay. Wait here, I won't be long.'

Only connect, only connect, only connect. Zoë rolls this mantra around her head as she runs down the steps to the book stacks. Now is the time. She can't wait in the wings any longer. She must act, she must ask. Ten minutes later, holding the books in one hand, Zoë takes the steps two at a time, reaching Alba out of breath.

'These are only a one-week loan,' she gasps. 'I think they're on the English Lit syllabus for the Freshers.' *Ask her now*, Zoë tells herself. *Now, now, now.*

'That's fine,' Alba says, hearing a strength in Zoë's words she's never heard before; they're edged with magenta, the colour of desire. 'I

156

won't take long. I'll bring them back in a few days.'

Just then, the other library assistant staggers toward the counter carrying an enormous pile of books. His messy hair is covered in dust and his baggy jeans reveal the top of his underwear. 'I've got 'em, babe.'

'Cheers, Andy.' Zoë glances at him with a quick smile.

Then Alba understands. She'd seen Zoë's aura tinged deep red, the colour of obsession, a few times before, and wondered who it was the librarian wanted. Alba's a little surprised at the object of her affection; she'd have afforded Zoë better taste, but who is she to judge?

'All right.' Alba picks up the books. 'Well, thanks again.'

'You're welcome.'

'Bye then.'

No, wait, Zoë thinks. *I haven't asked you yet. Give me a second. Wait! Run after her, you coward.* But instead she just gives Alba a little smile and a wave. 'Bye.'

'Do you fancy a film tomorrow night?' Greer lies across Blake's bed, her head nestling in his armpit while she strokes the golden hairs on his chest, gently twisting tufts around her fingers and humming.

'Huh?' He opens his eyes, having dozed off. A few days ago, mumbling something about office politics, he suggested they shouldn't have sex at work any more, in case someone should see them. So now they stick to his flat. Greer would like to take him to the house. But she has a funny feeling that it wouldn't welcome him, so she hasn't asked.

'*Adam's Rib* is on at the Picturehouse.' Greer glances up at him. 'We're both off, I thought we could go together.'

'Sorry, Red.' Blake starts to sit up, dislodging Greer from her crook. 'Not tomorrow.'

'Oh, okay.' She tries to sound nonchalant, though it isn't proving as easy any more. She's finding it harder to feign confidence or content-ment or whatever emotion she chooses, which is proving a little disconcerting. Excepting her mother, Greer has always been able to fool anyone and fake anything she wishes. But now she's losing her touch – just when she needs it more than ever. Greer can feel Blake starting to pull away, to withdraw little by little into a place she soon won't be able to reach him. And she knows that trying to chase him now will only push him further away. A slight sigh escapes her lips and, quickly, she swallows it. 'I'll ask Carmen, then,' Greer says lightly. 'She might fancy it. Or someone else, it doesn't matter.'

Blake doesn't react to Carmen's name. Not a flicker of guilt, surprise or even interest. Instead he smiles. 'Okay, sweetheart,' he says, his voice as sweet as sugar. He runs his hand through her hair. 'Sounds like a grand idea.' And though his tone is still kind and his actions still thoughtful,

Greer knows deep in her gut, even though she desperately wants to deny it, that something significant has changed, that while there may once have been hope of his loving her, there is no hope any more.

CHAPTER 12

Alba hates travelling. She hates staying in hotels, hates having to speak to strangers, hates not knowing where she is, hates being unable to find edible vegetarian food or a decent library. She's never wanted to go to exotic places and is more interested in historical times and fictional worlds than those she could actually visit.

After failing to find her father in the virtual world, and still a little too nervous to interrogate Edward or hire a detective, Alba finally decided to try to find him in the physical one. The sighting of Dr Skinner last week also made the idea of leaving the country rather more appealing.

Sitting on a sleeper train bound for Fort William, Alba bites her nails, trying to distract herself with books. She's already read *A Room with a View* and they're barely out of London. The scene of the bumbled kiss made Alba wonder if her own first kiss would be as unromantic. Considering her complete lack of experience and self-confidence, she imagines it might be. Although it also depends, she supposes, on the other party. Perhaps she'll find someone like George Emerson, full of passion and fervour. But in all honesty, Alba doesn't care how it happens, as long as it does. She's beginning to worry that she'll die a virgin, untouched, unloved and unkissed.

By the time the train passes through Yorkshire, Alba has read *Howards End, A Passage to India* and *Maurice*. And although *A Room with a View* is still her favourite, it's *Maurice* that makes her cry. She nearly misses the connection to Mallaig, pulling her book-filled bag behind her and falling through the train doors just in time. On this leg of the trip, Alba just gazes out of the window, running lines of her parents' letters through her mind. Somewhere in Scotland she falls asleep and dreams again of her mother. This time they sit together in the gardens of Ashby Hall.

'Are you finally happy now?' Alba plucks at a piece of grass. 'You always seem to be nowadays.'

'I am.' Elizabeth smiles. 'I truly am. What about you, my darling girl?'

'I'm fine.' Alba smiles. 'And every time I see you I'm better than I was before.'

Lady Ashby strokes her daughter's cheek. 'That's sweet, my love. But I hope you'll find happiness with someone you don't have to fall asleep to see.' She laughs. 'It's all I want for you, to be happy. Nothing else matters, only that.'

Alba reaches for her mother's hand and is still holding it when the train jolts to a stop and she wakes up. As she queues for the boat trip across

Loch Nevis, Alba is shivering so hard she almost can't pay for her ticket. Great gusts of wind whip the water into waves that crash onto the wooden pier, splashing the passengers. Alba watches as the waves spray mists over her head.

Alba grips the side of the small fishing boat, her fingers raw with cold, but she won't wear gloves, in case she loses her grip. When Inverie comes into view, Alba nearly passes out with relief. As they come ashore, a seal pops up in the water and Alba smiles. It's a good omen, she hopes: she will find her father, he will be overjoyed and they will get along brilliantly.

An hour later, when she's sitting on the edge of a bed in a twee little bed-and-breakfast, Alba's not feeling quite so confident. She has forty-eight hours to find him, that's until Monday morning, when the next ferry will take her back to the mainland. Her investigation is going to involve making enquiries of strangers, as well as, given the island terrain, physical exertion. Neither is a prospect she relishes. Alba kicks off her shoes, pulls off her jeans and drops them to the floor.

She looks up at the ceiling, at the pink wallpaper scattered with rosebuds, thinking that this is the craziest and bravest thing she's ever done in her life. And although thoughts of tomorrow still leave her trembling, she suddenly realises she's doing something so daring and different that her steady, staid life has just taken a sharp turn to the left. If she keeps this up, she might one day get that kiss after all. And for the second time that day, Alba smiles.

After getting up, getting dressed and swallowing three cups of strong coffee, Alba ventures downstairs with a list of questions. Last night she'd been greeted by a friendly, portly, middle-aged woman. This morning the woman has been replaced by a much younger version of herself: a sullen, pretty teenager who slumps behind the desk, scowling at her nails while she paints them scarlet. She reminds Alba of the gorgeous Cheltenham girls who made her childhood a misery. As Alba approaches the counter, map in hand, she tells herself that she's older now and, hopefully, braver. 'Hey.' Alba leans against the counter.

'Yeah.' The girl glances up. 'How can I help?' The words are rote, probably because her mother's been drumming them into her for years, resentful and dark brown: the colour of boredom.

'I'm looking for this house,' Alba says, displaying her father's address.

The girl gives it a cursory glance. 'Two miles down the road, past the Old Forge.'

'Oh, thank you.' Alba smiles. 'Is it easy to find? I don't have a street name.'

'Everything's easy to find.' The girl returns to her nails. 'It's fecking boring here. We only have, like, two streets, so the houses have names instead.'

'Oh.' Alba's suddenly slightly terrified. 'Okay.' Her father might be a few miles away; she might be just about to meet him. Alba grips the counter and the girl looks up at her.

'What you doing here anyway? You don't look like you'd make it up a mountain, and there ain't nothing else to do for fun. It's just fecking boring. I can't wait till I'm out of here.'

Most of life is fecking boring when you're fifteen, Alba wants to say, unless you're the youngest-ever student at King's College, in which case it's a bit fecking stressful and lonely. 'I'm looking for someone.'

'Okay,' the girl sighs, having lost interest. 'Whatever.'

It takes Alba twenty minutes to reach the house and another hour to walk up the short path to the front door. The house is small with a thatched roof and walls painted white. The curtains are drawn. When she knocks the sound is dull against the wood. Alba peeks in through the letterbox, but it's too dark to see inside. The weight of disappointment settles on Alba's shoulders as she sits down on the doorstep to contemplate her next move.

At first the sun is warm on her cheeks but then the wind starts to whip up. Alba slips her head and hands into her coat, shrinking like a turtle against the cold. But despite the chill and the disappointment, Alba is already quite captivated by Inverie, by the stark simplicity of the sea and the mountains, by the quiet, the muted colours of the sounds. In Cambridge Alba's vision was flooded with contrasting colours: the rush of traffic, people shouting, radios, sirens, horns . . . In Inverie all she sees are the trails of soft blue as birds sweep through the air, light green spray off the water, waves lapping against the stony strip of beach, streaks of white as the wind whistles through. Alba loves the solitude and wonders if her father does too.

'Well, hello there, little lassie.'

Startled, Alba looks up to see an old woman with short grey hair mostly hidden under a woollen hat. Suddenly scared she's trespassing, Alba jumps up and steps away from the house.

'What might you be doing here, then?' the woman asks, but her tone isn't harsh and her words are sky blue, the colour of kindness and friendship.

'I'm looking for someone.'

'Aye, well then, maybe I can help.' The woman smiles. 'Who is it you're looking for?'

'He's called Albert,' Alba says. 'I think he lives here.'

'Aye, Al Mackay, he used to, but not any more.'

'Oh.' Alba swallows her regret. But at least she now knows his surname. 'Where did he go?' Alba asks, desperately hoping she isn't about to hear her father is dead and gone.

'I couldn't tell you, lassie, I'm afraid. And no one's bought the house since Al left. Living here isn't everyone's cup of tea, wouldn't you know. Some seem to think it's the edge of the world.'

'When did he leave?' Alba asks. 'Do you know where he went?'

'Four years ago, or thereabouts. But no, he kept himself to himself, did Albert. I was the only one round here he ever said more than three words to.'

'Oh,' Alba says softly, tears gathering in her eyes. 'Oh, I see.'

After the woman leaves Alba returns to the doorstep to sit and soak up any remaining traces of her father, leaching the last molecules of his presence out of the stone, until the tips of her fingers are numb. When she pulls herself up to stand again, her legs are sleepy and leaden. At the gate Alba stops and turns to look at the low wall running back up to the cottage then continuing parallel to the house, leaving a passageway enough for a small person to squeeze through.

There must be a back garden. Alba can't believe she didn't think of this before. There might be an open window, or one with a faulty catch, or a back door unlocked. Glancing around, Alba turns and hurries up the path, then squeezes through the passage.

The back of the house looks very much like the front, but before she can examine it, something else catches her eye. The stone wall runs to the end of the garden, marking a square around the house and grounds. At the end, where the wild, overgrown lawn should continue, lies a blanket of colour that glints and sparkles in the sunlight.

From fifty feet away, Alba can't quite make out what she's looking at. As she gets closer, a sense of foreboding swallows her curiosity and she slows to step carefully through the scattered daisies and cowslips. And then Alba is looking down at layers of multicoloured glass, the fragments of smashed bottles forming a blanket of a dozen different colours. *Like a piece of modern art,* she thinks. Alba bends forward, her fingers hovering a few inches above the glass. Here and there, jutting out of the jagged edges are torn labels, historical evidence of the identity of individual bottles before they were sacrificed for the whole. Alba wonders if her father was an artist as well as a poet, someone who turns the ordinary into the extraordinary. She feels a flutter in her chest, a tiny, fragile connection to him across time and space.

Then she catches sight of something else. On the neck of a frosted pink bottle is a splash of dried blood, a shadow left behind, a clue. And, all of a sudden, the years fold together, showing Alba a truth she first missed. Her father must have drunk every bottle before he smashed them. Thousands of glasses of wine, whisky, champagne, cognac . . . She's looking at a graveyard of multi-coloured tombstones marking every hour of her father's alcoholism.

Alba stands, seized by an urgent desire to run, to be as far away from this display of pain and despair as it's possible to be. She's enough of a mess already, she doesn't want a father who is even worse than her. She needs one who is strong and brave, a man who can hold her in his arms and promise that everything will always be all right. After a lost and lonely childhood, Alba doesn't want another parent who really isn't one at all. She wants strength, dependency, endurance, courage.

Then, as she's about to turn away, Alba spots something else: the tip of a pen sticking an inch into the air, a little ship in a sea of glass. She bends down again and gingerly picks it up. It's a fountain pen: cream edged in black with a gold clip, faded from exposure, small enough to fit in the palm of her hand. It's weighty, expensive, the kind only a serious writer would own. Alba rubs it on her sleeve, then carefully places it in her pocket. And with her fingers still wrapped around the pen, she turns and runs out of the garden and past the house, leaving the layers of multicoloured glass far, far behind.

Peggy finds Greer ensconced in the back of her wardrobe, trying on an assortment of leather jackets with various cocktail dresses and cowboy boots.

'I thought I'd find you in here.' The old woman eases herself onto a pile of abandoned clothes with a soft sigh of effort. 'Hiding out with your safety blankets.'

'Yeah.' Greer smiles. 'I suppose so.'

'Well, there's nothing wrong with that, from time

to time.' Peggy fingers the hem of a dress, rubbing black lace between her fingertips. 'Though I'm afraid you can't hide your head in the sand forever, my dear, you don't have as long as—'

'You sound like my mother.'

'Well, I am a little like one, I suppose,' Peggy says. She picks up a moss green cardigan and absently slips it over her shoulders. 'At least, it's my job to help you find your way to happiness. And I rather think you're losing yours. Don't you?'

Greer slips a green leather jacket over red chiffon and gives a slight shrug. 'I haven't successfully auditioned for the Royal Shakespeare Company or found a prospective husband just yet, if that's what you mean.'

'Not exactly.' Peggy laughs. 'And I have a feeling that your acting career will sort itself out. But as for men, the one you're currently carrying on with will bring you nothing but heartbreak.' She discards one of her slippers and pulls on a pink cowboy boot. 'But then you already know that, my dear, don't you?'

It's a moment before Greer is able to look her landlady in the eye. 'Yes,' she admits. 'I know it and I still can't seem to stop myself.'

When Carmen wakes the next morning she feels a strange urge, an intuitive pull she's never felt before. Still in her nightgown she walks down to the kitchen, past the long wall of cupboards, the photographs of women who watch curiously, and arrives at a door she had never noticed. It stands ajar. Carmen pauses a moment, then pushes it open. As she steps through it and into the sunlight, a thousand tiny multicoloured butterflies sweep into the kitchen: a herald to the newcomer, a welcome. A second later, they are gone.

The beauty of the garden takes Carmen's breath away. She stands on the stone terrace for several minutes before seeing Peggy sitting at a table under an apple tree. Mog sits, invisible, at her feet. The old woman gives a small, resigned smile. The day has come. The garden is hers no longer, it has invited someone else in.

'*Paraiso*,' Carmen whispers. 'I can't believe, I live here two month, I think it just fields . . .' She steps off the terrace and onto the lawn. Blades of grass reach up to soften her soles. Flowers turn their faces in her direction, blossom-laden branches of the apple tree drop and settle close to her head. A puff of wind blows a shower of pink petals at her feet.

'*Meu Deus.*' Carmen sighs. 'It's like I step into a song.'

'It's always a little overwhelming the first time.' Peggy sticks her fork into a half-eaten slice of cake. 'I love chocolate cake for breakfast,' Peggy stalls, 'it sets me up for the day. A little decadence is good for the soul.' She's been eating more cake than usual, lately. Impending death does have compensations after all, then, if only chocolate-covered ones. She's also been thinking of Harry nearly every hour of every day. She knew she cared for him deeply but has recently realised that he might be the love of her life. The woman who never entertained regrets now finds herself facing a rather big one.

Mog jumps up onto the table to lick chocolate icing off the edge of Peggy's plate.

'So, my dear,' Peggy stalls, 'what brings you here?'

'I don't know. I feel something in my stomach and I follow it.'

'Yes,' Peggy says, 'well, the garden has invited you, which means . . . I'm afraid it's time to tell you something you won't want to hear.'

Carmen kicks her toes against the stone terrace.

'When you bury things instead of confronting them, they will haunt you until you do,' Peggy says. 'And I'm sorry to say that if you don't dig it up by Friday night, you will have to leave.'

CHAPTER 13

In the seven weeks since he last saw her, Albert has searched for his daughter everywhere. But she's apparently broken all her rituals and, as far as he knows, disappeared from the face of the earth. He can't understand why she'd leave in the middle of her MPhil. Of course no one at King's would tell him anything, and every other lead he had followed failed. Albert's at a loss. He can't afford a private detective, not unless he takes out a loan, so he roams the streets worrying about what might have gone wrong.

At times, when he's staring at an (as yet) unopened bottle of vodka, Albert actually contemplates going to Ashby Hall or calling Liz. It'd be a gross breach of promise, but should it matter any more now, given that Charles is long gone? Although Albert has thought about her so often, he thinks he might turn into a pillar of salt the moment he sees Liz again. Perhaps a letter would be best. He could write and ask about Alba, surely she owes him that, doesn't she?

Finally, Albert decides on a letter. Of course he knows her address by heart, but there is a tiny possibility she might have moved. So he turns on his computer to search for Elizabeth Ashby's whereabouts, just in case. And that is how he discovers that the love of his life is dead.

'You can't give up,' Stella says, 'you have to keep trying.' The kitchen ceiling sinks down then springs back up, twice, as if nodding in agreement.

'How?' Alba asks, fingering the pen in her pocket. She holds it now like a talisman, a good-luck charm. 'I only know his name and where he used to live.'

'Well, don't bother with the police, 'cause they'll do nothing,' Stella says. 'But you can pay a private detective because he will, I guarantee it.'

'I don't know,' Alba says, 'it seems a bit. . . seedy.'

'Don't be silly.' Stella laughs. 'They track down missing persons, too, not just philandering spouses. Anyway, what's the harm in trying?'

The disappointment, Alba thinks, *the absolute crushing disappointment of having hope dashed, obliterated, blown to smithereens. There* is *something to be said for avoiding all that.* 'Okay, I'll think about it,' Alba says, 'but can we change the subject, just for a bit?'

All right, Stella thinks, *enough pussyfooting around. It is time to be direct.* 'Well, if you want a little distraction, why don't you try fiction?'

'Yes.' Alba frowns. 'That's exactly what I do for—'

'No,' Stella says. 'Not reading it, writing it.'

Alba is struck dumb. The ghost has just looked straight into her heart to see the secret desire she's never admitted to anyone. Alba stares at the frayed sleeves of her T-shirt and fiddles with a loose thread.

'But I've got nothing to say, and no imagination.' Alba speaks softly, without looking up. 'That's why I've always written about facts, not fiction.'

'Except that you don't write now, either fact or fiction,' Stella says. 'Do you?'

Albert Mackay had clung to sobriety for twelve years, eleven months and six days. Until he learnt that the love of his life, the mother of his child, was dead. That night he drank half a bottle of vodka. It was cheap and tasted like paint-stripper. But it was enough to take the edge off his agony, to numb his suicidal urge, to slide him into a coma of no longer caring about anything any more.

But it didn't last. And the ache in Albert's heart hasn't ceased. He can't eat, he can't sleep for more than a few moments, he can't focus on anything. Instead he remembers. And, clearer than any other memory is the time he first saw his daughter. She was a week old and looked nothing like him, except for the little blue eyes. Those eyes were a perfect reflection of his. They blinked up at him as he held her. Since then, he always wondered how he could care so suddenly and so deeply for such a small, oblivious being. How could he feel that way for someone who had no feelings for him at all?

Now Albert drifts off in the middle of sentences, leaving his students staring at him. He'll be reading a scene from *Waiting for Godot* or *Antony and Cleopatra*, then stop halfway and forget to read on. When he has no students and is supposedly marking essays, he simply stares at the same page for hours. At some point he will look up at the clock and realise the day is long since over and the school is deserted.

Albert knows he has to do something. He can't go on like this. Last night he walked into a lamp-post and cracked his glasses. This morning he overheard his departmental head discussing Albert's descent into distraction in not altogether sympathetic terms. So he has to do something, or he'll lose his job. And that would be a tragic event worthy of Godot, Bovary, even Hamlet. Teaching literature is all he wants or knows how to do.

Since Carmen left Peggy's garden she's been worrying about what she has to do. She doesn't know if she has the courage to face again what she thought she'd got rid of forever. But right now, as she walks out of The Archer, she refuses to think about it. She has a few days left to decide what to do. And now songs from choir practise still echo joyfully in the air, and as she crosses the street she starts to sing – and then she hears Blake calling her name. Carmen turns back to see him leaning against the door and grinning. 'Where are you off to?'

'Home.' Carmen recognises his smile, it is the sort that bewitches women into doing foolish things, causing them to fall down rabbit holes into other worlds. But not her. She is safe from this, she won't fall in love. Tiago killed that possibility off years ago. Her heart is cold now, and numb. And in this, Carmen senses that she and Blake are a perfect match.

'Hey, sugar.' He crosses the street to reach her. 'Fancy a drink?'

Carmen laughs. 'I think I have enough of drink at work.'

'How about a cuppa, then?' The slang sounds strange on his southern tongue.

Carmen notices that he often asks questions as if they aren't really questions. He isn't requesting permission; he already knows that the answer will be yes. But she doesn't care. A gypsy woman in Bragança once told her that a man leaves his mark on the spirit of every woman he sleeps with. And Carmen is ready to have Blake wipe away Tiago's. So she shrugs. 'Okay.'

Instead of going to a coffee shop, Carmen asks him back to the house. She can't explain why she does this, but once the invitation has slipped out, she can't take it back. As Blake follows her across town, always half a step behind, she can feel him watching every curve of her body as she walks.

Thirty minutes later, in the kitchen, Stella, Vita Sackville-West, Dora Carrington and one hundred and fifty-seven other women eye Blake suspiciously.

176

Oblivious to this, he leans back in his chair and slides his feet onto the table. With a pang of guilt and remorse, he thinks of Greer, working until midnight at The Archer. For her sake he regrets what he's doing. But he still has to do it. He can't fall in love with Greer and if that means sleeping with Carmen then so be it. In this life, Blake has to protect himself. He must put his own needs first, just as his mother did.

'You want Earl Grey or English Breakfast?' Carmen interrupts Blake's thoughts and he looks up, then remembers to smile.

'I'll drink whatever you're drinkin'.'

'Milk?'

'Black, plenty of sugar.'

Carmen drops the tea bags into cups.

'After two years, I'm finally starting to understand the English obsession with tea,' Blake says. 'Down south we love ourselves some iced tea, but it's so stifling down there most of the time that we don't go in for the hot stuff. But anyway, you aren't English.' His gaze lingers on Carmen's hands, her hair as it falls over her face. Carmen watches the kettle, waiting. Stella watches them both.

'In Portugal,' she says, 'we drink tea usually just for fever or flu.' She pours boiling water into their cups. 'But here is different, here I like it.'

'I like it too. You got any cookies?'

'I think so.' Carmen opens the cupboards again and rummages around. Blake fixes his eyes on her bottom, the strong curves of her thighs. She tips some slightly stale ginger biscuits onto a plate and sets it on the table next to Blake's cup. Then Carmen sits down next to him, cradling her cup of tea.

Stella floats across the floor to stand between them. She studies the American with narrowed eyes. She can see right through him, past his dazzling smile, his seductive words and straight into the heart he strives so hard to keep far from prying female fingers. She sees that he hasn't let himself love a woman since the day his mother left. From that day he hasn't shed a single tear, or slept a single night through without waking.

Stella's fingers skim the air an inch from Blake's neck and he shivers.

'Do you feel that?'

'Sorry?' Carmen looks up.

'The chill in the air.'

Carmen shakes her head. Stella looks closer into Blake's heart, so broken that shards stick through his chest, creating heartbreak all around him. She runs her finger along his spine, watching as his muscles twitch. She knows what he's feeling now, because she's making him feel it. Everything that he's always striving so hard not to feel, everything he suppresses with sex: longing, despair, fear . . . Stella stands behind Blake as this cocktail of emotions sinks into his bones, deep into the marrow, until they are so brittle they could snap.

Suddenly Blake pushes his chair away from the table. He glances around the kitchen, at the photographs of all the women on the walls, now terrified they are about to leap out of their frames and attack him.

'I'm so sorry, sugar.' He chokes on the words. 'I, I . . . there's somethin' I've gotta sort out. I'll see you later.'

Carmen frowns. 'You don't finish your tea?'

'No, sorry, another time.' He shakes his head, edging toward the door. And is gone.

It's three o'clock in the morning. Greer sits inside her wardrobe wearing a T-shirt and short black taffeta skirt and clutching a bright pink minidress to her chest. At times like this her couture always brings her comfort. When she'd walked into the house, long after midnight, she'd felt the presence of Blake, so sharp and strong that it had driven her straight to her clothes. Now he won't leave her: his smile, his touch, his unreachable heart. And whenever she tries to replace him with happier thoughts, he is replaced only by Lily. Her daughter would be almost Alba's age now. Waves of sadness wash over her as she wonders what Lily would have been like. The idea of adoption, something she discussed with the ex-fiancé, returns but Greer pushes it away. She knows it'd be a struggle to be approved. She's single, broke, works in a bar and, in less than a month, will have nowhere to live. She can barely support herself, let alone another human being.

⋆   ⋆   ⋆

The desire to be a writer, to create fiction instead of rehashing fact, is one Alba has held hidden in the depths of her heart since she was a child. After being admitted to King's College she suppressed it completely, allowing herself to read only novels relevant to her historical study: all the Victorians and their European counterparts: Balzac, Dumas, Flaubert, Goethe and the like.

But despite this willpower and focus, Alba has always secretly loved fiction more than fact. She didn't cry over the death of Darwin's daughter or the millions killed by the Great Plague, but sobbed buckets at the fates of Emma Bovary, and Beth in *Little Women*. She loves books more than life and, for that very reason, she never tried to write anything of her own. Who was she, after all, to think that she could create something brilliant and beautiful, something that wouldn't simply be a waste of the paper it was written on? Alba never dared to dream it was possible. Instead she buried the longing deep in her soul where it wouldn't trouble her too much. But now it's risen again. Stella's suggestion won't leave her alone. Finally, this morning, Alba thinks – Why not? She might just give it a try. What, after all, does she have to lose? Nothing, except her heart, and there's not much left of that anyway.

Alba sits up in bed and rubs her eyes. Thousands of books blink back at her. But they've changed. They've shifted around and re-shelved themselves. They must be misbehaving, she thinks.

Perhaps they know that their historical facts are no longer needed. Curiosity gets Alba out of bed. Then she sees her mistake. The books haven't moved, they have been replaced. The histories and biographies of great Victorians have become the novels they read: *Wuthering Heights*, *Tess of the d'Urbervilles*, *The Death of Ivan Ilyich*, *North and South*, *The Picture of Dorian Gray* . . . Alba walks across the room to study the titles on the opposite wall. This time they are plays from the same period: *The Cherry Orchard*, *Peter Pan*, *A Woman of No Importance*, *Pygmalion*, *The Woman in White* . . . then poems: *Tintern Abbey*, *The Rime of the Ancient Mariner*, *Ozymandias*, *La Belle Dame sans Merci*, *The Maid of Athens* . . .

Alba's alarm clock beeps. She hurries back to her bed to turn it off – and there on the table is a note, the words curling across the paper in black ink:

Take one step back and two steps forward.

She reads it twice, then once again, but still doesn't understand. Alba pulls a moth-eaten cardigan off her bedpost and slips it over her pyjamas. She'll have to ask Stella. Opening the bedroom door, she sees a bright yellow notebook on the floor. A lurid colour, like radioactive egg yolks. Alba fingers the pen in her pyjama pocket, then picks up the notebook and walks slowly toward the stairs. Reaching the first step, she stops.

On the wall is a photograph she's never noticed before.

'Emmeline Pankhurst.' Alba smiles at another of her historical heroes. The suffragette nods at the notebook. 'I see you're about to embark on an adventure.'

'I don't know,' Alba says. 'It's just something I wanted to do a long time ago. I don't even . . .'

'Hardly so long ago, you're still a teenager, a tadpole.' Emmeline laughs. 'You're far too young to give up on yourself or life yet. And my own experiences should certainly teach you never to give up at the first hurdle. Or, indeed, the second. Wouldn't you say?'

'Yes, I'll bear that in mind.' Alba smiles. 'Thank you.'

'You're welcome,' Emmeline says. 'Anytime.'

A few minutes later when Alba opens the kitchen door she hears her mother's butterfly song and stops in her tracks.

'Well.' Stella materialises in the sink. 'You look like you've seen a ghost.'

'Very funny.' Alba sits at the table. 'But I did just meet one of my idols. I can't quite believe Emmeline Pankhurst just gave me life advice.' She smiles.

Stella eyes the notebook. 'So are you going to start writing now?'

Alba ignores the question. 'The song you were singing just now, the one I heard the first night I came here, how do you know it?'

'I'm sure I don't know what you're talking about.'

'Come on, I know you do. Why won't you tell me?' But Stella just smiles.

Alba scowls. The mystery of the ghost and the particulars of her life gnaw at her like an Agatha Christie novel with the final pages ripped out. She's been searching for Stella's picture in the hope that it might yield clues. She's also been searching for a photograph of Miss Christie. Alba has a theory that, when the author disappeared for eleven days in 1926, she came to Hope Street. She just needs to find the photo to prove it.

'Why *are* you here?' she persists. 'Why have you been here all these years?'

'I told you – I was waiting for you.'

'Yes, there is *that* great mystery, but I mean, I wasn't born until twenty-three years after you died. So, for all that time, how did you even know I was coming and why—'

'I told you.' Stella interrupts her. 'Time isn't the same for me as it is for you. Waiting isn't the point. When I died I wanted to be useful. So I hung around here to help out until you showed up.'

'But why?' Alba frowns. 'Why me?'

'Well, now,' Stella says, 'if I just told you, what would be the fun in that?'

Charles Ashby had been searching for stamps when he found the letters. His wife's office was open. He strode across the room, disgusted by the mess: papers strewn everywhere, piled up and sandwiched between books. He wasn't interested in looking at any of it, but when he found a locked box in her desk drawer, he was suddenly intrigued. No one kept secrets from Charles Ashby. At age five he was the first of his friends to uncover the true identity of Father Christmas and was singlehandedly responsible for disillusioning his entire class. He was the only one who knew about all his father's affairs, the first to discover his mother's drinking. And if his wife had a locked box, he would be the one to open it.

Twenty minutes later, after he'd found the key, he sat in her chair and read her letters. Charles reflected that, if the box hadn't been locked, he would never have known. Now, although he cared that his wife loved someone else (he still loved her despite his own infidelities), he would have over-looked it if not for the other discovery. It didn't take Charles long to realise, the date on the last letter being Alba's seventh birthday (along with the fact that he'd had sex with his wife only once the year that she conceived), that Alba wasn't an Ashby at all. And having his wife cuckold him was one thing, but raising another man's child was something else altogether. He simply wouldn't stand for it.

As he sat and considered his options, Charles contemplated making the scandal public but, considering his own innumerable indiscretions, quickly decided it wasn't an option that favoured him. He thought of the address on the last letter, of visiting the bastard and beating the hell out of him. But being a tall, skinny man, Charles never courted physical violence, and with no idea what Albert looked like, he wasn't really prepared to risk a confrontation. After a few hours of musing on the matter, Lord Ashby came up with the perfect plan of retribution: one that ensured himself maximum gain and minimum pain, and his wife just the opposite.

CHAPTER 14

'I only know his name,' Alba explains. 'And that he lived in a remote Scottish village for sixteen years, and used to be a teacher.'

'Nothing else?'

'I have these letters.' Alba pushes the shoebox across the desk. 'But they're personal. They don't have any information that'll help you find him.'

'I'll be the judge of that.' The detective takes the box and opens the lid.

'I went looking for him in Inverie,' Alba says, 'but he'd left four years ago and no one knew where he went. Or maybe they did and just wouldn't tell me. Either way . . .'

'It doesn't matter,' the detective says. 'I'm quite sure I won't need to go there. But if I do, you'll cover all expenses, in addition to my time. Are you fine with that?'

Alba nods. She still has the rest of her student loan fund and nothing else to spend it on. Of course, in five weeks she'll have to find a new place to live and something to do with the rest of her life, so there is that to consider. But for now finding her father is all that matters.

'It's a shame you don't have a photograph,' he says, 'or a bit more to go on. But I'll do my best and we'll see where it takes us.'

'And you'll give me weekly updates?'

'Yes. Or call you as soon as I get anything concrete.'

Yesterday Albert lied his way into King's College, then tracked down and interrogated Alba's former supervisor about her whereabouts. Dr Skinner was suspicious and obtuse, claiming to have no idea where she could be, claiming to hardly remember Alba Ashby at all.

'I don't know. One day she just up and left—'

'Two months ago,' Albert said, 'April thirtieth was the last day I saw her.'

'Yes, something like that. Must have cracked under the pressure. Quite a few of them do. Probably went running home to mummy—'

'No.' Albert suppressed an overwhelming desire to knock Dr Skinner down. 'She didn't do that. Her mother is dead.' It was the first time he had spoken the words out loud. They tasted black and bitter as soot.

'Well, then, I'm afraid I can't help you. Now, if you'll excuse me, I have somewhere else to be.' And with that, Dr Skinner had turned and walked away, leaving Albert standing on the stone path next to the lawn, seething with a fury he'd rarely felt before, a sadness he knew only too well, and wondering what the hell he was going to do now.

★　★　★

187

Carmen heaves her weight against the chapel door and falls through the doorway. Excited laughter floats toward her as she runs down the aisle to Nora and Sue, skidding to a stop in front of the altar, pausing for a split second to cross herself, then joining them. 'Sorry I am late,' she gasps, catching her breath. 'Stuck at work, I run all the way.'

'Oh, don't worry . . .' Nora smiles.

'. . . we haven't started yet, we've been too busy . . .' Sue giggles.

'. . . planning our television debut.' With this, Nora lifts her arms toward the chapel ceiling, then takes a deep bow, dipping her head toward her toes, as far as her girth will allow. 'Oh, dear,' she splutters, 'I'm stuck.' Nora waves a chubby hand toward Sue. 'Help me.'

'Come here, you silly diva.' Sue steps forward and lifts Nora so she's upright again.

Carmen drops her bag onto the nearest pew. 'Television?'

'Yes.' With a flourish, Nora hands Carmen a piece of paper. 'There's a televised talent contest coming to Cambridge . . .'

'. . . we're seizing the opportunity for fame, fortune,' Sue declares, 'and, in Nora's case, public humiliation—'

'If you remember rightly,' Nora says a little frostily, 'my Queen of the Night went down a storm last year.'

'Yes, a thunderstorm that sank your ship.' Sue

giggles. 'If only you hadn't insisted on wearing that helmet with the horns, I think you might not have been laughed off the stage—'

'Yes, well, that's not quite how I remember it,' Nora huffs. 'Anyway, I'm sure she gets the idea.'

'No, not really.' Carmen stares at the press release. The show is on July 21, ten days before she has to leave the house. And that's assuming she's allowed to stay all of her ninety-nine nights, which is only if she digs up the midnight glory tonight. The thought sends a shot of panic through Carmen. 'We are really doing this? But, it is only three weeks away. This is a bit crazy, *nao*?'

'Not entirely,' Nora replies. 'It's an opportunity. A very remote one, yes . . .'

'. . . but this year you've inspired us to try again.'

'Me?' Carmen looks at the two women, wide-eyed.

'But of course,' Sue says. 'Without you we're just two fat ladies on a stage.'

'Speak for yourself. I lost two pounds last week,' Nora declares. 'And I've got a fabulous idea for a costume this year, lots of silk and taffeta—'

'I predict a fiasco,' Sue sighs, 'but it's bound to be fun. You will join us, won't you?'

Carmen is about to shake her head when the last shafts of sunset shine through the stained glass. Squares of coloured light fall on her face, lighting her up like a Christmas tree, and something inside her stirs. Despite everything that happened with Tiago, despite her memories and her fears, she wants to feel that excitement again, the pure, unadulterated joy of standing onstage and singing to an audience.

'*Sim*.' Carmen nods. 'Okay, I will.'

Blake Walker has a sixth sense about women. He knows when they're still madly in love and when they're on the verge of giving up. Halfway across town he feels Greer's decision to finally dump him. And he can't let her. No, if he has to swim all the way to Savannah, he'll be the one to leave first.

Blake lifts the female arm draped across his torso and places it back on the bed. He glances at her face, the long dark hair spread out like a fan on the pillow, but can't remember her name. Barbara? Bridget? Something beginning with B. Or possibly G. It doesn't matter. He went home with her only to get Greer and the Spanish singer out of his head.

Looking at the alarm clock on the girl's bedside table, he curses. He's an hour late. He slips out from under the duvet and, quickly pulling on his jeans and T-shirt, ducks out of her bedroom and into the street. He runs to The Archer, pausing only to nip into a newsagent's and buy Greer the best bunch of flowers they have.

Peggy sits at her kitchen table sipping Earl Grey and listening to the radio: a dramatisation of the abdication of Edward VIII. She remembers hearing his speech when it first aired in 1936. She was six years old, watching her mother washing dishes. She can't recall now where her sisters were but remembers the house was silent, except for the radio.

Today her tarot card is the Six of Cups: the card of simple blessings, family and innocence. Peggy closes her eyes to listen, but instead she's back in her mother's kitchen, splaying her tiny hands into starfish on the shiny plastic tablecloth.

'You all know the reasons which have impelled me to renounce the throne . . . but I want you to know that, in making up my mind, I did not forget the country or the Empire.'

'What does "impelled" mean, Mummy?' Peggy kicked her legs under the table.

Milly Abbot turned and smiled at her daughter. 'It means pushed, or forced. It means he doesn't really have a choice.'

'But he does.' Peggy frowned. 'He doesn't have to abandon us, does he?'

Milly wiped her wet hands on her apron. She pulled out a chair and sat down. 'He's in love with a woman,' she explained, 'but she's not allowed to be queen. And he can't marry her unless he stops being king. So—'

Peggy interrupted. 'But why can't he just find another woman to marry?'

'My dear, I'm afraid you can't simply choose who you fall in love with. And, when you do, you can't give them up so easily.'

'Oh.' Little Peggy stared at her fingers, considering this. It made sense, she supposed. But she still felt she'd been let down somehow, that a grown-up had done something selfish.

'. . . *and he has one matchless blessing enjoyed by so many of you, and not bestowed on me; a happy home with his wife and children* . . .'

Peggy looked up, suddenly curious. 'Are you happy, Mummy?'

'Yes. I am, very.'

Because her mother never lied, Peggy knew this was true, but she still wondered. Her sisters – all born exactly two years apart – were forever fighting. And her mother never seemed to do anything but look after everyone.

'Do you ever want to run away?'

'Sometimes.' Milly laughed. 'But I also know that not everything I want every moment will actually make me happy. This is my circus, I'd miss it after a minute.'

Peggy regarded her mother with a suspicious squint. 'I want lots of different things. How do I know which one will make me happiest?'

Back in her own kitchen, a song bursts out of the radio and Peggy jumps. Still caught up in the past, she wonders where she is, and where Milly has gone. Unable to summon the energy to stand and switch off the music, Peggy shuts her eyes and attempts to return to 1936, to remember her mother's answer to the question.

But no matter how hard she tries, she can't. It's gone.

★   ★   ★

Greer stands at the bar, polishing glasses. She holds each one for a few seconds over a bowl of hot water, watching the steam fill the paper-thin bulb, then gently rubs the smudges away with a cotton cloth. Every now and then she's seized by the urge to smash one against the marble counter and watch it shatter. Today she's wearing a black miniskirt with red leather boots. It's her power outfit, the thing that will give her the confidence to break up with Blake. It must be done today.

Greer has finally decided to heed Peggy's nudging and take action. It's time to get back to the business of addressing the mess that is her career, and for that she'll need all her energy. No more white nights and slept-through days. She must focus. She must really apply herself, line up auditions and not stop until she succeeds at something. She should probably move to London and set her sights on the RSC. Greer feels strong. Resolute. This time she won't cave in to his seductive southern ways, she won't lose her will to the pull of mind-blowing sex.

Less than an hour later Blake stumbles in to the bar, out of breath. Nearly knocking over a table on his way to the counter, he stands opposite Greer. She doesn't look up.

'Hey, Red.' He gives her his best grin. 'How you doing today?'

'I'm fine.' Her voice is controlled and cold.

Panic tugs at Blake's heart. It's worse than he

thought. He'll have to do some damage control, quickly.

'I missed you, Red.' He holds out the flowers, red tulips and roses, toward her.

'You didn't call.' Her words are sharp as flint. 'You haven't been to the bar in days.'

'I know, I'm sorry, sweetheart, I had a heap of stuff to sort out. Let me take you to dinner tonight.' He reaches for her hand but she pulls back. 'I'll make it up to you after.'

'No.' Greer feels tears threatening. She must be quick. 'This isn't . . . we're not right—'

'Don't say that,' he says, 'please, don't.'

She hears the crack in his voice and is surprised. He must care more than she realised. For a moment she wonders. Seeing she's wavering, Blake reaches again for her hand and, this time, she doesn't flinch away. It is her fatal mistake. As his warmth flushes her skin, Greer's resolve weakens.

'Give me another chance.' Blake gently lifts her chin until their eyes meet. 'You won't regret it, I promise.'

'The flowers are lovely.' Greer surrenders a little smile. 'My favorite colour.'

'I know, Red, I remember.' He fixes her with his most alluring smile. And she is trapped, helpless, as he leans over the counter and kisses her so deeply that her cheeks glow, her heart swells and her womb begins to throb.

* * *

194

Alba lies across her bed, Albert's pen in her hand, the yellow notebook open, trying to come up with something to write – fiction, not fact. But her mind is completely blank. And she keeps getting distracted, wondering if the private detective has made any discoveries yet. The pen is beautiful, which is something. Letters flow out of it, silky across the page, dark blue on white. But so far Alba has only three sentences. Crossed out.

~~Fireworks explode, scattering light like fistfuls of stars. Esme tucks her head under the pillow. Everyone is celebrating in the garden but she escaped hours ago.~~

Seeking inspiration, Alba glances up at her books, catching sight of *Great Expectations* snuggled between *North and South* and *Tess of the d'Urbervilles*. Dickens was Dr Skinner's favourite author. With a sigh Alba thinks again of that day. The day everything fell apart.

She found out about Dr Skinner's betrayal while sitting in her favourite place on earth: a table underneath a south-facing window in the university library. There she could pretend she was alone in the world with only eight million books for company. A cast-iron radiator fixed to the wall toasted her ever-cold feet when she slipped her toes between its ridges.

It was Zoë who brought her the news. She snuck up behind Alba and tapped her gently on the shoulder. 'Sorry,' she said when Alba flinched, 'I didn't want to disturb you, but I've just got something I thought you'd want to see.'

'Oh?' Alba closed *Pitt and Peel: The Legacy of Youth on Victorian Britain* and looked at the *Journal of Modern History* in Zoë's hand: edition 8312.

'Your supervisor just published a paper. It's brilliant.' Zoë nodded at Alba's notebook. 'You know, you must be the only one in here without a computer—'

'What? But the article—' Alba looked suddenly startled. 'What's the title?'

'"Mona Caird and the Marriage Question in 1888: A Revisionist History".'

'Really?' Alba wondered if Dr Skinner had been meaning to surprise her with it. She took the journal and flicked through its pages until she found the title in bold and, underneath, the author's name: Dr A. Skinner.

One name. Alone. Single.

It must be a mistake. She stared at the black letters standing out against the white page, trying to suppress her rising panic. Perhaps this article was a precursor to the real one, perhaps Dr Skinner had written it to prepare for their joint paper so that it would have the impact it deserved. Entirely forgetting Zoë, Alba began to read. Although she was an extremely fast reader with a nearly photographic memory, it took her two hours to read the article's ten pages. Ten pages of what would now be known to the world – at least the world of academic historians – as Dr Skinner's brilliant revision of Victorian marriage mores in the late nineteenth century. It was a perfect, word-for-word account of her initial notes, crafted into elegant, brilliant paragraphs that followed every line of her reasoning exactly.

When she'd finished reading, Alba stayed at the desk, still holding the magazine, staring at the wall. Her world had turned on its axis, tipping so far that she could no longer see straight. And Alba sat there, until the library closed at ten o'clock and a concerned Zoë had to ask her to leave.

Carmen kneels in the dirt, carefully scooping out handfuls of soil with her fingers. Twilight sinks slowly into night, but the sky is still light enough for her to see by. Carmen wishes she'd never done it, wishes she had never brought it with her to England. It was a stupid mistake. And then it started to smell so strongly of Tiago, of sex and cigarettes, that it began to choke her. So Carmen tried to get rid of it, and burying it seemed the most sensible option. Though of course it hasn't worked.

The midnight glory was the first plant Carmen saw when she came to the house. Its nearly black flowers reminded her of Tiago, how everything around him turned dark, so it had seemed appropriate. And she thought, once she buried the last piece of him, that she could get on with her life, that she could forget. But it's just the opposite, and now he's poisoning everything around him.

As Carmen digs she prays to a Catholic God she no longer worships that she's doing the right thing – not burying her problems but facing them. She thinks of the night it all went wrong, the night their love turned sour. Tiago had invited Carmen up on stage to sing a duet with him, something he wanted to serenade her with. But when she sang, the audience fell silent, totally enchanted. And when she stopped they cheered so loudly, begging for an encore, that Tiago couldn't hear himself singing his part. He stared at her. A light had flicked on inside Carmen, one he'd never seen before, not even when they made love. But it went out the moment she saw his face. That night he slapped her, warning her not to take on airs or think she was anything special to anyone but him. Carmen never sang after that. Indeed, she hardly ever left the house again.

'*Foda!*' Carmen's knuckles hit the box and she winces, pulling her hand out of the ground and rubbing away the pain. She glances up at the sky and the black shadows of the trees as the last patch of light slips away. She doesn't have any more time. Carmen wraps her fingers around the wooden edges of the box and pulls it out of the soil. She places it next to her on the grass, hurriedly fills the hole, stamps down the dirt, spits on it, then turns back toward the house with the box in her hand.

CHAPTER 15

The next morning Carmen wakes feeling lighter than she has in years. And she knows, before she even opens her eyes that, for doing as it asked, the house has given her a gift. She has no idea what it is, but she has a sense of where. Slipping out of bed, Carmen pads across the room, steps into the corridor and hurries into the living room. And there, by the bay windows overlooking the front garden, stands a baby grand piano.

She walks to it slowly, postponing the moment of joy, savouring every juicy second. She slides her fingers along the smooth golden wood, sending sparks of excitement through her hands. Carmen smoothes the back of her nightdress and sits on the black leather bench. The moment she touches her fingers to the keys she begins riffing chords, jumping octaves, speeding up and down the notes.

At last she stops, her hands held in midair as a shaft of sunlight slips across the wood. She stares at the line of dust motes that dance in and out of the light, mesmerised by the way they move. Gradually a memory rises up inside her, a flicker, the shadow of a dream. And as she starts to play again, Carmen sings a song remembered from long ago. And then she thinks of Alba, knowing what she has to do now.

'I need help.'

'With what?'

'Writing,' Alba admits. There isn't any point in keeping her desire a secret any more, since she can't seem to do it anyway. And today is the first of July. She can't wait for too long; in six weeks she'll never see Stella again. This thought brings tears to Alba's eyes and she blinks them back.

'Well, okay. What do you want to write?'

'I don't know.' Alba holds the pen between her fingers, clicking the lid. 'I wanted it to take my mind off . . . things. But it's not really working.'

'That's because you need some inspiration first,' Stella says. 'You need to live a little. You need to get into mischief, fall in love . . .'

'Mischief?' Alba repeats, as if the ghost is speaking a foreign language she's not sure she wants to learn. 'Love?'

'Exactly.'

'Did you do that, then?' Alba shifts the subject. 'When you were alive?'

'Oh, absolutely.' Stella smiles. 'All the time.'

Alba snaps on the pen lid with a triumphant click. 'You said you couldn't remember anything.'

'Did I?' Stella asks, unabashed. 'Well, maybe some of it's starting to come back to me now.'

Alba sits up. 'Like what?'

'Just things.'

'What things?'

'You don't want to hear debauched tales of my misspent youth. It's all too sordid. It'd shock you.' But Stella smiles, knowing it's time.

'Please,' Alba says, 'stop teasing me.'

'Oh, all right, then.' Stella feigns a sigh of surrender. 'So, I grew up rather like you, amidst a great deal of material wealth but very little love. I was sent to Cheltenham Ladies' College just after my sixth birthday—'

'Really?' Alba's surprised at the coincidence. 'I was eight.'

'You were luckier than me, then. God, how I hated it, I ran away a dozen times. I was an only child 'til I was nine, then I came home one day to a baby sister. My parents hadn't said anything. It was a bloody shock, to say the least.'

'Did you like her?'

'No.' Stella laughed. 'I wanted to kill her. Once, I tried to smother her with a pillow, and I would have if her nanny hadn't walked in.'

'Oh.' Alba thinks of her half siblings, how they must have hated her even more than that. She wonders when they found out the truth. She wonders if she'll ever dare to speak to them again.

'Exactly,' Stella says. 'But, luckily, Beth was a rather forgiving sort of girl and we made friends, until I loved her more than anyone else in the world. She was twelve when I died. She still looked for me around every corner and in every room, poor thing. But of course I wasn't there, I was here.'

'How did you die?'

'Drugs, drink . . . all very clichéd, I'm afraid.' Stella shrugs. 'But then it was the sixties, all the cool people were dying that way.'

'You died here, in the house?'

Stella nods. 'Pills. Like Joplin and Monroe and Morrison . . .'

'But I thought . . .' Alba thinks of her mother and takes a deep breath. 'Peggy said the house helps everyone—'

'With a few tragic exceptions, remember?' Stella says. 'Well, I was one of those.'

'But,' Alba whispers, 'what, how . . .?'

'I wanted to be a singer,' Stella says. 'Not a star. I just dreamt of writing songs and singing them. In clubs and cafes, that sort of thing.'

'Why didn't you?'

'I didn't have the guts I suppose. I didn't think I was good enough to start with and I didn't try to be any better. Maybe I was just lazy or terrified, or both.' She sighs. 'So instead I fell in love with a few musicians, and followed them around the country and listened to them play and let them write songs about me, and pretended I didn't know when they were fooling around. And I pretended to myself that it was good enough, that it was a life close enough to the one I really wanted. It wasn't until I found myself here that I knew it wasn't.'

'So why didn't you change, when you came here?'

'Like I said, I was one of those exceptions. I didn't—'

'But why couldn't the house help you?' Alba's voice starts to crack. 'I thought it was supposed to take care of people, I thought it was supposed to help.'

'It does its best,' Stella says. 'But it can't save everyone. It shows people the way, it gives them a little nudge now and then, but the house can't do everything. And some people don't have what it takes to be happy. It's not an easy thing, you know. It takes great courage and determination, to keep looking for light in all the darkness of life.'

'And you didn't have it?'

'No, not then, I didn't,' Stella admits. 'But don't worry about me. I had my chance, and it was a good one. I didn't suffer massive deprivations or diseases. I had a pretty comfortable time of it, all in all. Just like you. That's why I'm a perfect example for—'

'Me?' Alba frowns.

'Exactly,' Stella smiles. 'Most of my misery was self-inflicted, too, so—'

'Hey! That's not—'

'Fair?' Stella interrupts. 'Harsh, perhaps, but entirely fair. You didn't have the best childhood, admittedly, but it wasn't hideous. And you're all grown up now, so it's up to you to decide if you're going to at last let go of all that and get on with your life.'

'But,' Alba protests, 'you just said it wasn't easy.'

'Not for some, true. Not for Sylvia and Dorothy' – Stella nods at the ceiling – 'and the one in the tower.'

'Who?' Alba's frown deepens. 'Peggy?'

'No, of course not,' Stella laughs. 'Never mind, the point is that some people don't have what it takes to live happy lives, but you do. You've got everything you could possibly need. You've got greatness inside you, and love ahead of you, if only you'll stop running from it.'

Alba chews at her fingernail.

'Speaking of which, I know what'll give you some inspiration to write. Go to the library.' She nods at Alba's notebook. And, although the pen is still capped in Alba's hand, a list of titles and authors is now written down on the page.

'The library?' Alba frowns again. 'But I'm sure I can find them upstairs.'

'No, you won't.' Stella hides a smile. 'You'll have to go to the library for these.'

'I've come for more novels.' Alba hands Zoë the list. She still can't understand why, given the few thousand novels that had recently materialised in her bedroom, she couldn't find them at home. 'Oh, and to return these.' She places the small stack of Forster novels on the counter.

'Did you love them?' Zoë asks.

'*A Room with a View* was my favourite. I loved *Maurice*, too, it made me cry,' Alba says, a little surprised at herself for admitting it. She thinks back to the train journey, Inverie and her father. The detective hasn't been in touch yet, but it's been less than a week, so she keeps telling herself not to worry.

'Really?' Zoë asks, hopeful, wondering if the fact that Alba loved *Maurice* might be a sign. She glances down at the list: *On the Road, Reality Sandwiches, Nowhere Man* and *Other Voices, Other Rooms*, then turns to Andy, who sits behind the computer.

'Will you cover me while I nip down to the stacks?'

Andy shrugs and grunts his acquiescence.

'That's great.' Alba leans against the counter. 'Thanks.'

As Zoë disappears, Andy turns to Alba. 'Don't you wonder why she never makes you wait for books, just like every other silly bugger?'

Alba is surprised by his tone. Perhaps their love affair has gone sour, perhaps Zoë broke his heart. She shrugs and steps away, pretending to be absorbed in reading announcements pinned to the notice board on a nearby wall: Violin Concert of Vivaldi's *Four Seasons*, Tiddlywinks Championship at Corpus Christi, Guitar Lessons in Exchange for Spanish Lessons. Alba remembers Stella saying she once hitchhiked all the way from Spain to England.

Someone taps her on the shoulder. Alba turns in shock.

'*Desculpa*,' Carmen says. 'Sorry, Peggy tells me I find you here.'

'Oh.' Alba stares, slightly nervous. Since that night in The Archer, after the embarrassment of running away, she's been sneaking around the house, studiously avoiding Carmen.

'I want you to help me write a song.'

'A song? Me?' Alba stares at her, incredulous. She wonders if Stella has set her up, somehow planting the idea in Carmen's mind. Or the house. The house is full of tricks. 'But why?'

'Because I want to be a singer.'

'Oh,' Alba says. It doesn't surprise her that Carmen should be a singer. It's a suitably glamorous ambition for someone so sexy. Even if Alba could sing she'd never do it in public. The very idea of standing on stage while people stare makes her feel faint.

'*Sim*.' Carmen says, 'I have a audition, a television show. With these two crazy ladies I meet. They will want to dress with horns and sing operas, if I don't do anything different. So I must find something. I play piano, I have tune, but I don't write words. Especially not English words, and . . .'

Alba stares at Carmen, wondering what on earth she's talking about.

'Anyway, I need some song – *qual e a palavra?* – lyrics. I need a writer,' Carmen says. 'I hope you might try.'

'Just the words.' Alba muses on the possibility. 'A bit like a poem, you mean?'

'*Sim*.' Carmen nods, recalling Peggy's suggestion. 'A love poem.'

'Love?' Alba frowns.

'Yes.'

Alba thinks of Charles, who told her she shouldn't waste her time on something she had no talent for. Then she thinks of Albert, the poet, and ponders if perhaps she has some untapped abilities she can draw on. It's the thought of Albert that decides it, the thought of creating a connection, however distant, between them. 'Okay,' Alba says. 'How long do we have?'

'Three weeks.'

Alba's eyes widen. She has absolutely no idea if she can do this. She's almost entirely certain she can't. But she gives a little shrug, attempting nonchalance even though her heart is beating so hard in her chest Alba can barely hear her own voice say, 'I'll try. I can't promise, but I'll try.'

'*Excelente, excelente.*' Carmen grins and kisses a very startled Alba on the cheek.

Two days later they stand in the living room at the piano. The pipes rattle and shake with excitement, the lights flicker on and off and Alba smiles.

'It's beautiful.' She runs her finger slowly along the honey-coloured wood. 'I've never seen anything like it before.'

'*Sim.*' Carmen nods. 'It is very rare. Steinway. Roses wood. Very rare.' She sits, then pats the black leather. 'Sit with me, *por favour.*'

Alba inches onto the stool. They sit side by side in silence as Carmen gazes at the piano with a reverence reserved for religious relics. Alba waits. 'So, um,' she says finally, 'what do we do now?'

Instead of answering, Carmen starts to play, pressing the keys so that the notes reverberate in the wood and echo softly through the air. Shivers of excitement run down Alba's spine as if she's being given tiny electric shocks, rooting her to the spot. The music sweeps around her in a thousand different hues: red notes in every shade soar above her head, yellow notes sink to her feet, green and blue notes linger in the air between them. At last, the piece reaches a crescendo and, as she hits the highest note, Carmen stops. Alba exhales, suddenly realising she's been holding her breath.

After every echo of every note has evaporated, leaving a multi-coloured mist that settles and slowly disperses, Alba finally speaks. 'My God, did you write that?'

Carmen nods, her fingers still resting on the keys.

'It was completely . . . utterly, purely magical. Your music, it made me feel . . .' She's never heard anyone play anything the way Carmen just did. It filled her with emotions she's never known before, like an empty glass filling with wine: sweet, fruity, intoxicating. She has to taste it again.

Carmen smiles. 'I think you do like music, then, no?'

Alba's momentarily confused, then remembers the lie she told.

She thinks of how afraid she'd been of Carmen

then. Now it seems like years ago. 'Oh, yes,' she says softly, 'sorry about that.'

Still a little dizzy from the music, Alba glances at the wall above Carmen's head and there she sees it – the photograph that, with the exception of Stella, she's been most keen to find: Agatha Christie is standing in the front garden, a tiny smile on her lips as she glances toward the midnight glory. It's a sign. Discovering the author who's supposedly sold more books than any other writer in the world except Shakespeare is a sign she should do something equally brilliant and bold. Or at least take a baby step in that general direction.

'So,' Alba says, realising she hasn't spoken for several minutes, 'why don't you tell me about this song?'

Later, Alba glances around at all the books in her bedroom, wishing she could imbibe their brilliance through osmosis. How can she write a love song when she's never been kissed, when her only experience of romance has happened entirely in her head?

It had taken Alba a week to find the courage to confront the object of her affection. She had hurried across the quad, clutching *The Journal of Modern History*, her eyes on the ground, for the first time not admiring the intricately carved turrets and spires above her, the sculptures of gargoyles and saints, flowers, crosses and coats of arms. She scuttled past the chapel with its dozen stained-glass windows reaching fifty feet to the roofline, its delicate lattice of stone that took nearly a century to build. Her shoes slipped on the cobbled paving as she ran.

When Alba reached Dr Skinner's office, she stopped. Perhaps it had been a mistake after all. Perhaps her supervisor had submitted her name and the editors forgot to use it. Maybe she should wait, maybe she should come back when she's calm and quietly ask what had really happened. There would be a sensible explanation, Alba was nearly certain. But she needed to know it or she wouldn't sleep for another week.

So, very softly, Alba knocked and waited. She heard the voices inside the room stop talking, and imagined her supervisor scowling.

'Come in!'

Alba nudged the door open, poking her head into the room. Dr Skinner sat behind a desk. A student sat on the battered leather sofa across the room.

'I need to talk to you,' Alba whispered into the silence.

'Can't it wait?'

She held the magazine up.

'Oh.' Dr Skinner turned to the student. 'Bugger off, Nick.' Nick scowled, apparently sorry to miss the particulars, but picked up his bag and hurried out.

'Sit.'

Alba sat.

'So, I suppose this is about my not crediting you.'

Alba stiffened, her last pinch of hope extinguished. The room went white, bleached of all colour, as if she was looking through fog. So it was intentional. Calculated. Cold. Alba was speechless.

'Your research was good,' Dr Skinner said, 'but not enough to credit your name alongside mine. That would suggest we wrote it jointly, which wasn't the case. Now, if you felt you deserved more than that, I'm sorry, but that's how these things go.'

By the end of this ridiculous speech, Alba had found her voice again. 'Yes, you're right,' she said, biting each word between her teeth. 'We didn't write it jointly. I wrote it. And you copied every word.'

'I did nothing of the sort.' Dr Skinner laughed.

'You did,' Alba said, barely audible. 'You did.'

'Are you certain of that?'

'Of course I am. I've got, I've got . . .'

'What?' Her supervisor leant across the desk. 'You've got what?'

'My . . . Give me my notes back,' Alba begged. 'Give them back.' For the first time in her career she deeply regretted resisting technology. If she'd written it all up on a computer instead of only on paper, she'd now have backups, files, proof.

'I'm afraid I really don't know what you're talking about.'

'I'll go to the dean,' Alba mumbled.

'By all means.' Dr Skinner gave a wry smile. 'An excellent idea. In fact, I'm having lunch with the dean this afternoon. Would you like to join us?'

'I don't believe . . . How could you steal from me?' Alba felt tears pricking. In a moment they'd be spilling down her cheeks. And if she could do nothing else, Alba wouldn't allow that. She wouldn't let Dr Skinner see her broken.

'I'm getting a little tired of this now,' Dr Skinner sighed. 'And if you insist on this behaviour, it'll be impossible for me to keep supervising you.'

'How can you say that?' Alba asked. 'I, I . . .' *I did it all for you, I didn't ask for anything, and I loved you, I love you.*

'Well, we need to reconsider our situation, don't we? I don't think this is quite working, wouldn't you agree?'

'What?' Alba gaped. 'What do you—'

'Us. This.' Dr Skinner gave a small shrug. 'I think it is time to part ways.'

'But my MPhil, my . . . what am I supposed to do?'

'You could find another supervisor, dependent on my recommendation, of course. Which, after your accusation, I'm afraid I couldn't possibly give you.' Dr Skinner turned away to shuffle through papers, as though it was already over and they had never known or meant a single thing to each other.

'You, you . . .' Alba shook, unable to get the words out. 'I, I, I . . .' But she couldn't find words that came within a thousand degrees of how she felt.

So instead she turned and fled.

It's been a week since Blake and Carmen worked the same shift. He's arranged it that way, taking a little time out to focus exclusively on Greer. But now he's ready to get back in the game. Having waited until after closing time on Greer's day off, and sending everyone else home, he finds her in the wine cellar.

'Hey, sugar.' He grins from the doorway. 'How's it going?'

Carmen just shrugs and lifts another box onto her pile for re-stocking.

'Look, I'm sorry it's been a while. I had some personal stuff to sort out. But now it's done I'd love to see you again.'

Carmen looks up at him: the green eyes, the blond curls, the creamy complexion: white swan to Tiago's raven, perfect for erasing his black imprint from her body and soul. But she can play this game, too, and contrition is called for. Grovelling.

'I don't think so.' Carmen turns away.

'Look, I know I don't deserve it.' Blake steps toward her. 'But give me another chance. It won't happen again. You have my word.'

Carmen raises an eyebrow. 'And how do I know you are worth it?'

Blake tries to gauge whether she's just toying with him. But he can't read her. Unlike Greer, she seems to be able to see through his smile and into his cold, dark heart. 'Try me and see,' he says. 'I'm well worth it.'

Carmen holds Blake's gaze, then steps forward to kiss him. For a second he's too shocked to respond but, quickly recovering, he presses his chest against hers and kisses her back, strong and deep and desperate.

'Ow!' Blake steps back, his finger to his lip where she bit him.

'*Desculpa.*' Carmen laughs. 'I not mean to hurt you, at least not like that.' She gives him a wicked smile. She wants to scratch him, to tear at his skin and draw blood. She's full of fire and fight. All she can think of now is Tiago, how much he hurt her, how much she wanted to hurt him. Fury burns through her body, lighting up the tips of her fingers as though she's been ignited and could singe his skin. 'I want to—'

'Yes,' he whispers, stepping forward to kiss her again. 'I know exactly what you want.'

CHAPTER 16

Peggy can sense what's happening with her girls, how events have taken a sharp downward turn, but she knows that intervening right now, especially with regards to Blake and Greer, will do no good. Sometimes a surrogate mother has to know when to step back and let her kids learn their own lessons. So instead she thinks of herself and Harry.

Whenever she misses him during the week, she arranges a rendezvous in the bathroom. A decade ago, Harry bought a flat around the corner, the bedroom window of which overlooked her bathroom. Of course the other inhabitants of Mill Road Mews, in the absence of need or invitation, can't see the house at all. Unfortunately, buying the flat didn't halt Harry's campaign for cohabitation. Sometimes he hangs homemade posters in his windows with *Come To Me* written in letters two feet tall. On their anniversary he writes *Marry Me*, not bothering with a question mark, but leaving it as a statement of interest, a declaration of intention.

When she's feeling frisky Peggy performs a little striptease at her bathroom window. Nothing very risqué – she wouldn't want to give Harry a heart attack – just a suggestion of what's to come on Sunday. For his part, Harry would gladly risk a coronary. What better way to go, after all? But he looks forward to these teases enormously. He is so in tune with the rhythm of Peggy's heart that he's always ready and waiting just before she appears at the window.

Peggy can't now pinpoint the exact moment she must have fallen in love. Unlike Harry's almost instantaneous tumble down the rabbit hole, her feelings crept up gradually. For their first anniversary they returned to the cinema to celebrate, watching *Robin Hood: Prince of Thieves*. Peggy thought the film dreadful, but refrained from saying so when she saw Harry with a tear in his eye at the end. That was the moment she first loved, although she'd refused to fully admit it to herself until now. Having never known real love before, she has taken a while to recognise it. But she recognises it now.

'How are your lyrics coming along?' Stella sits cross-legged at one end of the table, elbows balanced on her knees, cupping her chin.

'They aren't, really,' Alba admits.

'How long until the show?'

'Two and a half weeks.' Alba puts down her pen. 'I'm not sure I can do it.'

'Don't underestimate yourself,' Stella says. 'Have you heard from the private dick yet?'

Alba shakes her head, caught by a sudden longing for her father. She wonders if she'll ever find him. Then she thinks of her mother. 'Please tell me about the song you were singing the night I came,' Alba says. 'How did you know it? I'm going to keep asking until you tell me, so it may as well be now.'

Stella smiles at Alba's tone, at the new injection of strength and determination. 'All right then, yes. I heard it in the air, on the breeze.' Stella tells a half-truth. 'I heard your mother singing that night. The recently departed are easy to hear.'

'But she didn't die that night; it was a week after I came here.'

'No, that was when Charlotte called you,' Stella says, 'but that wasn't when she died. She walked into the woods to take the overdose. They didn't find her for five days.'

'No,' Alba says, 'that's not true, they didn't tell me that, it can't be—' Shock and disbelief shiver through her body as if she was walking barefoot on ice.

'They didn't tell you a lot of things, though, did they?'

'I don't believe you.' Alba forces the words through her frozen lips. 'How do you know?'

'The dead know a lot more than the living,' Stella explains. 'It's one of the perks.'

'I don't believe you.'

But they both know that she does. Alba thinks of all the secrets her siblings have kept from her, she thinks of the father she never knew was hers and the one she thought was. Charles Ashby was hardly a model dad. In fact, he was so rarely home when Alba was young that it had taken a few weeks for her to realise he'd gone for good, though many months passed before anyone actually confirmed it. Her brothers were travelling in Europe and her sister found her in the playroom. An hour after she broke the news, Alba was still asking questions.

'He isn't coming back,' Charlotte had said. 'That's what I'm trying to tell you.'

'But where has he gone?'

'I don't know.'

'Why's he not coming back?'

'I told you, Al, I don't know.'

'But he didn't say goodbye. Won't he come back to say goodbye?'

'That's not how it works. You just have to accept it, okay?' Charlotte said. 'That's how life is. It doesn't always go the way you want it to.'

'Where's Mummy? I want to see her.'

'She's resting.' Charlotte sighed. 'I already told you.'

'No, she's not. I went to her room. She's not there. I waited until dark.'

'Yes, well, she went to have a little rest in a hospital.' Alba held her breath. She knew what hospitals were for.

'Is Mummy going to die?'

'Oh God, no.' Charlotte laughed. The sound

spun out of her mouth in grey curls, collecting in clouds above Alba's head. 'Of course not. It's not that kind of hospital. She's . . . unhappy, they're going to help her. We'll visit her next week, so you can see her then.'

'Are you going back to school at the end of the summer, like last year?'

'Of course I am.'

'So, who's going to look after me?'

'Well, it's been decided that this year you'll come to Cheltenham with me.'

Alba frowned up at her sister. She hated school, hated the teachers and the other pupils, and the only saving grace of the one she went to now was that she could run home when the day ended and be in her bedroom in ten minutes. Then at four o'clock their cook would bring her tea and home-made ginger biscuits. She didn't imagine that this new school would have better teachers and students, ones who wouldn't treat her like a leper, and this one she wouldn't be able to run home from.

'Don't expect me to watch out for you, though,' Charlotte said. 'You'll have to learn to take care of yourself, okay?'

Alba nodded, wishing her mummy were there. Because even though Elizabeth hadn't talked for months, didn't respond when Alba hugged her, didn't stroke her hair or sing the butterfly song any more, Alba still wanted her. Right then she would have given anything for a hug, heartfelt or not. Because a hollowed-out mother was better than no mother at all.

'This is nice.' Greer smiles. 'We've not been out in public for ages. I was starting to think you might be hiding me.' They're sitting in Blake's favourite restaurant, and to celebrate the occasion she's wearing her favourite outfit: a turquoise velvet version of the iconic Marilyn Monroe dress, along with red slippers.

'Hiding you?' Blake returns her smile, his tone light, nonchalant. 'I like to be discreet, is all. So,' he quickly shifts the subject, 'you're looking particularly ravishing tonight. I don't think I've ever seen a more delicious-looking female.'

'Thank you.' Greer blushes. She wonders if it's too soon to be talking about the future, about maybe moving to London, about what he wants to do with his life and whether or not they might do it together. He's been so attentive since she nearly broke it off, but for all his honeyed words and gentle caresses, Greer still senses she has to tread very softly with this subject. She bites into a tiny potato and chews slowly. 'Hey, do you still want to write something for me to star in?'

'What?'

'Don't you remember?' Greer asks, tentatively. 'You said you might.'

'I did?' Blake pours them each a little more wine. He's been with Carmen nearly every night since that first time in the wine cellar – in parks, in alleyways, on benches. He can't call what they do making love, it's far too ferocious for that. They meet, fuck, then part, and he can't get enough of it. He's in no danger of falling for Greer now.

'I don't remember,' Blake says, a little confused. 'But yeah, sure, it shouldn't be a problem.'

'I'd love to read some of your work,' Greer ventures. This is another subject she's been longing to broach. She'd been waiting for him to offer but doesn't think he will. 'I didn't want to ask, but . . .'

'Oh, right.' Blake nods, cutting up his steak. 'Sure.' Then he remembers. The writer line is something he sometimes uses in the early stages of seduction. It sounds sexy and the women never last so long that he has to worry about them actually wanting to see his nonexistent work. Until now.

'I bet it's great,' Greer says. 'I wish I could write, then maybe I'd have done a one-woman show and starred in that, instead of having to audition for everything else, along with five hundred other likely candidates.'

'Don't worry, Red,' he says carelessly, without looking up, 'I'm sure it'll all figure itself out.'

'Do you think so?'

'I surely do.' Blake swallows his steak. He's never been with a woman like Carmen before, someone who kisses as if she wants to bite off his tongue, who touches him as if she'd rip the skin from his bones given the chance. She'll never look him in the eye and won't cuddle afterward, not for a

221

minute. And every time they have sex it is like she's shaking him awake.

'So.' Greer is as careful as if she's stepping on glass. 'Do you think you'll ever . . .?'

This time Blake listens, not hearing the words she actually says but the ones he knows she wants to say: love, marriage, babies. The Holy Trinity. Waves of Greer's longing hit Blake across the table and, with a twinge of guilt, he looks up. He wishes she were made of stronger stuff so she wouldn't hurt so much. He doesn't want to hurt her, and it's a shame that he must.

To soften the blow he's about to give, Blake offers Greer a piece of himself he's never offered anyone before. 'You know—' He pauses, pulling the words up from the deep well he'd long ago dropped them into. 'When my mama left, my father locked himself in the restroom for three days. The noises he made, I'd never heard noises like that before, like . . . the sounds of hell. When he came out he told me, "Your mom's gone and she's never coming back." And that was the last he ever said of it. I cried 'til I threw up, every night for a year. And when I stopped I promised myself, I promised myself that I'd never let it happen to me again.'

Greer gazes at him. 'God, I'm sorry—'

'It's not that.' Blake stops her. 'I'm trying to tell you, I won't let myself . . . Do you see?'

She thinks she does, but it's not what she wants to hear. 'No, not really.'

'I'll never marry,' Blake says, sorry that he has to spell it out so crudely. 'I'll never have kids.'

In the silence Greer grips her fork so tightly that her fingernails cut into her palm.

'Do you understand?'

Greer nods.

Alba spends the rest of the evening with Carmen, listening to her play, writing down words that float into her head along with the notes. The living room walls silently shake in appreciation of the music and, during a particularly splendid piece, all the lights in the house flicker on and off, then blow a fuse at the crescendo. Carmen plays for hours without stopping. Sometimes Alba puts down her father's pen and closes her eyes, letting herself be carried away with the music, drifting, soaring and falling, entirely forgetting herself. Two sentences drift into her head, perfect and complete. She writes them down, then reads them to Carmen, who smiles and nods and continues to play. At eleven o'clock, when the phone rings in the hallway, it's Alba, having nipped into the kitchen for a bedtime hot chocolate with cream (Peggy's influence), who picks up. 'Hello.'

'Hello. Is this Peggy Abbot?'

Alba stiffens. It's her brother Edward. What should she do? *Put the phone down. Hang up and flee.* 'Hi, Ed.'

'Al?' Edward says, relieved at the sound of his sister's voice. 'Is that you?' It's taken him weeks

223

to pluck up the courage to call, knowing that she'll ask questions that will unravel all the secrets he's been struggling to keep.

'Yes,' Alba says. 'How did you know my number?'

'Charlotte gave it to me.'

The phone line is silent. All Alba can hear is static and she wonders if Edward's hung up. 'How did Charlotte get the number?'

'Your landlady called up a week before Mum died to say you'd moved in,' Edward says. 'Didn't you ask her to?'

'Yeah,' Alba says, because it's easier that way. 'Yeah, I did. How's my little niece?'

'Tilly's okay. She still cries for her mother most nights. I'm afraid I'm a poor substitute. I never learnt much about being a good father.'

'I'm sorry,' Alba says, and she is. 'I miss her.' And she does.

'Perhaps you could visit us in London sometime,' Edward says. When she doesn't respond, Alba hears him take a quick breath. 'Al, we need to talk.'

'What's wrong?' Alba feels a shot of panic in her chest. 'Is everyone okay?'

'Well, Til and I are coping. And, apart from being a couple of prats in need of heart transplants, Charlie and Lotte are still alive.'

Alba smiles. 'So, what is it?'

'I want to see you, Al,' Edward says softly.

'Okay.'

'It's nothing urgent. I just thought . . . I have

some things to tell you, about our family, about our – my – father. You ran away before we could talk about it all. I thought maybe you'd have questions I could answer.'

Alba thinks of her mother's death, the disappearance of her original father, and her biological father still at large. 'Yes,' she says. 'Yes, I do.'

Alba sits on the edge of the bath, notebook in hand, reading the first few lines of her lyrics to Sylvia Plath and Dorothy Parker, who listen from their vantage points on opposite walls. She didn't want to, but they've been asking every day how her writing is progressing, so eventually Alba succumbed.

'Not bad,' Dorothy says. 'You have potential.'

'She's overly critical,' Sylvia says. 'You have a natural flair, but you need to be bolder. Your writing is too tentative, you care too much for the reader—'

'Which will kill you quicker than anything,' Dorothy interrupts. 'The eyes of others are our prisons; their thoughts our cages.'

Alba frowns. 'Really?'

'Dismiss that warning at your peril,' Dorothy says. 'Literature is strewn with the wreckage of writers who have minded the opinions of others.'

'You must be completely alone when you write,' Sylvia adds. 'Cast out everyone else from your mind so you can sit down and write the truth.'

'Okay, all right.' Alba nods, scribbling down their

thoughts, still unable to believe she's getting writing tips from her two literary heroines.

'But all this is moot if you've never been in love,' Dorothy says. 'To write about love you first need to know it.'

Alba bites the end of her pen and glances at the floor. 'Well, I, um . . .'

'Go out and live,' Sylvia says. 'Then come back and write about it.'

'I thought writing was all about imagination,' Alba protests. 'I thought—'

'Poppycock,' Dorothy snaps. 'If you pass the rest of your life in this bathroom, you'll never find anything worth writing about, nor the talent to do it.'

'Well—'

'She's right,' Sylvia says. 'You won't be able to write anything true until you've felt it first. And I'm afraid it doesn't seem as if you're very willing to do that.'

'Hold on,' Alba says through gritted teeth. 'Now, I'll very gratefully take literary advice from you, but not life advice. I hardly think either of you is qualified to give it, since you killed yourself' – she nods at Sylvia – 'and you tried to.' Alba nods at Dorothy before striding to the door. 'So, thank you and goodbye.' And, with that, she's gone. The bathroom door slams behind her, shaking every photograph on the walls.

'My, my, that was fun.' Dorothy laughs. 'I think our girl is starting to get some fire.'

'Yes,' Sylvia says, her teeth still rattling, 'though I do worry about her, I've never known anyone so scared to feel anything.'

Five minutes later Alba's sitting in the kitchen reading her lyrics to Stella. When she's finished Alba looks up, her heart in a holding pattern, waiting for Stella to speak.

'I like it. It's a good beginning. Now you just need a little more—'

'Life experience, yes,' Alba snaps. 'I know.'

'Especially since you're writing about love, but you've never actually . . .'

'Felt it.' Alba sighs. 'I know.'

They sit in silence until Alba nods nervously, biting a fingernail.

'What's it like?'

'True love will rip your heart right open and knock you for six.' Stella smiles. 'But you'll also feel safer than you've ever felt in your life.'

Alba considers this, still biting her nails.

'No.' She shakes her head at last. 'I don't think so. Not me.'

'Oh, yes,' Stella says. 'I promise you will. Even you.'

CHAPTER 17

'He's here.'

'Where?'

'In Cambridge.'

Alba looks at the private detective, incredulous. He'd called that morning and invited her to his office. 'No, he can't be, are you certain?'

'Of course I am. He lives on Gwydir Street. Number twenty-one.'

Her world is spinning. The green-striped wallpaper blurs. She closes her eyes. Her father lives less than a mile from Hope Street. They could have passed on the pavement. She might have seen him.

'He's an English teacher. Has a part-time job in a bookshop on King's Parade too.' The detective sits back in his chair. 'He has strange habits, spends most of his time walking around, waiting outside certain places for hours. Still. I expect—'

'King's Parade?' She went there months ago, the cashier told her to read . . . Him. It was him. And then, all of a sudden, it hits her. 'Oh God. It's not a coincidence that he's here, is it? It can't be. I just—'

'It's not unheard of.' The detective shrugs. 'Occasionally parents who abandon their children will find them again and move to be close to them. I've seen it before.'

'But how did he know, how did he find me?'

'It's easy. If you're ever in the paper, if you make the news, it'll most likely be on the Internet . . . Everyone's an amateur detective nowadays. Fortunately most people are thick as two short ones, no offence, so I'm not out of a job just yet. Anyway . . .'

'But what should I do now?' Alba whispers. 'What will I say?'

'Oh, I'm sure you'll think of something,' the detective says. He's always a little uncomfortable when his clients threaten to get emotional. 'Start with hello. Go from there.'

'Yes, I suppose so.' Tears cloud Alba's eyes and she swallows.

The detective fixes his own eyes on the piles of paper covering his desk. 'Don't worry, I'm sure it'll be fine. Now, my next client's due any minute now, so . . .'

'Yes, sorry.' Alba forces herself to stand, though the room seems to be spinning.

'Ms Ashby?' says the detective, stopping Alba as she reaches the door. 'Good luck.'

'You've got to give her up. It's time to let go.'

Zoë sighs, staring at the computer, refusing to look at him.

'And I'm not saying it 'cause I want you so desperately,' Andy deadpans. 'I'm totally over us now. It took a lot of therapy, grief counselling, prayer; but I'm finally okay.'

'Shut up.' Zoë giggles. 'You're an opportunist and you know it.'

'You think so little of yourself, eh? Sounds like someone else needs therapy. I've got my counsellor's card.' He pretends to reach into his pocket.

'Stop being so pathetic.'

'Pathetic? *Moi?* Pot. Kettle. It's been, what, two years?'

'Three years, four months . . .'

'You know the minutes too?' Andy laughs. 'You are seriously screwed.'

'Of course I don't. Shut up.'

'Why the hell haven't you just asked her out?' Andy leans against the pile of books they're supposed to be cataloguing. 'You don't even know if she . . .'

'What?' Zoë interrupts. 'Plays for the other team, bats for the other side, swings the other—'

'I was going to say, "is attracted to spineless, blue-haired pixies."' He shrugs. 'But whatever.'

'"Spineless"?' Zoë scowls. 'Have a little sympathy. You've obviously never been rejected, never had your heart stamped on.'

'No.' Andy grins. 'I can't say I have. But then I am a love god. You know, I could probably cure you of your little problem, if you gave me half a chance.'

'Hey.' Zoë swivels around in her chair to face him. 'Are you saying that my—'

'No, touchy. I meant your hideously heavy crush on that bookish midget, not your particular brand of sexuality.'

'Oh.' Zoë huffs. 'Well, anyway, don't call her that. She's lovely.'

'She must be. You've been celibate for practically a decade.'

'I haven't.'

'Have you had sex since you fell in love with her?'

'Not exactly, no.'

'Well then,' Andy says, returning to the computer. 'I rest my case.'

Albert must find Alba again. If he can't find her himself, he'll sell his signed first edition of *A Moveable Feast* and hire a private detective. If only he could knock on every door in Cambridge, if only he could put up posters. But of course he can't. He has to keep himself a secret from Alba – he has to keep his promise. Even though her mother is dead, it's still not his place to destroy her memories, to tell her what she might otherwise never know.

Albert sips his second glass of vodka and thinks about the night Alba was conceived. It's the memory he's visited most often over the years, so much so that he no longer remembers what was real and what he's imagining. Was the wallpaper

231

sky blue and Elizabeth's dress deep red and dotted with roses? Were her nails painted to match her dress? Or are those details he has added? He'll never know.

What Albert knows for certain is that, at the time, he had no idea he was creating his only daughter.

It was the second anniversary of the day they met. Albert rented a cottage in Brighton for the weekend. Elizabeth told her family she was visiting a friend in London. It was the first time they'd spent an uninterrupted forty-eight hours together. They walked along the beach, crunching stones beneath their bare feet, getting tiny pebbles caught between their toes. They stood in the sea, kissing as the cold water soaked their clothes. They sat in restaurants, holding hands across the table, forgetting to pick up their forks and actually eat anything. They walked along the pier, watching the waves pulling back and forth in the gaps between the wooden slats beneath their feet. When the sun went down they looked out at the ocean as the horizon turned pink, orange and red. They walked hand in hand back to the cottage, their faces lit by the flashing lights of fairground rides and casinos, and made love until morning.

That night Albert pretended Elizabeth was his, that he could let her go and she'd come back to him. He lay in the dark and stroked every inch of her as if he had all the time in the world. He gave her soft kisses, whispered her name until it was all he could say, until his mouth couldn't make sense of the word any more. Usually, in their stolen afternoons together, she napped afterward and he loved to look at her. But that night he slept when Elizabeth did, pretending that they could take their time for granted. If he'd known that it would be their last night together, he would have stayed awake. But of course he didn't.

When they met again after that weekend it was always during the day and only for a few hours at a time. Elizabeth quickly started to show and had to begin telling the great lie, a lie that included sleeping once more with her husband. Secretly Albert hoped that Charles wouldn't be fooled, that he'd divorce his wife and allow them to be together. Sadly, and rather surprisingly, when he was given the news Lord Ashby experienced a sudden surge of devotion brought on by impending fatherhood and hardly let her out of his sight. So, in the snatched hours Albert shared with Elizabeth after that, he could only close his eyes and remember what it had once been like to hold her as though she was his forever.

Peggy kneels in her garden, plucking dead flowers off plants and pulling out weeds. It's the eighth of July. The sun is high in the sky and hot on her back. Perhaps she should put on sunscreen, but what does it really matter now? In the corner of her eye she catches sight of her beloved black roses. The day they first blossomed, nearly twenty years

233

ago, Peggy felt overjoyed to have created something so beautiful. Now she focuses on the dusky velvet petals until all she can see is darkness, death, suicide and murder, which reminds her of that mystery writer, the one who enjoyed extolling the virtues of matrimonial bliss. But, being as yet untouched by love and filled with the ignorance of youth, Peggy hadn't listened.

Agatha Christie had stayed in the house for a week back when Esme was in charge. Years later she returned for a surprise visit, interrupting Peggy having afternoon tea in the downstairs kitchen. So they sat together, eating chocolate cake and sipping Earl Grey tea.

'Oh dear, I'm sorry,' Agatha said after her cup slipped out of her fingers and spilt tea across the table. 'Old age is embarrassing.'

'Don't worry.' Peggy mopped it up and poured her another cup.

'If you get a chance you should marry an archaeologist. I don't suppose there are too many to go around, but it's the best sort of husband to have. The older a woman gets, the more he's interested in her.' Agatha laughed.

'I'll remember that when I'm in my seventies and looking for a lover.' Peggy smiled obligingly. 'Cream?'

'Absolutely, thank you.'

'So,' Peggy said, 'why are you back?'

'Well . . . my days in this house were some of

the most significant of my life, I appreciated every one of them.' Agatha glanced down at her plate. 'I think I'm starting to lose my grip. Words often escape me, plots are more difficult to remember. I'm starting to wonder how many more books I'll be able to complete before I lose . . .'

'I see.' Peggy nodded. 'And what are you working on now?'

'I don't know yet.' Agatha tapped the side of her head and her helmeted coiffure of curls quivered. 'These little grey cells, it's up to them.'

Regarding the old woman carefully, Peggy dipped her finger into the cream and slowly licked it off. 'You'll be fine for another fifteen years,' she said. 'You'll write another ten books or thereabouts. I'd have to check upstairs to be certain, but I think so.'

'Ah, the infamous tower.' Agatha smiled. 'A very intriguing matter, all in all. I confess I tried to sneak in once but that damn door refused to budge.'

'Yes, I'm afraid it won't open for anyone but me.'

'Oh well, some mysteries remain unsolved.' Agatha sat back in her chair. 'Another decade of books, then? That does lift my heart a little. So, tell me, how are you enjoying life as a landlady? It's surely a lot of responsibility for someone so young.'

'Well, I've already been here ten years,' Peggy

said, 'so I'm quite used to it, and I'll be here until I die, so—'

'A lifetime without marriage or motherhood?' Agatha sighed. 'Well, if you want my advice, ditch your duty and find yourself that archaeologist. You're not the queen, you can abdicate without anyone kicking up a fuss.'

'It's not like that.' Peggy stuck her finger in the cream again. 'I want to do this, it's not only a duty, it's an honour. And it's not without its compensations.'

'Oh, well.' Agatha sipped her coffee and shrugged. 'I see good advice is always certain to be ignored, but that's still no reason not to give it.'

Peggy returns to her black roses. She hadn't met Harry then, when Agatha had come to visit. So what could she know of love and marriage? What does she know now?

When Charles Ashby found out about his wife's affair and her love child, he wanted to rip out her heart. He was hurt, though he'd never admit it. Also, Charles was certain he'd never been cheated on before, and the humiliation threatened to overwhelm him, to push him beyond rationality. But deciding he'd rather spend the rest of his days living a privileged life than rotting in jail, he came up with a plan that would instead drive his wife to rip out her own heart.

That Elizabeth had never stopped loving Albert was clear enough. Now that Charles looked back over the last eight years he could see the signs: the way she sometimes gazed at Alba as though remembering something else, how she spent endless hours staring at nothing with a secret, sorrowful smile on her face. The fact that she'd named the damned girl after him. It was hardly the child's fault, of course, but that didn't stop Charles hating her with the same passion with which he now hated his wife. Her bright blue eyes weren't his, nor her black hair. Indeed, her colouring was so opposite to her blond, brown-eyed siblings he couldn't believe it hadn't made him wonder before. Pure ego and pride, probably, he simply never thought Elizabeth would stray, though he'd given her every reason to.

Charles planned his disappearance with precision. He thought about all the possible consequences and accounted for them. The first thing he felt certain of was that, once he was gone, Elizabeth would reply to Albert's letter. She would call him back and they would spend the rest of their days in unadulterated bliss. Unless, of course, he never received her letters, and so never replied. Then, not only would they be separated, but Elizabeth would believe Albert no longer loved her. And that, Charles guessed, would go halfway to breaking her already fragile heart.

Being several miles from the village, Ashby Hall had its own post box and Elizabeth would use it, just as she'd always done, of that he was certain. And so, one morning, Charles went out to meet their postman, a middle-aged Scot who'd worked the same route for the last twenty years and would no doubt continue doing so until he died. With a check for ten thousand pounds, Charles bought assurance that no letters going to, or coming from, Inverie would ever reach their destination.

Then he just had to take care of the children.

Since she'd given up her lover for their sakes, to ensure their clueless father would continue to clothe and feed them and subsidise their over-priced educations, Charles imagined that, were he to turn them against her, it might be enough to finish her off. In her depressive episodes, Elizabeth would cry for hours if she ran over a rabbit on the road, so just think how she'd react if three of her four children suddenly stopped loving her.

One evening he took Charles Jr, Edward and Charlotte into his office and told them that their mother had betrayed the family, that she loved another man – that Alba wasn't really their sister. He told them that for those reasons he was leaving. He was going away and never coming back. But they must never tell Elizabeth or Alba. It was their secret. It would be their duty, as the only true Ashbys left in the house, to hate these interlopers, the ones responsible for the dissolution of their family. And he promised he'd keep in touch, as long as they kept his secret.

The final parting gift of Charles Ashby to his wife, the thing he hoped would break her mind as well as her heart, was a letter to the police telling them he feared his wife meant to kill him. He knew she'd never actually go to jail – which was a shame – since they'd never find a body. But the stress of it all, the interrogation, the malicious gossip, the cruel press, the lifelong suspicion might just be enough to send her right over the edge.

For the first time in her life, Alba takes more than five minutes choosing what to wear. In two hours she's tried on six black sweaters, three white shirts, ten navy T-shirts and four pairs of faded jeans. The books strewn across Alba's bed watch her procrastinate, flapping their pages impatiently. After she decides on the black sweater with the least number of noticeable holes, and the darkest pair of jeans, a dozen books open and snap shut a few times, applauding the fact that she's finally dressed.

An hour later she's standing outside iron gates looking up at the words *Park Street Community College* on a sign high above her head. She watches the teenagers shouting in the playground, thinking they look like hardened street kids who know much more about life than she does. It's a long way from the sheltered, uniformed students of Cheltenham Ladies' College. Alba tightens her grip on the letter in her hand. Then she takes a deep breath, pulls herself up to her full height of five feet, two and a half inches and strides through the gates and into the playground.

'Excuse me.' Alba stops a fairly normal-looking

boy and addresses him in what she hopes is a friendly yet confident tone. 'I'm looking for Mr Mackay's classroom, do you know where it is?' The child just stares up at her. 'Do you have any idea? Or perhaps you could just point me in the right direction?' Alba waits but is only met with the same blank stare. Alba gives up and keeps walking.

Once inside she wanders through the corridors, hoping no one asks why she's prowling around a secondary school, hoping the school isn't too vast and contains no deserted corridors where she might be cornered by a gang of knife-wielding teenagers. A bell rings. Instantly the halls are flooded with frantic bodies, their high-pitched voices and squeals setting Alba's nerves on edge. Being surrounded by hundreds of children, scuttling past her like scorpions, makes the hairs on the back of her neck twitch. She stiffens and pushes through the crowds.

At the end of the corridor a door stands ajar and, though she can't explain how, Alba knows this is the one. This is his door. When she reaches the classroom she sees his name etched on the wood:

MR MACKAY
11A

Alba stares at the letters, until they start to swim in front of her eyes. Just then the door opens, hitting her in the face.

'Ouch!' Alba stumbles back, rubbing her nose as a young girl runs off, laughing. A man steps into the corridor and, for a moment, Alba's vision is compromised and she can't see him. At first, he doesn't see her.

'Oh goodness, oh dear, I am sorry, are you—'

Then Alba looks up and Mr Mackay stares at her. And Alba stares at him. She's studied every one of the photographs the private detective took and knows every line of his face, every inch of him. But she still can't believe that he's really standing before her. 'Oh,' he gasps. 'Oh, my . . .'

Alba blinks a few times and focuses on her father. He is short and stocky with gold-rimmed spectacles and a mop of messy brown curls. He's only a few inches taller than Alba and when she looks into his eyes she sees they're exactly the same as her own. She glances at his clothes: cheap polyester shirt and tie, grey cardigan with holes at the cuffs, polyester trousers frayed at the edges.

His bright blue eyes, wide behind his glasses, are slowly filling with tears. A dark mist comes off him in waves and his pain is so vivid, so substantial Alba could reach out and touch it. The memory of layers and layers of broken glass rises up and, all at once, she sees her father raw, broken, flawed. Alba feels a surge of panic flood over her and suddenly it's all too much too soon.

Albert reaches a chubby hand out toward her. 'Alba.'

His words are royal blue and dark red: sorrow mixed with obsession.

Alba stares at her father, and he stares back at her. Then she turns and runs.

CHAPTER 18

Greer lies naked across her bed, face up, spread out like a starfish, wondering what to wear. Usually this is the most delightful moment of her day, but today she's just too tired to care. Acting onstage is one thing, it's hard enough – but acting every day of your life is bloody exhausting. Greer spends so much time lying lately – to Blake, to herself, to her mother – that she's losing track even more than usual of who she actually is and how she really feels.

With a sigh she gazes up at the ceiling to see a crystal chandelier she's never noticed before. It's large with heavy, glittering droplets of glass hanging in tiers around six light bulbs. Sunlight bounces off the crystal, scattering rainbows across the room. Balanced between two lights is a piece of paper folded in half. Greer stands and reaches up for it, then flops back onto the bed again.

At first, turning the paper to examine the diagrams from different angles, she can't make any sense of it. And then, suddenly, it's clear. The page has been torn from a dress pattern, showing the cut of fabric, the lines to stitch and sew. She can't tell what it would make, but the design is old-fashioned and the paper worn, as if ripped out of a 1950s copy of *Good Housekeeping.*

Greer glances at the wardrobe, the inkling of an idea simmering in the back of her mind, and feels suddenly hopeful.

For once Alba's not in the mood to see Stella. She doesn't even want to fall asleep and see her mother. Tonight she just wants a break from everything: her father, the love song, her family, the question of what she's going to do with her life. Tonight she just wants to lose herself in a book and forget. Alba sits in the living room, propped up on sofa cushions reading *On the Road.* The photographs try to engage her in conversation, but she studiously ignores them. So Vivien Leigh and Vanessa Bell resort to holding an open conversation about her.

'She'll never be a great writer,' Vivien declares, 'or a great woman, if she keeps running from life like that. No guts, no glory.'

'Cliché,' Alba mutters to herself.

'And all the truer for it,' Vivien retorts. 'Why did you run from him, what were you so scared of? I can't quite understand it.'

'Well, what do you know?' Alba hides behind the book.

'Watch your mouth, missy,' Vanessa says. 'We certainly know a lot more about the ins and outs of life than you do.'

'I remember being young and naïve,' Vivien says. 'It had its perks, but there is nothing quite like experience, trust me. Of course, for that you have to throw yourself into the fray.'

'Indeed you must.' Vanessa nods. 'You cannot find peace by avoiding life, only by diving in and finding you can swim. Peace comes from conquering your fears, not running from them.'

'Please,' Alba snaps, 'just leave me alone, okay?' She returns to her book, trying to focus on the story, but no matter how hard she tries to block them out, Vanessa's final words linger in front of her eyes, the floating letters a bright, shining green.

To avoid more preaching from the photographs, Alba escapes to spend the rest of the afternoon with her book on a park bench. She's had enough of the house for now, or rather, all the know-it-alls who inhabit it. She appreciates getting advice when she actually asks for it. But when she's purposely trying to avoid something, she wishes everyone would just leave her alone.

It's a new phenomenon for Alba, having so many people who care enough to constantly offer their opinions about her life. Having grown up among entirely uninterested (or clinically depressed) family members, Alba can't quite get used to it. Her own mother never gave advice, and now she has a hundred replacement mothers wanting to do nothing but dispense their own particular brand of wisdom. As the sun sets Alba thinks of Elizabeth, her rare moments of mania and joy and the long winters of darkness that blacked out everything else, even her youngest daughter.

Elizabeth's fragile mental state passed the point of no return when she was arrested for the murder of her husband. The day the police came to take her mother away, Alba had answered the door. The two tall, dark figures in black uniforms stared down at her.

'Is your mother home?' the taller one asked, his voice so gentle it seemed to suggest that if she gave him the answer he wanted, he might give her a lollipop.

For a long moment Alba just looked up at him, thinking that his hat looked like a big beetle that might, any second, scuttle off his head. Her mother was upstairs, writing another letter, and Alba wasn't sure she'd want to be disturbed. But the men weren't going away; they wanted an answer, and she knew the answer they wanted.

For years afterward, Alba replayed the scene over and over in her head, this time with her saying no instead of yes. She blamed herself, believing that if she'd sent the policemen away that day her mother would never have been arrested. She believed Elizabeth's breakdown was her fault. Because when Elizabeth Ashby finally came home from the police station, the cloud of darkness that before had come and gone never lifted again.

They kept her for forty-eight hours. When they dropped her back on the doorstep of Ashby Hall,

246

Alba knew they'd taken her mother and left a zombie in her place. She'd once spied on Edward watching *Invasion of the Body Snatchers* and knew what was possible. And when she saw her mother – the hollowed-out cheeks and vacant eyes, the curve of her back and her shuffling steps, the dense clouds of dark blue in the air around her – the little girl understood that the mother she'd known had been snatched away.

It was a while before Alba learnt that Elizabeth was suspected of her husband's murder, when children started saying things at school. Her siblings had always refused to talk about it. Alba screamed at her classmates and cried in bed at night. She was certain her mother was innocent. But, after two terms of taunting, Alba began to wonder. As she stared up at the ceiling of her dorm room, trying to block out the whispers of the other girls, Alba knew she could never really know anything for certain.

Edward waits for Alba at the back of the coffee shop. She's fifteen minutes late and he's worried she isn't coming at all. When, ten minutes later the door bangs open and Alba falls in, wearing a woollen coat even though it's July, Edward's face lights up with relief and delight. She walks over to his table. 'Sorry I'm late.'

'Hello, Al.' Suddenly Edward wants to hug her, but he can't. They've never shared that sort of affection before and he's embarrassed to try now.

'Do you want a drink – tea, coffee? Some sort of cakey thing? They seem to have everything one could possibly want here.'

'No thanks, maybe later.' Alba sits. 'I thought you might bring Til.'

'I wanted to, but . . . I'll bring her next time. That is, if . . .' His words are bright silver, so glowing with hope that it makes Alba's heart ache a little. Edward leans forward. 'Are you okay?'

She shrugs. 'Fine, sane, sleeping through the night.' A moment of her mother's last nocturnal visit floats up inside her and Alba offers a small smile. 'Progress is being made.'

'That's good.' Edward smiles in return. 'I'm glad.'

They fall into silence. Customers pass by, inching around their table, ordering their afternoon hits of caffeine and sugar. Alba picks at the frayed edges of her sleeve.

'You knew, didn't you?' she says.

Now Edward wants a cup of coffee. He isn't ready for this. He doesn't have the right answers, the sort that will keep Alba sitting in front of him, the sort that won't reveal him to be a bit of a bastard. Of course he knew the question was coming, but he'd hoped for a little preparation time, half an hour of small talk to pave the way, to strengthen the bond between them and cushion the blow. But the question is in front of him now and he must answer it.

'Yes, we all did.'

'And did he . . . did' – Alba isn't quite sure what to call Charles – 'your father know too?'

'Yes, he knew.'

'When did he find out?'

'When you were eight.' Edward remembers the day he promised to hate Alba forever, as though it were only a moment ago. 'He found her letters. But it wasn't your fault he left. It would have happened eventually,' he says, without any idea of whether or not that is actually true. 'They were never really happy together. They were a bit like Charles and Di. He was stepping out on her long before she stepped out on him.'

Alba nods, as if he's not telling her anything she didn't already know. She bites her lip, staring down at the table and plucking again at the edge of her sleeve.

'And he disappeared so he could punish her, didn't he?' Alba asks.

This time Edward nods. 'Yes,' he says, trying to look her in the eye, but she won't look at him. 'I know we should have told you everything,' he says softly. 'I know it's unforgiveable that we didn't. But I'm hoping, I really hope that you might be able to, one day—'

'So he could frame her for murder and ruin her life, right?' Alba looks up.

'Yes,' Edward admits. Rationally he knows full forgiveness and immediate reconciliation were too much to hope for, but he still couldn't help wishing for it. 'Yes, I believe so.'

'Do you know where he is? Do you know where he went?'

This is the question Edward's been waiting for. And he had promised himself he would tell Alba the truth when it came, but now he can't. It will hurt her. It might make her run and he'll do anything to prevent that, even betray her trust again.

'No, I don't,' Edward says, hating himself for it. 'I'm afraid I don't.'

His words hang in the air: black, the colour of dishonesty. Alba looks at her brother, frowning slightly, wondering what he's keeping from her now. They fall into small talk, Alba, not being very good at confrontation in general, and not knowing how to confront Edward in a way that'd get him to tell the truth, and Edward, being only too happy to take refuge in safer subjects. After a while Alba stands, excusing herself with imaginary errands. Edward walks with her to the street and as they part, they almost hug. But Alba steps back at the last moment, and Edward catches himself just before he stumbles.

'We've made a decision,' Nora says.

'An executive decision,' Sue adds. 'So it's not up for discussion.'

'Exactly,' Nora says, 'that's what that means.'

'Oh, hush,' Sue says. 'I was just being clear. Anyway, she's foreign, so she might not know that.'

Carmen watches the two of them going back and forth. She was late for choir practice and found Tweedledum and Tweedledee bickering good-naturedly next to the altar. She waits for a pause in the action before speaking up.

'Okay, what is your decision?'

'You're to go on alone,' Nora declares quickly, leaving Sue with her mouth open.

'Alone?' Carmen asks. 'Where?'

'You might have put it a little more gently,' Sue says. 'At the television audition, my dear. We've decided that we would only hold you back. You must have the stage all to yourself—'

'Unencumbered by two fat ladies,' Nora adds, 'however magnificently well dressed we might be.'

'Let it go, Pavarotti,' Sue hisses. 'We've already discussed this.'

'I'm not that large!' Nora retorts. 'I lost three pounds last week, I—'

'You want me to do it all by myself?' Carmen asks, trying hard to keep her voice steady. 'No, I can't. This was all your idea in the beginning anyway. I would never do it without you.'

'But you must,' Sue says. 'It's the chance of a lifetime. You simply must.'

Nora walks to Carmen and takes her hand. 'You have a gift, my dear, a gift from God.' She squeezes Carmen's hand as tightly as she did the first time they met. 'And when you sing that is your gift back to Him.'

'To us all,' Sue adds.

'Exactly,' Nora nods. 'And it's up to you to share it with as many people as you possibly can.'

'Which brings us back to the beginning,' Sue says.

'Yes.' Nora smiles. 'And the fact that you must do this alone.'

Edward forces himself to walk all the way to the train station, though he'd much rather have caught a taxi. It's a pathetic effort at self-punishment, he knows, but it will have to do for now. He thinks of his sister, how her distrust of him hung in the air, how she couldn't look him in the eye, how she wouldn't let him touch her – and how much he deserved it all. He'd helped to ruin her child-hood. He'd been trying to make up for it with Tilly, to give her the best of everything, and then her mother died. Edward thinks of his own mother and how he might have saved her.

It was Charlotte who initiated it. Three days after their father left, she pulled her brothers into Elizabeth's study, interrupting her first letter to Albert.

'Daddy told us what you did,' she'd hissed. 'We're going to make you and your daughter pay, we're going to make you suffer for the rest of your lives.'

'We hate you,' Charles added, 'and we want you to die.'

At first their mother had denied it all. But under intense interrogation she finally admitted every-thing. Charlotte and Charles continued to torture her while Edward, unable to bring himself to indulge in such cruelty, said nothing. Yet he didn't defend her and he didn't stop it. In fact, he barely spoke to his mother again. This he now regrets more than anything.

Edward remembers the first hospital they committed Elizabeth to: the tiny grey rooms, the virtually catatonic patients, the irritable nurses and inattentive doctors. Sometimes he forces himself to imagine what it must have been like for her to be left alone with nothing but her own broken heart for company. Edward crosses Trumpington Street, promising himself he'll find the courage to tell Alba the truth, that he'll do everything in his power to make it up to her.

The night they left Elizabeth, she'd stared out of the window, wondering what had happened to her garden. Her trees and flowers had disappeared. Behind her someone bustled into the room, muttering. Elizabeth didn't look up.

'Time for your pills, dear.' A nurse thrust a plastic cup of water into her hand. 'Get them while they're nice and hot.' She laughed, her chins wobbling. She had said the very same thing that morning. Elizabeth looked up at her name tag – *Gina* – and took the three pills: two green, one white.

'Drink up, drink up.' Gina folded her arms over her enormous bosom. 'They'll make you nice and strong.'

Elizabeth swallowed a pill and stared up at her. 'Are Alba and Ella coming today?'

253

'I don't know, dear, but I'm sure your kids will come soon.'

'No.' Elizabeth frowned. 'Ella's not my daughter, she's—'

'Take the next one, there's a good girl. I can't be waiting for you all day now, I've got plenty more visits to make before dinnertime.'

Elizabeth swallowed and gazed back at the window, the last pill in the palm of her hand. 'Aren't the colours beautiful? Alba loves the colours.'

The nurse glanced out at the bare fields blanketed in snow under a slate grey sky. 'No, dear, there aren't any colours now. It's winter. You'll have to wait for spring to see flowers.'

'There are thousands of colours,' Elizabeth said. 'When birds fly the noise of their wings leaves trails of dark blue in the air. They sing in green, except when they're complaining, and cows fart pink bubbles.' Elizabeth laughed.

'Very nice, dear. Now take that last pill for me, please.'

'And your words are dark brown, the colour of boredom.'

The nurse let out a long sigh, her eyes on the pill. Before she could ask again, Elizabeth swallowed it. 'There's a good girl,' Gina said, thinking she wasn't being paid enough to endure the craziness of these people. 'Now give me the cup.'

'You think I killed him. Don't you, Ella?'

'I'm not Ella, dear.' The nurse scrunched the

cup in her hand and dropped it into the bin. 'I'm Gina. Geena.'

'She's calling to me.' Elizabeth murmured. 'I can hear her singing. She wants me to come home.'

Alba hurries to the university library to return the novels she's read and collect the others, also absent from her home library, Stella has insisted she read for inspirational purposes. List in hand, she crosses the four-hundred-year-old wooden boards of the Bridge of Sighs, worrying about Carmen's love song and the fact that she hasn't written anything wonderful yet. When Alba reaches the counter, Zoë's face opens into a grin. 'Hey.'

'I've brought these back.' Alba slides the books over to Zoë and hands her a list: *The Golden Notebook*, *The Grass is Singing* and *The Feminine Mystique*.

Zoë says, 'Yep, we've got these. Do you want to wait?'

'Yeah, that'd be great, thanks.' Alba leans against the counter and watches Zoë scurry away. She reminds her of a pixie: perky and petite, short spiky hair dyed dark blue, eyes always heavily kohled. She thinks again how similar they might seem at first glance, except that Zoë's appearance is clearly the product of careful thought, and to good effect, while Alba's is accidental and to no effect at all.

Zoë returns a few minutes later. 'I'm afraid we didn't have *The Golden Notebook*. It's hardly ever in. But I can reserve it for you.'

'That'd be great, thanks.' Alba slips the books into her bag. 'Well, I suppose I'll—'

Zoë nods.

'Bye then.'

'Bye.'

Alba turns and walks toward the door.

'Wait.'

Alba turns back. Zoë's brow is furrowed with anxiety, her eyes are wide, her aura edged in silver. Alba waits, wondering what she's hoping for.

'Um, have you ever read this?' Zoë reaches under the counter and produces a tattered book. She hands it to Alba.

'*Chocolates for Breakfast.*' Alba takes it. 'No, I don't know it.'

'It was a bestseller in the late fifties, sort of trashy, but amazing. I read it when I was thirteen and, well, it opened my eyes to some things.' Zoë looks into Alba's bright blue eyes and holds her gaze, not letting her look away. 'That book means a lot to me. And . . . um, well, I'd like to know if you love it as much as I do.'

'Okay,' Alba says, a little shaken by this sudden intimacy. She hasn't shared a look like this with anyone before, excepting Dr Skinner, and those looks were invariably one-sided.

Zoë takes a deep breath. *It's now or never.* She opens her mouth and runs to the edge of the cliff.

'Would you . . .' Zoë jumps. 'Would you like to go for a coffee, a walk, or something?'

Alba swallows. She's never had a real friend

before. She thinks of Stella. Not a flesh-and-blood one, anyway, but much as she'd like one in theory, everything is moving a little fast. First her brother and now her librarian. 'Thanks.' She scrambles for an excuse, an easy lie. 'But I've got to go, my dad's expecting me for dinner.'

'Okay.' Zoë shrugs, feigning an uncrushed heart. 'Sure, fine, no problem.'

'But thanks anyway . . .' Alba moves toward the glass doors. 'Bye.'

'Bye.' Zoë offers a small wave in return, but Alba has disappeared into the darkness before her hand is even in the air.

CHAPTER 19

Albert twists the cap off his fifth bottle of
vodka in five days. He pours a glass slowly,
watching the liquid slice through the air
and splash up the sides. Then he closes his eyes
and sees Alba as a baby, the first day he saw her,
the only time he ever held her.

They met in London, in a dark little cafe in
Covent Garden where no one would know Lady
Ashby. But still they didn't kiss or give any
indication that they were anything more than
acquaintances. When Elizabeth handed him his
daughter, Albert took her as if she were made of
glass. From the moment he held Alba he never
wanted to let her go. He wanted to kidnap his
daughter and lover and take them somewhere
they'd never be found. But of course he gave his
little blue-eyed girl back. He watched Elizabeth
walk away and finally felt the hope he'd been
holding on to so tightly shatter inside his chest.

When Albert blinks again the vodka is over-
flowing and spilling onto the floor. Albert rights
the bottle, bends down, sips an inch out of the
glass, then picks it up and takes it to the sofa.

For his first anniversary with Elizabeth, Albert planned something spectacular. He stopped writing for a few weeks, worked extra shifts at his part-time jobs at the cinema and corner bookshop to save what he needed for his surprise.

Elizabeth met him at the cinema at midnight. Charles was spending the weekend in London with his latest socialite, the nanny was at home with their children. Elizabeth was dressed in dark blue silk, the colour of her eyes, her blond hair twisted up in curls. Albert met her in the foyer with a dozen roses and a tub of salted popcorn shaken up with chilled chocolate drops. He'd paid Tom, the projectionist, to stay late and show the film he'd ordered, couriered from the capital at great expense.

'Can you guess what it is?' he asked, as they snuggled down in their seats.

'I think so.' She smiled. 'And I can't believe you did it.'

'Anything, anytime.' He slipped his hand into her lap. 'If it's within the realm of my magical powers, you've got it.'

The titles flickered onto the screen. Elizabeth squeezed Albert's hand as Miss Bartlett appeared:

'*The signora had no business to do it, no business at all. She promised us south rooms with a view close together, instead of which here are north rooms, looking onto a courtyard, and a long way apart. Oh, Lucy!*'

Albert glanced at Elizabeth to see her mouthing the lines. He knew she wouldn't leave her husband while her children were young; they'd lose all their privileges, relocate to a council estate and probably hate her forever. Albert, having grown up on a council estate, can't see what a disaster that would be, but he understands about the children and is quite prepared to wait until they have left home, or whenever she's ready, as long as it takes.

With Elizabeth's eyes still fixed on the screen, Albert kissed her.

Without turning to him she whispered: 'I'll love you, Al, for the rest of my life.'

Snapping out of the memory, Albert sees that his glass is empty. He heaves himself off the sofa and shuffles back to the sink. As the half-empty bottle comes into view, he stops. What the hell is he doing? Is he really going to give up on Alba as he did on Elizabeth? Will he let her run away, or will he find and fight for her? Will he drink himself into a coma, or search and not stop until he's looking at his daughter again?

Albert picks up the bottle and watches his hand – seemingly of its own accord – skim over the glass and tip the rest of the vodka down the sink. As Albert watches the last few ounces slip down the drain, he's suddenly hit with an idea so simple he can't believe it hasn't struck him before. He doesn't have to go from place to place, seeking out Alba in her regular haunts, hoping one day he'll see her. He can go to one place and wait until she comes. And if Alba is still in Cambridge, then there is one place she's sure to visit eventually, even if he has to wait a very long time.

Having left Harry upstairs waiting for her, Peggy knocks on Greer's bedroom door. She holds a new note in her hand, one she found on her pillow this morning. She knows it was meant for someone else, which means it's clearly time to stop stepping back and start interfering again. When no one answers she pushes the door open and crosses the room to the wardrobe. She finds Greer buried in the back. Peggy stands outside and softly calls her name until Greer pokes her head through the curtain of couture.

'Oh, hello, Peg,' Greer says, a little flustered. She's holding a silk tea gown as shiny and pink as the inside of a shell.

'Sorry to burst in like this.' Peggy runs her fingers through the beaded tassels of a black sequined flapper dress. 'I have something for you.' She offers the note.

Greer unfolds it and reads,

As soon as you trust yourself, you will know how to live. – Goethe.

'It came to me. For the second time this month,' Peggy says. 'And I believe that, this time at least, it was meant for you.' Peggy notices the sea of shoes on the floor. 'Goodness, how lucky you are, I do so love shoes.'

Greer picks up a pair of velvet heels the colour of Peggy's earrings. 'Try these on.'

'Oh, no.' Peggy laughs, slipping them on. 'I gave up heels years ago.' She thinks of how much Harry would enjoy them.

Greer glances at the note again. 'So, what do I need to trust?'

'Your instincts,' Peggy suggests. 'The truth about the things in your life.'

'Is that what you do?'

Peggy frowns. 'Yes.' Though she's not nearly as certain about that nowadays as she used to be.

'But,' Greer says, 'I don't think I know what my instincts about things are.'

'Oh yes, you do.' Peggy looks at her. 'You know exactly, you just don't want to believe it.'

'Won't you move in with me, Peg?' Harry asks. 'You don't have to marry me, just live with me. Haven't I paid my dues? Haven't you paid yours?'

Peggy bites her tongue. The temptation to say yes is so strong in her now that she can hardly hold it back. 'You know the answer to that,' Peggy says softly, 'it's the same one I've been giving for the last twenty years.'

'Yes,' Harry agrees. 'But I'm not sure if I believe you any more.'

There is no point in marrying me, Peggy wants to tell him. *You'd be a widower before we were even on our honeymoon.*

They're sitting at the kitchen table, sharing a slice

of post-coital chocolate cake with cream. The characters on the crockery are suspended in the poses they were in when Harry sat down at the table. On Peggy's plate Rumpelstiltskin is lifting the Lady of Shallot's skirt above her head. On Harry's, the Red Queen is engaging in a little light bondage with Dopey. They've been spending nearly every night with each other recently. Peggy doesn't care any more about the rule against overnight visitors. If the forbidden room is locking her out, if the house is ignoring her, then she will jolly well ignore it in return. If she's going to be selfless and sacrifice the remaining days of her life to the house, then she'll also be selfish and cram in all the mortal joy she possibly can while she's still breathing.

'It hasn't been that long.' He takes another bite of cake, while Peggy licks the cream off her fork. 'Are you sure?'

'Yes,' Peggy says, 'quite sure.' The desire to run away with him swells up but with some effort she pushes it down again.

'I don't understand.' Harry takes her hand. 'You've given up everything to be here, to do this. You haven't had a husband or a family—'

'These girls are my family, they're my daughters,' Peggy says, wanting to end the conversation.

'But they leave after ninety-nine days, which isn't quite the same, is it?'

'It's always suited me fine,' Peggy lies. 'I told you that.'

'I'm not going to drop it, Peg. I know you're

hiding things from me. What about that door, the one that won't open?'

'It's just stuck.'

Harry, who has tried several times to pry open the door with a crowbar, knows this isn't true. 'I love you, Peg, so I've accepted your lifestyle. But it's different now. Something's changed – you want to leave, I can feel it.'

'Don't.' Peggy holds up her hand to stop him, but Harry just enfolds it between his hands and places it on his chest, not letting her go.

After Harry has gone home, Peggy finds a hammer in a long-forgotten cake tin (along with a very mouldy piece of cake). She's decided to take drastic action; waiting clearly hasn't worked, so she's going to resort to brute force. She lifts the hammer high over the door handle and brings it down hard. This makes a little dent in the gold-plated knob, but nothing more. So she does it again.

Downstairs, in the living room, Carmen stops playing and wonders at the rhythmic banging above her, which is punctuated ten minutes later by an exasperated scream.

Alba lies in bed, unable to sleep. She'd been practising with Carmen earlier, testing out the first verse of their song. They'd agreed it was okay, but far from brilliant. Finally she'd come to bed and picked up *Chocolates for Breakfast*, curious to see why Zoë loved it so much. Now that she's finished it, the book lies next to her, open at one of its most well-thumbed pages, and Alba is a little nervous.

She looks back at the book, thinking about its sensual scenes. Is it ridiculous that she's never touched herself before? Surely it's something she should have done at puberty, but she was just too self-conscious. Every time she got the urge, she blushed. Alba's never read anything as sexy as this before and the parallels of the book's plot with her own life are shocking: the protagonist is a rich teenager with a crush on her teacher. Alba wonders if Zoë might be psychic.

Tentatively, Alba picks up the book again. She glances down at her tiny breasts under her T-shirt, studying them, then takes a deep breath and slowly begins to stroke her hand along her body, her touch as light and soft as the cotton. Alba shivers a little. She slides her hand along her ribs, gathering her T-shirt until it settles in folds over her belly. She licks a finger and strokes it across her skin as the lights in her room begin to flicker.

Air rushes through the pipes, rattling as Alba gasps. Soon every wall of every room in the house trembles, shaking the photographs in their frames so that eight hundred and twenty-one women giggle. Whispers on the lips of every woman rush along the corridors. As Alba's body contracts, every light in the house flickers and every flower of the midnight glory bursts open. Every fuse in the house blows. And then, one by one, the streetlamps on Hope Street explode, scattering thousands of golden sparks into the night.

At two o'clock in the morning Carmen leaves the piano and returns reluctantly to her bedroom. She's been practicing until her fingers went numb. Since she's agreed, or at least surrendered, to the crazy stubbornness of Nora and Sue, Carmen is determined not to make a fool of herself, if she can possibly help it. She walks slowly across her floor and stands in front of her dressing table. Finally, she opens the drawer and peers inside, half hoping the box will have disappeared. But of course it hasn't moved. It sits among the clothes, partially hidden by the sleeves of a silk shirt and the hem of a red dress. Every time Carmen enters the room she's compelled to check on the box, though she still hasn't flipped the lid and looked inside.

The smell of Tiago is overwhelming, rising off the little box in waves of sweat and spice as it sits in the drawer. The smell has sunk into Carmen's skin and, no matter how many showers she takes, she can't seem to wash it off. She's soaked herself with perfumes, rubbed her skin raw with scented soaps, but nothing works. If Blake were to kiss her now he'd taste nothing but Tiago. For the thousandth time she wonders how the hell she'll be able to get rid of him for good.

An hour later Carmen is sitting on her bed, the box in her lap, willing herself to pry it open. She can feel it feeding on her fear. Her room has lost all of its colour. The view of the ocean has disappeared, replaced by grey skies that never shift no matter what the weather is outside. The box is slowly draining the life out of everything, and if she doesn't do something soon, it will have her too. She's already off her food and her clothes aren't fitting as tightly any more. Next her heart will start to shrivel, her lungs will dry to dust and, worst of all, her voice will evaporate. She can't allow this to happen. She has to do something to stop him.

Carefully, as though fearing it might unleash the Apocalypse, Carmen picks up the little box and forces it open half an inch. The spring catch snaps back, nearly grabbing Carmen's fingers, but she pulls it open again, all the way this time, until she can see the glint of a band of gold. Very slowly, Carmen lifts the ring and places it in her palm, staring at it as if seeing her husband again for the very first time. Tiago's hands were delicate, the hands of a guitar player, his fingers long and thin. So the ring looks as though it might fit her; but Carmen knows it'll slip right off if she tries it on. Not that she has since their wedding night. She curses herself for bringing it to England. Why couldn't she have left it? Why did she have to be so sentimental?

Carmen stares at the golden circle, at the

engraving inside, at the drop of blood that covers the T of Tiago's name. It grips the gold like a limpet, still as red and fresh as six months ago, when she pulled the ring off her dead husband's finger.

CHAPTER 20

Alba lies across her bed, playing with words and sentences, trying to finish Carmen's song. It's far from perfect, but the show is in less than two weeks, so she can't mess around forever. She'd hoped working on it would help her forget about her father for a few hours, but it hasn't. She thinks of his bright blue eyes, his tatty clothes, his sorrow, deep and dark, weighing down the air, seeping into her name when he said it, colouring the letters the darkest blue she'd ever seen. Is that what scared her so much?

Alba bites the end of his pen and glances up at the thousands of books lining the walls. And there it is: *A Room with a View*, the title bright in gold letters, sandwiched between *Howards End* and *Maurice*. On the shelf above sit the other books she'd borrowed.

Alba frowns. 'So, you can provide anything, a grand piano, a thousand books, but not the ones I need until I've already read them. Why is that?'

The pipes in the room rattle, as if giggling. Alba's frown deepens. What is the house playing at? She thinks of Dr Skinner and the words that ignited her obsession, words that sweep into her head even now, mixing with and muddling her own. Alba had never heard anyone speak with such passion before. She remembers the very first lecture, on Gladstone and the Great Gordon Debacle, as she watched the words flow forth:

> When Gladstone abandoned General Gordon at Khartoum, allowing him and his remaining troops to be massacred by the invading Mahdi army, the public, goaded by a saber-toothed press, turned against him. And the Grand Old Man became the murderer of Gordon. Because he couldn't play the political game as well as Disraeli . . .

Dr Skinner's words had poured forth in dozens of different hues: puce for passion, violet for joy, bright green for truth, scarlet for dedication, deep purple for wisdom, orange for insight, bright yellow for inspiration. Alba had never before seen so many brilliant colours all at once. And by the time her teacher fell silent, she was in love.

At least, she'd thought so then. She understands now it was just infatuation, addiction, obsession. She was as obsessed with Dr Skinner as Dr Skinner was obsessed with becoming an acclaimed academic, even if it took cheating, lying and ruining other people's careers to get there. But the pain of all that is dull and muted now, almost entirely eclipsed by thoughts of her father and by her preoccupation with Carmen's song, the current version of which is definitely lacking something.

'Have you ever . . .?'

'What?' Stella asks, though she knows what's coming.

'Well . . . what I mean is,' Alba says, fumbling for the right words and not quite sure why the subject embarrasses her so much. 'That is, I wonder what . . .'

'Yes?' Stella asks, knowing Alba needs to be able to say the words herself, to talk about it, if she ever stands a chance of actually experiencing it.

'Love,' Alba says. 'Tell me about being in love.'

At last. Stella smiles. 'Of all the musicians, Ellis was the one I loved the most. We read together. I've never done that with anyone, not before or since. I like to be alone for certain things . . .'

'Yes.' Alba nods, shocked at the thought of sharing something so intimate as reading. She isn't sure what scares her more: the possibility of reading with someone else, or sex.

'Oh, but it was wonderful.' Stella laughs. 'We'd lie on the sofa together, or in bed, and share a book. We would take it in turns to read aloud. Sometimes we'd both silently read at once. But I was always so much faster than him, and I'd get impatient to turn the page, so that was rare. Ellis had a beautiful voice . . . I could have shut my eyes and listened to him forever. I'm not sure which was better, soaking in his words or his sweat.' She giggles again, and it ripples along the kitchen walls as Dora, Vita and a few hundred other women echo her. Alba blushes.

'I can still hear his voice,' she says, smiling. 'It rather makes me feel all—'

'What happened to him?' Alba interrupts to avoid hearing a potentially embarrassing revelation.

For the first time Stella's eyes fog over and she puts her chin into her palms. 'Pills.'

Alba doesn't have the right words so she says nothing. They sit in silence.

'Do you want to know what love feels like?' Stella looks up, her eyes shining again, though whether with tears or excitement Alba can't quite tell.

Slowly, Alba nods.

'Well,' Stella says, 'if you're sure you're ready, then I can show you.'

'You can?'

Stella nods. 'There are certain abilities the dead have. Give me your hand.'

Alba reaches out. Holding her own hand a few inches above Alba's, Stella looks at her more deeply than she ever has before. Her gaze is two parts joy, one part hope, one part compassion, with a sprinkling of pure adoration. At first Alba feels nothing, then a sensation tingles her skin. A deep, sudden rush of warmth seeps into her, into every inch and every cell. It's the softest, strongest, most wondrous thing she's ever felt – as though every single cell in her body is bursting with light, being born again. And she feels her heart as intimately as if she were holding it in her hands.

There is one thing Zoë has done in her life of which she is truly ashamed. But she's been excessively punished for it, and that's served to ameliorate her guilt a little. Nearly three years ago she found a story of Alba's slipped between the pages of a very tattered copy of *Rebecca*. For seven days Zoë kept it in her bag, telling herself she'd return it unread. But, as the days passed and Alba came and went, Zoë held on to it. Until she finally had to admit the truth, that she was going to read it and wouldn't give it back.

In an attempt to soften this betrayal of Alba's privacy, Zoë read the story (six pages, handwritten and obviously autobiographical) in the library, sitting behind the stacks after everyone else had gone home, pretending it was a book that Alba had published, that anyone might pick up and read. It was a difficult self-delusion to pull off, as Alba's tiny scrawl was nearly impossible to read and clearly not intended to be seen by any eyes other than her own. Deciphering the story required immense concentration on Zoë's part, along with a flashlight and a very powerful magnifying glass.

It was nearly two o'clock in the morning when Zoë finally finished and, just as Alba had fallen for Dr Skinner's words, so Zoë fell for Alba's. Reading that story tipped Zoë off the cliff of superficial attraction onto the rocks of complete

273

adoration. In Alba's scrawl she found a mind that mirrored her own, a soul that spoke the same words, a heart that kept the same beat. In Alba's secret thoughts and feelings, Zoë found herself. Some of Alba's sentences were so lyrical that Zoë spoke them aloud just to hear the words. She didn't understand it all – the references to the colours of sounds and smells were particularly strange and intriguing – and Zoë wished she could ask Alba to explain, but of course she couldn't. Not then, not now, not ever.

In the years of private longing that followed, Zoë has often wondered whether or not she'd have fallen for Alba without the story. She thinks probably not, that without it she would just have lusted, rather than loved. So she's got her comeuppance for this moral lapse, suffering a prison sentence of unrequited love for three years, four months, two weeks, twelve days and counting . . .

Carmen sits at the piano, absently trailing her fingers up and down the keys. She's supposed to be practicing the first verse of Alba's song but she can barely keep her eyes open. Since opening the box, Carmen has been out every night trying to dispose of it. But when she buries the ring it pushes up through the dirt, when she hurls it into rivers it surfaces again, floating up as soon as Carmen turns her back. Only in the house or garden does the ring stay where it's put, but even then Carmen can't wash the drop of blood away, not if she scrubs until her nails bleed and her fingers are raw. She wishes it were possible to burn gold and knows that, even if she had the ring transformed into something else, its smell would never leave.

For a moment she forgets Tiago and thinks instead of Blake and what she's going to do now that he's starting to want what she doesn't want to give. Memory-obliterating sex is all well and good but she won't let it get in the way of her survival and her song. She needs to focus, completely and without distraction. She'll tell him tonight.

In twenty-one days she has to leave Hope Street to find another home, one that won't protect her or hide the evidence connecting her to Tiago's murder. Fear pollutes her blood, infusing her bones – until she begins to play. A little Tchaikovsky, then Beethoven and Mozart. She plays with a gusto that overtakes her entirely, her fingers moving faster than she could ever speak or sing or run; sometimes soft, sometimes strong, filling the room with a heavy smoke that sinks into her lungs. Carmen swallows the music until the sound is all she can taste, hear and feel. It's the best medicine she's ever had, able to banish memories, sorrow, sleepless nights, and leave only the notes.

Having failed to force the door open, Peggy simply stares at it, trying to shame it into submission. She stands at the stove, peeling chocolate biscuits off a tray. The sweet scent of cooked sugar and melted chocolate rises into the air, briefly soothing her nerves. The first time she made these biscuits was in the downstairs kitchen, and she slowly consumed the entire batch while chatting with Mary Somerville and Caroline Herschel, who had just spotted each other from opposing walls.

'I was just extolling the virtues of love to this young lady,' Mary said, 'though she's not heeding a word I say.'

'If you're appealing for support,' Caroline replied, 'I can't give it. I was never in love, and I never missed it. I always preferred mathematical equations to men.'

'How ridiculous.' Mary laughed. 'There's nothing like marriage and motherhood, it's quite the best thing in the world.'

'Oh, well.' Caroline shrugged. 'I suppose small things amuse small minds.'

'I have a magnificent mind,' Mary snapped, 'and you know it.'

'Mary.' Caroline smiled. 'You always were too easy to tease.'

'I've missed you, you old bat.' Mary said. 'I can't believe you never noticed me before, all those comets you spotted over the years. You've probably been too busy staring out of the window.'

'And you've been too preoccupied reminiscing about babies while doing complex algebra.'

While the two women bickered pleasantly, Peggy had eaten the entire batch of biscuits. Now she's staring down at a full tray, remembering. It's funny, she thinks, how she spent eighty-two years believing she was just like Caroline Herschel, not needing love in her life, except on Sunday afternoons. And now, in the light of death, she sees how wrong she was. She didn't know herself at all. How could she have seen into the hearts of more than a thousand residents over sixty-one years and not seen her own? Which isn't actually funny, Peggy thinks as she bites into a biscuit, but quite the opposite.

Greer stands in the shower, engaged in the time-consuming process of washing her long, tangled hair. Now that each evening brings her closer to the day she'll have to leave the house, she can't help thinking about the future. Her job at the bar is clearly a dead end, her acting career is at something of a standstill, Blake is growing ever more distant. Greer is seriously contemplating giving up men and acting altogether, finding a real job and a flat and trying to adopt a child.

She steps out of the shower. Perhaps she could train to be a teacher; the government is always desperate for them, hurling generous grants at anyone foolish enough to think long holidays and short hours mean an easy life. But although it isn't something she'd love to do, if it means finally becoming a mother, Greer thinks she could handle it.

She wraps a towel into a bright blue beehive around her head and pads over to the bathroom mirror to examine her wrinkles. She still looks fine, though faint lines remain on her forehead, even when she isn't frowning – as she is now. Greer thinks again about the potential job and the potential child. But she's torn. Is it right to give up on one dream in order to fulfil another?

Alba dawdles along Trinity Street, on her way to the library. Since reading *Chocolates for Breakfast*, she's been feeling rather embarrassed at the thought of seeing Zoë again. What if she starts discussing specific paragraphs? By the time Alba finally reaches the counter, she's too nervous to say hello. And then the look on Zoë's face stops her short.

'Hey.' Zoë nods in the direction of the doors. 'That man's been waiting for you three days in a row. He asked for your address.'

Alba turns to see her father sitting on the wooden bench under the notice board. Slowly he stands, then walks toward her one slow step at a time, as if she might at any moment turn and run. He stops a few feet from his daughter. 'Were you ever going to come back? I didn't, I'm sorry . . . I'm afraid I had to know.'

Yes, of course, Alba thinks, *of course I was. I just needed time.* But she can't speak the words.

'Do you want to punish me?' he asks, in a tone that suggests it's no more than he deserves. 'I know how much you must hate me—'

'No, I don't,' Alba manages to say. 'I just, I couldn't . . .'

Feeling dazed, she stumbles over to the bench where Albert was sitting. He follows and sits a few feet away from her, close enough to speak softly and still be heard. Zoë watches from behind her computer screen.

'Alba,' he whispers, 'I loved your mother more than anything and . . . I've thought about you every day of your life. I didn't—'

'Then why have you never even spoken to me' – tears fall into her lap – 'when all this time you were living right next to me?'

'I wanted to, every single day, but I couldn't, in case . . .' Albert says, wishing he could wipe away her tears and hold her. 'It would have been selfish, it wouldn't have been fair.'

'How did you know I was here?' Alba asks. He wanted her. He really did. *She was loved.*

'You were the youngest undergraduate at King's College. You made the news.' Albert bows his head, momentarily exposing his bald spot. 'I'm sorry, so sorry you had to go through all this. I wish it hadn't happened, I'd give anything if it hadn't.'

'She named me after you.' Alba stares at the stone floor. 'Didn't she?'

Albert nods. 'Liz was always generous. I gave her nothing and she gave me you.'

'Well, not exactly – she made you go away.'

'She did what she thought best.' Albert longs to reach out to Alba, just a fingertip on the cuff of her shirt. 'Even though it broke her heart, and mine.'

Alba sees his words in the air: royal blue edged with silver: sorrow and hope.

'Why didn't you come back, after he left, why didn't you come back?'

'I wrote to Liz, but she never replied. I thought she didn't want me any more, what could I do? I only discovered she died when you went missing.'

They sit in silence, as tears run down Alba's cheeks. When her father can't take it any more, he slips his fingers tentatively over her hand. Tears fall down his own cheeks and, never taking his eyes off Alba, Albert pulls her into a hug, finally holding his daughter for the first time since she was a baby.

CHAPTER 21

'Hi, Mum.'

'Hello, my darling.' Alba takes her mother's hand and they walk together across the rooftops of King's College, clambering over chimneys and stepping over loose tiles. They talk as the sun, hot at first on their faces, sinks lower and illuminates the edges of the stone spires rising up all around them. Alba and Elizabeth sit overlooking the meadows at the students punting in the river, laughing bubbles of champagne as they bump into each other. Behind them the fields are lined with oaks and scattered with geese. Halos of soft light around the trees dim and eventually disappear, and then everything is dark.

Elizabeth slips her arm over her daughter's shoulder. Alba smiles at the tingling on her skin and the warmth that slowly seeps into her body, hoping she'll be able to feel the sensation when she wakes.

'Now, my dearest girl,' Elizabeth says, 'I have something for you to tell your father.'

When Alba opens her eyes she remembers, for the first time, every word her mother said. An hour later, after trying in vain to forget again, she called Albert. Two hours after that she's sitting with him in the back of a small cafe on King's Parade, dreading the moment of spilling her mother's secret, torn between hoping he believes her and hoping he doesn't. It's a choice between his being devastated or thinking her mad. Neither of which Alba wants. She fiddles with the cinnamon bun in front of her, picking out the raisins and scattering them around the plate. Albert watches, rather wishing that he, too, had a cinnamon bun to fiddle with and take the edge off his nerves.

'So, um,' he begins, not looking up from his teacup, 'why did you leave King's?'

When he sees the look on Alba's face he instantly regrets the question. 'But, anyway,' he quickly backtracks, 'what are you doing at the moment?'

'I'm writing a song. But it isn't quite finished, there's something missing, I don't know how . . .' She shrugs it off, not really wanting to explain. She trawls her mind for topics that might impress her father and make him proud, but comes up blank.

'Well, the most important thing is to have fun.' Albert takes a gulp of his tea. 'In the end, it's all that really matters.'

Alba is so surprised she laughs. A few moments later she can't stop, and starts spluttering. She grips the edge of the table, trying to catch her breath.

'Are you all right? Shall I get a glass of water?'

'It's okay,' she gasps between words, 'I'm okay. It's just so funny.' She giggles. 'All my life, everything I've ever done, it's always been so . . . sensible. The idea of doing something just for fun seemed ridiculous. And now my father is telling me that enjoying myself is all that really matters. It's like I've stepped into an alternative universe, and I've got no idea what to do next.'

'Oh.'

Alba shrugs. 'It's just a little hilarious, that's all.'

'I wonder if you'll find all of my fatherly advice hilarious,' he smiles. 'I hope so.'

Alba catches her father's eye and this time she doesn't blink or glance away. They look at each other, two pairs of matching blue eyes, for a long time. And as they do, something deep inside Alba, some torn little piece of her, heals.

Carmen stumbles down the stairs, heading for the bathrooms and hoping she makes it in time. It's been a really busy shift at the bar and she hasn't had a chance until now. All night she's been avoiding Blake, who's been trying to catch her attention, and sneaking sips of vodka to give herself courage. When she reaches the last step she stops to steady herself against the wall. The door to the men's opens and Blake walks out. He sees her and grins. 'Hey, sugar.'

'*Ola.*' Carmen swallows a sigh.

Blake moves toward her. 'You look especially stunning tonight.'

'No.' Carmen steps back against the wall. But it's too late, before she can say anything else he's pressing up against her, his lips on her neck.

When Greer opens the door at the top of the stairs, she doesn't immediately realise whom she's looking at. She'd popped into the bar to surprise Blake, to take him out to dinner and sit him down for a proper talk about their future. And then, she sees Blake's face buried in Carmen's black hair. Greer screams.

For a moment Blake's paralysed, then he springs away from Carmen and starts to sprint up the stairs. Greer turns, pushing through the small crowd that has collected, and disappears. Carmen gazes after them before she suddenly understands what's happening. Huge brown eyes wide with fury, she shouts after him. '*Foda! Foda! Tu mais que foda estas a fazer? Tu e a Greer, e ele esta apaixonada por ti? Mais que foda que fizes-te?!*'

Blake runs through the bar after Greer. He finds her slumped against the wall outside, staring at the pavement. Blake hurries to her.

'Fuck you.' Greer looks up. 'And fuck off.'

'She didn't know,' Blake says. 'So you shouldn't hate her, only me.'

'Oh, I will,' Greer snaps, 'don't worry about that. Now fuck off.'

'I'm sorry,' he whispers. And he's shocked to

discover he actually means it. Seeing her here like this, on a public pavement with her heart exposed again, makes Blake wish he were a different man, one capable of taking care of someone other than himself. But he isn't. So the kindest thing he can do now, after all his cruelty, is remove himself from her sight and her life.

'I'm sorry.'

After he's gone Greer sits for a long time. She rests her head on her knees and weeps – not because she loved Blake and not because she's lost him. But because she didn't take care of herself. She *knew* Blake's nature the moment she met him, just as she knew the philandering fiancé. She knew them and she knew herself. Greer thinks of the story of the scorpion and the frog, and she knows that she cannot blame these men for her messy life, they only did what she always knew they would do. No, this is not about crushed hopes and broken dreams. This is about trusting her own heart. Hope doesn't even enter into it.

Two days after their cafe meeting, Alba and Albert meet again at the Fitzwilliam Museum. For the last two nights Elizabeth hasn't visited her daughter's dreams, and Alba, feeling a little guilty that she hasn't yet passed on her mother's message, hasn't slept much anyway. Now they're at the Vermeer exhibition, squeezing between the crowds. Alba is babbling incoherently about Dutch painters and Albert is trying to make sense of what she's saying while also wondering what's wrong with her.

When they're standing in front of *Girl with a Pearl Earring*, Alba, quoting passages from the book with the same title, starts fiddling with her frayed sleeves and chewing the ends of her fingernails. When he notices her missing her fingers and biting the air instead, he has to ask.

'Are you all right?'

She studies the painting. 'I'm fine.'

'Are you sure?'

Alba nods. 'Beautiful, isn't it?' She wanders over to *The Milkmaid* and feigns absorption in it too. An hour later, in front of *The Music Lesson*, Alba turns to face her father.

'Okay. I have to tell you something.' Conscious of the crowds, she whispers. 'It's going to sound a little strange, you might not believe me, but—'

'If you tell me,' he says, 'I'll believe you.'

'I had a dream about my mother,' Alba says. 'That's to say, she visited me; well, anyway . . . She told me to tell you she replied to your last letter. She wrote to you every week for a year, asking you to come back. She thinks Charles had them destroyed, so they never reached you.'

Albert stares at Alba, unable to move or speak. He starts to shake.

'She never stopped loving you,' Alba says softly. 'She loved you right up to the day she died, and even after that.'

Albert nods, tears falling down his face. Alba

rests her hand on her father's sleeve and gives him a small, hopeful smile. And, when she slips her hand into his, his heart swells until it fills his whole chest.

That night Albert sits on the sofa in his small, dingy flat, staring at the flickering television, but not really watching it. Next to him, on a scuffed cushion, is a TV dinner he's barely touched. The over-cooked carrots and slightly burnt sliver of white chicken glisten with congealed gravy. He plucks at the cuffs of his cardigan, widening the holes in the wool. He misses Alba already. If he loved his daughter before, it's nothing to how he feels now. The feeling is so deep, so infinite, so strong that it never fails to shock him. Albert thinks how lucky he is, that this love for his daughter fills the jagged hole inside him left by the loss of Liz.

He wonders, for the hundredth time that evening, if his daughter would consider moving in with him, if she might let him be a real father to her for a few years. It would be the greatest gift, so great, in fact, that he's scared to ask for it. The idea entered his head when Alba told him she has to move out of Hope Street in a few weeks and has nowhere to go. But he doesn't want to put her under any pressure. Perhaps, he thinks, gazing at the carrots, he should just stick with what he's already got and be grateful. After all, it's much more than he ever thought he'd have.

★   ★   ★

When Carmen stumbles into the kitchen in the early morning Peggy is at the table, sipping a cup of tea. She lifts a delicate hand. 'Sit.'

'Okay.' Carmen nervously slides into the nearest chair.

'I'm afraid, my dear girl,' Peggy says, 'the time has come for things to be faced.'

With a little sigh, Carmen closes her eyes and waits.

'I'm sorry, but you must leave,' Peggy says. 'That ring holds your husband's spirit and it clearly can't be destroyed. You have to face what you've done. If you stay here and hide he'll soon suck the life out of you.'

'But I can't leave yet. I can't, I don't want—'

'I'm sorry, sweet girl, I really am.' Peggy takes Carmen's hand, which is trembling and cold. 'But his spirit is getting stronger. The house can't contain it any more. So you must. You must turn yourself in and face what you've done. You will get through it, I can promise you that. Have faith and you will be fine. And, when it's all over, you'll be much better than that. You'll be free.'

'Faith?' Carmen whispers. 'You can give me no more help than this?'

'You must trust me,' Peggy says. 'It's the only way to be rid of his spirit. As long as you run, he will chase you. He'll feed on your fear and, eventually, it will kill you.'

Carmen closes her eyes. She can't fight this. Staying at Hope Street has been a gift, the old woman could throw her out of the house right now if she wanted to. But the thought of faith, of putting her trust in the God she believes abandoned her is rather more than she's ready and able to do.

'How much longer I can stay?'

'I think we can hold him off for another seven days,' Peggy says. 'Until you've sung your song, my dear. And then you must go.'

CHAPTER 22

Later that evening Carmen tries to focus on the piano and the new verse Alba has given her, but her mind keeps returning to two things: the fact that she has to leave the house, and to Greer. Greer has barricaded herself in her bedroom, ignoring the notes Carmen slips under her door. No matter what Carmen writes, Greer isn't listening. Which is a shame. But she understands. Surprisingly, the thought of leaving the house fills her not just with terror but also with a sense of calm determination, determination to do the one thing she wants to do: to sing in public – her swan song. She wants it to be the most brilliant thing she's ever done, so beautiful that the memory of it will light up all the dark nights to come.

Perhaps she should ignore Peggy and just run, leave Cambridge for that remote village Alba mentioned, or emigrate to Australia. She could start a new life there. But what about the ring? Crazy thoughts circle Carmen until she starts to feel slightly mad, but then she gave up any claim to sanity a long time ago. That went out of the window the day she killed her husband.

Tiago Viera wasn't a mean drunk. In fact, alcohol calmed him down rather than riled him up. But he was always sure to be stone cold sober on the nights he beat his wife. He wasn't set off, triggered by something that suddenly made him snap. He wanted her to know he meant it. It wasn't an accident, a mistake, something he'd regret in the morning. No, Tiago's punches came with purpose because he told her she deserved every blow.

Different things decided him. And before long Carmen could feel it coming: the heat of his gaze on the back of her neck, the twist of his mouth, the look in his eye. She knew what to expect and she braced herself for it. For hours on end, Carmen would think about leaving. Sometimes just the idea of escaping was all that got her through one day, and then the next. Before she knew it, a year had passed. But she never planned anything, because she didn't have the first idea where she'd go. She'd never been out of Bragança, had never seen Lisbon or been to Spain. And she'd have to go much farther to stand a chance of not getting caught. Tiago had friends, he warned her, friends everywhere. There was nowhere she could go that he couldn't find her. One day, Carmen's cousin left for England to take a job in a Portuguese restaurant in a city called Cambridge. After that, when she fantasised about escaping, that was where Carmen went.

On the last night of his life, Tiago decided his wife might be pregnant by another man and he was going to beat the baby out of her. 'You're fat,' he'd said first, spitting the words out over his supper, as though this was something she'd done intentionally, to annoy him. In the past, before jealousy had deformed him, Tiago had adored Carmen's curves. He'd spent hours smoothing his hands over her breasts, her soft belly, her bottom and thighs. 'All this,' he'd whisper reverently, 'all this just for me.'

'You're fat,' he said again, and she waited.

'You're pregnant, aren't you?' he snapped. 'Who've you been fucking?'

He accused her of sleeping with every member of his band, and not just one at a time. It all happened very quickly after that. Carmen stood up, walking to the sink with her plate, her food untouched. He reached her before her hand touched the stainless steel tap.

He leant into her ear. 'This time I'm going to kill you – kill you and bury you in the back garden.' And, even though it was almost comical – the soap opera sentence and the way he said it – Carmen didn't laugh because she suddenly knew, deep in her bones, that he meant it. This time he was going to kill her.

The first blow was always the worst. This time Tiago grabbed her hair, yanked her head back, then slammed her face into the sink. He held her down, punched her in the back, then let Carmen slide to the floor. She gasped for breath, blood dripping into her eyes, pain firing through her body, and then she surrendered. It was enough. She didn't want to live any more. The last thought she remembers passing through her mind was a prayer: *Please may it end quickly.*

She was slipping into a merciful darkness when Tiago pulled her back up to her feet and shoved her against the wall, holding her with a splayed hand pressed to her chest. And then he did something that Carmen had never understood at the time, and can't even now. With his free hand he reached into the sink for a frying pan, still coated with scraps of fried egg, and held it in front of her face. Carmen flinched, expecting another blow, but instead Tiago wrapped her fingers around its handle one by one.

'Hit me,' he whispered. 'I'll give you one hit.'

For a moment she just looked at him, unable to make sense of what he was saying. He gripped her hand, digging her fingers into the metal. 'I won't tell you again, bitch.'

And so she did. With every last bit of her strength, Carmen lifted the pan and brought it down on Tiago's head. He slumped to the floor and she waited for him to get up, to see if she'd done what he wanted, still praying he would kill her quickly.

It was a while before Carmen realised Tiago wasn't getting up. It had happened at last. One of them was dead. Only, shockingly, it wasn't her. It was over.

Carmen fell to her knees and wept, choking Hail

Marys through her sobs. When at last her tears dried up she looked at her husband, at the blood on his head and his beautiful face and the eyes that would never look at her again. And then, in a moment of sentimentality she'd always regret, she took his hand and slid the ring off his finger, still stained with blood, and slipped it into her pocket. She ran from the house, taking nothing with her but money, and hid in the shadows of the streets. The next morning she boarded a bus out of Bragança, then hitchhiked from Madrid. Carmen rode for six days and nights, by land and by sea, until she reached the grey skies and sandy shores of England.

Something in the house is beginning to shift. Peggy can't put her finger on what, exactly, yet she can feel it brewing. Something in the forbidden room is beginning to stir, even though it still refuses to open for her. And something is stirring in Peggy. Something that has been stirring ever since she learnt she was going to die is now whipping itself up into a storm in her heart. Her regrets. Her longing. Her hope. But it's too late now. It's too late to do anything about all that now. She can feel herself fading. Her edges are starting to dissolve, her breath is becoming lighter and lighter, until she can barely feel it flowing in and out of her lungs. She wants to run to Harry and hold him tight, to have his arms around her. Peggy never minded the thought of death. Especially since she knows it's not so very different from life, excepting the critical absence of sex, cream and chocolate. But now that Death is so close she can almost smell him, she's getting a little scared.

Peggy sits by the fire with Mog drooling in her lap. It's nearly the middle of July but chilly tonight, with a cool wind. There have been pitifully few of the sunny days they'd been promised. Bad weather makes the house irritable and Peggy has to put up with the rush of its wheezing breath through the walls, the shuddering and sneezing of the pipes.

She's written Harry a letter. A goodbye letter. She'll leave it for the house to deliver after her death. And until then she'll spend the remaining weeks giving Harry wonderful memories, showing him boundless amounts of love. She hopes that when he's turning them over and over like pebbles in his pocket, they will bring him comfort.

HOPE STREET,
MONDAY 17TH JULY, 2011

Harry,
I love you. I know I never say it, but I do. I hope you've always known it. I'm going to die. I don't know exactly when, but it'll be soon. Don't worry, I'm all right with it, as right as I could ever be, anyway. I'd love to have longer with you. But we've had twenty years' worth of Sundays together. Every one of them perfect

295

and wonderful which, I imagine, is a lot more than most people ever get.

I hope you understand why I didn't tell you. You'd have probably thought me mad if I had and, anyway, I didn't want to spoil our last few months together. I know you could never understand why I didn't leave the house, why I didn't marry you. I hope it brings you comfort, rather than sorrow, to know I wish I had.

I love you. I love you with all the words I never gave you, I love you with all my heart.
Peg

'Dad.'

'Yes?' Albert glances up, failing to suppress an enormous grin. It's the first time she's called him Dad. He turns the word over on his tongue, soft and sweet as toffee. *Dad. Dad. Dad.*

'I, um . . . there's someone I want you to meet.'

'Oh?' Albert swallows another enormous grin. He's being introduced to the boyfriend. A landmark ritual in any father–daughter relationship. He wonders if Alba would mind if he takes pictures.

They are sitting together on a bench outside Trinity College, eating fish and chips out of newspapers, watching the punts glide past. Students knock into each other, the occasional tourist loses his pole to the river and falls into the water trying to get it back.

'Her name's Stella,' Alba says. 'But, well, you

might not be able to see her at first. She's sort of shy and it might . . . take a little while.'

'Oh, okay,' Albert says, slightly disappointed it's not a boyfriend after all, but glad Alba has friends. He's a little confused about why he might not be able to see this particular friend at first, but asking for clarification might make him seem uncool, ignorant of the particular ways of young people today. Trying hard to cultivate the air of a fashion-able modern father, he's even bought a new cardigan, a red one. It's the first time he's ever owned something so bright.

'I've got to tell you something,' Alba blurts out, 'and maybe you'll hate me, but I can't keep lying to you. And I—'

'Alba.' He places a hand on her knee. 'I could never hate you, no matter what.' And he knows, absolutely and unequivocally, that this is true.

'So.' Alba stares down at the cold fish and chips in her lap. She affects a detached tone, as though she's talking about someone else, just telling him the facts. 'You know I'm supposed to be doing my PhD now, but I failed my MPhil? Well, I didn't actually fail, I was set to get ninety percent, but . . . I was researching a paper for my supervisor and I discovered something amazing. I spent three months writing the paper and it was brilliant. Then Dr Skinner took it and published it.'

'But that's incredible!' Albert beams. 'How wonderful.'

'No, no – it was published without my name. Without any acknowledgment that *any* of it was mine, no matter all of it. And when I threatened to go to the dean, the honourable Dr Skinner dropped me.'

'Oh.' Albert can't say anything more for the moment, because he's not sure what the appropriate words are. What is a father supposed to say?

'I didn't say anything,' Alba goes on, 'I didn't fight. Not just because I didn't have any evidence, which I didn't, but because . . .' Alba holds her breath. This will be the first time she's ever said it out loud. 'Because I was in love with her.'

Her.

The word burns brightly between them, three letters ablaze, a startling green, lighting up in the air like fireworks. Alba wants to run, but she can only wait for him to say something.

'With who?' Albert frowns, not quite following.

'With Dr Skinner,' Alba says.

'Dr Skinner?'

'Yes.' Alba nods. 'Dr Alexandra Skinner.'

'Alexander?' For a moment Albert is confused. He has met Dr Skinner, he knows she's a woman, but he doesn't immediately understand.

'No.' Alba's heart thuds in her chest. 'Alexand*ra*.'

Albert isn't sure what to say next. In his rather limited preparations for hip fatherhood he hadn't expected this. He needs to read a book, or take a course. He needs to be told what to say and what to do. But Alba is waiting; his daughter wants him to speak. So Albert says the first thing that comes into his head.

'I love you,' Albert says. 'More than I've ever loved anyone in my life.'

'You do?' Alba whispers. 'Even—'

'Of course.'

'But—'

'My dearest girl,' he says. 'You've given me back my heart.'

CHAPTER 23

Greer's breasts ache, her skin tingles, her whole body throbs. It's protesting that it's lonely, that it longs to be touched again. And it's betraying her because, right now, she doesn't want to think of men ever again. And now that she's firmly set on her idea of adoption alone, she doesn't need to. Greer hasn't dressed since the night with Blake, instead remaining perpetually clad in a pair of flannel pyjamas she found stuffed at the back of the wardrobe. For the first time since the fiancé, she doesn't give a damn about how she looks. Which doesn't matter because she just spends her days staring at the ceiling and muttering, her words floating up to the chandelier and disappearing into the air, unheard.

'Okay.' She places a hand on her chest. 'I hereby vow that my body will remain untouched by male hands until I can trust my instincts.' Slowly she sits up to gaze at her magical wardrobe; simply seeing it always lifts her spirits. Its clothes give her comfort. In fact, right now, they are the only things that do. Lately she holds them like safety blankets.

Last night she fell asleep in a pile of blue satin ball gowns.

Greer pulls herself off the bed, pads across the floor, and walks in through the wardrobe's open doors. There she spends the rest of the day, sitting among her clothes, rubbing fabrics across her face. Then, when Greer buries her head in her favourite little black Audrey Hepburn dress, something falls through the air and lands with a thump at her feet.

It's a book, two inches thick and bound with brown leather. Greer picks it up to find it's actually a collection of papers, hundreds of dress patterns ripped from magazines, much like the one she found a week ago. Greer flicks through the pictures, wondering if they're supposed to be a clue to something. But she can't find a sequence or connection; they seem random, unorganised.

'What am I supposed to do with this?' Greer mutters, self-pity clouding good sense. 'You want me to make dresses? When I'm nearly forty and will soon have nowhere to live?' She stands. 'If I'm going to do anything, I'm going to raise a child. And for that, I need a real job. All right?'

With that, she drops the papers and marches out of the wardrobe.

Walking up the path, Edward hesitates. He stops a few feet before the door, glancing up at the dozens of windows above him. It's a magnificent house, as big as a church, and he can't believe he never noticed it when he was a student at Trinity. Not that it matters now, because as he rings the bell, Edward's feeling torn in half. He's overjoyed Alba has invited him over, having feared after their last meeting that she'd never want to see him again, but now, at some point he'll have to tell her the truth, and he's dreading it.

An hour later, after the exchange of a great deal of small talk, Edward sits at the kitchen table with Alba, drinking coffee and eating ginger biscuits. Stella watches them from her favourite spot in the sink.

'Do you want something else?' Alba asks, wondering why her brother seems so distracted. 'I could make toast and jam.'

'What?' Edward fiddles with his watch strap. 'No, I'm fine.'

'But you don't seem to like the biscuits.'

'Oh, they're fine. I'm just a little distracted, that's all.'

'What's wrong?'

'Oh, nothing, just work stuff.' Edward shrugs. 'It's okay.'

They shift to talking about their childhood memories: the tree house with two floors the gardener built in a three-hundred-year-old oak, the secret cupboard under the stairs in the south wing they'd both used as a hiding place. They talk about Tilly, who's not visiting with him because she's still recovering from the flu, and they even talk about Edward's late wife, much to Alba's surprise. She talks about Peggy, and tells her brother a little about Albert, but stops short of mentioning Stella.

'It's not really work,' Edward blurts out at last. 'I'm not fine. I'm sorry, I lied to you. When you asked me about father's disappearance and . . .'

'And you told me you didn't know where he was.' Alba waits.

Stella, watching them both, leans forward in the sink. Edward slowly snaps five ginger biscuits in half, one by one, releasing little puffs of dusky orange vapour that float between them. He takes a deep breath. 'He was living in Italy – Sicily. Until two years ago we visited him every year in spring.'

'We?' Alba sits up and stares at her brother.

'Lotte, Charlie and I.'

Alba can't quite make sense of what he's saying. She hears the words but their meaning – the implications – momentarily elude her. 'Why two years?'

'He died, the Christmas before last. Heart attack.' Edward gazes down at his plate, at the discarded biscuits.

'Oh.' Alba's still confused. 'So, wait . . . he didn't leave *us*, he only left *me*.' She grips her coffee cup. 'But I thought . . . I even . . . but, how the hell could he do that? And how could you not tell me, after all these years, how could you not?'

'I'm so sorry, Al, I really am.' Edward is on the verge of tears. He wishes he could reel back his words, unsay them, have them disappear. It was too soon, too fast. He should have waited until more time had passed, until he and Alba had a chance to create a less fragile bond, one that couldn't so easily break. But it's done now. It's said. There's no going back now. 'He was cruel, and we shouldn't have gone along with it. At the time we were angry, we blamed you and Mum for his leaving. We swore never to tell, but now they're both gone and I wanted you to—'

'And what about Mum?' Alba can hear her voice sounding shrill. 'You let her go through all those interrogations, the whole village treating her like a leper, you saw what it did . . . it broke her, it killed her!'

'I know,' Edward says. 'I've regretted what we did every day.'

'But not enough to undo it? You had, what, ten years to tell Mum the truth. Why didn't you?'

But Edward doesn't have a satisfactory answer. It's something he's asked himself over and over again. 'I'm so, so very sorry. I hope one day you might forgive me.'

Alba just stares at him. 'I think you should go.'

'Please,' Edward says, 'please . . .'

Alba can hear the crack in his voice. She can see the desperation in his eyes. But she shakes her head. She hears a small sigh from the kitchen sink, but Alba ignores Stella too.

'Now,' she says softly, 'leave now.'

Edward wants to beg her to let him stay, to say he can't bear to lose her again. He wants to weep and plead for the forgiveness he doesn't deserve. But instead he stands and walks slowly out of the kitchen and out of the house. Alba, her eyes fixed to the floor, doesn't watch him go.

When Alba ventures into the kitchen two days later, the ghost is sitting in the kitchen sink, as if she hasn't moved an inch. Of course, except for reading, Alba has no idea how Stella otherwise passes her infinite time, so perhaps she hasn't.

'Don't talk to me about my brother,' Alba says before she sits down. 'Whatever advice you have, I don't want to hear it, okay?'

'Okay.' Stella shrugs. The problem of Edward will have to wait; she's got a more immediate issue to address first.

'Why are you looking at me like that?' Alba reaches her chair by the stove, frowning at the ghost. 'You look like you're up to something. I don't like it.'

Stella smiles with exaggerated innocence, then says:

Does it seem reasonable that she should play so wonderfully and live so quietly? I suspect that one day she will be wonderful in both. The water-tight compartments in her will break down and music and life will mingle.

Alba listens to the words from her parents' favourite book, suspecting Stella is attempting to make some sort of point, but since she hasn't touched a piano in twelve years and doesn't play anything at all 'wonderfully', or even well, that point isn't entirely clear.

'So.' Stella raises her eyebrows. 'What do you think of that?'

'I'm not sure what you mean,' Alba admits.

'You are exceptionally intelligent, talented and will no doubt be successful at anything you choose to put your hand to,' Stella says. 'But so far you only apply your brilliance to the study of life's retelling rather than life itself.'

Alba says nothing.

'My hope is that you, like Lucy Honeychurch, will allow your passion for literature to leak into life,' Stella says. 'And for that, you have to act.'

'Take to the stage?' Alba jokes. 'How will that help?'

'Yes, very funny,' Stella says. 'But I have a feeling that if you don't do it now—'

'What's the rush? I'm fine. I'm not even twenty. I've got a whole lifetime.'

'So you think,' says Stella. 'But if you don't do it now, with the power of the house behind you, then I'm afraid you probably never will.'

'Do what, exactly?'

'It's time to face the things you really want. Not just in your fantasies, but in your life.'

'What do you mean?' Alba asks again, hoping that Stella doesn't know about the *Chocolates* book but rather suspecting she probably does. Her heart quickens.

'You know exactly what I mean,' Stella says. 'That girl loves you. And it's time to find the courage to love her back.'

It's time. Alba grabs a summer jacket from the coat rack and sees Florence Nightingale wink at her from the opposite wall. Alba stops.

'What?'

'You're finally doing it, well done.' Florence smiles. 'You certainly took your time about it.'

Alba pulls on her jacket. 'We aren't all blessed with the courage of an army, you know. Some of us need to deliberate on the best course of action before—'

'Oh, what rot.' Florence interrupts. 'Not acting when one should act is a waste of life. Feelings ought always to be distilled into actions that bring results. Now, go!'

'Okay, okay,' Alba snaps. 'I'm going!'

With that she slams the door and runs down the path toward the street. Behind her, the door opens again as the house watches her go. At the window, Peggy smiles.

Alba runs all the way to the library, dashes through the doors and up to the counter, but Zoë isn't there. Instead Andy sits at the computer with a look of bored resignation. Alba's heart drops into her belly. If she doesn't do it now, she might not conjure up the courage again. Maybe a few years down the line, with someone else?

Just then Zoë comes running up from the rare book room.

'I've got it, Andy boy, I've got it!' Zoë sees Alba and stops. 'Oh, hello.'

'What is it?' Alba asks.

'A signed first edition of *The Jungle Book*. It's a new donation.' Zoë holds it out as Alba inches forward for a closer look. 'Here, you can touch it.'

Alba takes the book with great care, handling it as though it's the most precious thing she's ever held. She slowly turns the pages. 'The illustrations are so beautiful.'

'They're painted by Kipling's father,' Zoë says. 'My favourite is Shere Khan.' She leans over the counter to find the chapter. Her fingers brush Alba's and, for one single, eternal moment, neither one of them moves. Alba stares solidly at the tiger while her fingertips tingle as if she's just had an electric shock. She can feel Zoë's gaze on her face and her cheeks are as hot as if she'd just stepped into a pool of sunlight. Alba looks up. It's now or never. She loosens her hold on the book and lets it settle in Zoë's hands.

'I liked that book you loaned me, you know. The chocolate one, I mean—'

'Oh?'

'It was very . . .' Alba takes a deep breath,

wishing Stella were there to hold her hand. 'I've been thinking . . .'

Zoë waits.

'Yes, well,' Alba mumbles, 'I was thinking, wondering if you still wanted to go for coff—'

'Yes.' Zoë grins. 'I'd love to.'

CHAPTER 24

Tomorrow is her date with Zoë, but there is someone else Alba keeps thinking of. Since the day she threw her brother out of the house she's been regretting her harshness to him. So yesterday she called Edward and invited him back to Hope Street. When he rings the bell she's in the bathroom brushing her teeth and arguing with Sylvia Plath and doesn't hear it.

Greer, having graduated from pyjamas to jeans, has left her bedroom to roam the house and stretch her legs, after spending the day reading teaching prospectuses helpfully procured for her by Alba. Striding along the corridor, slowing to smile at Elizabeth Taylor, she hears the doorbell and stops, realising she's never heard it before.

'You should answer it,' Elizabeth says.

'No,' Greer says, rather reluctant to be seen by anyone. 'It's not for me.'

'I wouldn't be so sure.' Elizabeth winks. 'I have a feeling he might be.'

Greer frowns, wondering if she's heard correctly, when the bell rings again.

'Oh, go on,' Elizabeth cajoles. 'Don't be such a scaredy-cat.'

Greer opens the door to a tall, dark-haired man with big brown eyes, holding the hand of a little green-eyed girl. Forgetting to say hello, Greer just looks from one to the other. Then she notices the man's expression change from one of friendly curiosity to bemusement. She says, 'Oh, I'm sorry. Hello.'

'Hello,' Edward and Tilly respond in unison.

'Hi.' Greer smiles at the little girl, who fixes her with a wide-eyed stare, then hides behind her daddy's leg. 'What pretty red shoes,' Greer addresses the girl. 'What's your name?'

'Tilly,' Tilly squeaks from behind her father's legs. 'Matilda Jane Ashby. Miss.'

'What a lovely name,' Greer says. She can feel the man looking at her. When she glances up he holds her gaze. She feels drawn to him in a way she's never really felt before. It's not lust, nor a desperate desire to be loved. Instead it's a gentle lifting of her spirits, a soft stirring in her chest.

As Alba walks down the corridor toward them, she sees sparks of silver that fire up the air, and smiles. At the sight of her aunt, Tilly gives a little shriek of delight and runs into the house, crashing into Alba's legs and clutching them tightly.

'My little monkey.' Alba picks up her niece and squeezes her tightly. 'I've missed you.'

'Miss you.' Tilly presses her face into Alba's neck. 'Miss you much.'

To her surprise, Alba feels a lump in her throat. 'You've grown . . .' She swallows. 'You've grown so big.'

Realising he's still staring at Greer, Edward turns to his sister. 'She grows like a beanstalk,' he says. 'She's going to look just like her mother.'

'She's beautiful.' Alba smiles. 'Absolutely beautiful.'

Edward steps forward so he's only a few feet from his sister and his daughter. The sight of them hugging makes him want to join in, to tuck them both against his chest. 'I'm sorry,' he says softly.

'I know.' Alba, a little embarrassed that Greer is watching them, starts walking toward the kitchen, Tilly still in her arms. 'I know, and you don't have to be any more, okay? Now, come and have a cup of tea and some more of those ginger biscuits you don't like.'

Almost overcome with relief, Edward starts to follow his sister, then stops and turns back to Greer. He holds up his hand and gives a little wave. 'Bye.'

'Bye.' Greer leans against the wall, watching Edward disappear down the corridor. The photographs remain perfectly still until he closes the kitchen door behind him.

'Well, well.' Florence Nightingale grins. 'Now, what was that?'

'I'm not certain,' Emily Davies says, 'but I do know it made me tingle all over.'

'Oh, don't be silly.' Greer shakes her head,

dislodging the fantasies that have collected there, ignoring the thump in her chest. 'It was nothing.'

Edward sits at the kitchen table, still a little distracted. Tilly slides into his lap while Alba makes two cups of tea and, as his daughter amuses herself with the buttons on his shirt, Edward thinks of the woman in the corridor.

'That was Greer.' Alba hands him a cup and Tilly a ginger biscuit. 'She's single.'

'Sorry?' Edward frowns.

'Oh, don't bother.' Alba laughs. 'I'm not blind.' She won't tell him about the colours, not yet. And perhaps he doesn't realise it right now, but she knows that she just saw her brother falling in love.

Edward blushes. 'So . . . how are you?'

'I'm okay. I'm better, much better.' Alba sits and Tilly, clutching her biscuit, switches allegiances and laps. 'So, how's the job? Designed any great monuments to capitalism lately?' She pushes the plate of biscuits toward him. 'They're a few days old but still delicious, I promise.'

Edward obligingly takes one. 'Actually I'm doing some pro bono work at the moment, building a community theatre in Camden.'

'So we're both broke right now.' Alba tickles Tilly, who giggles. 'How inspiring.'

Edward dunks his biscuit in his tea and chews. 'And what are you up to?'

'I'm not sure.' Alba shrugs, attempting nonchalance. 'I have to leave here in three weeks.'

'Where will you go?'

'I don't know. I suppose I should get a job. Goodness knows what I'm qualified for.' Alba smiles, pretending she's not as worried as she is. The questions of where she will live, and what she will do with her life, have been taking up far too many of Alba's thoughts.

'You can do anything you want to,' Edward says, 'of that I'm quite certain.'

'I should probably just get a proper job, like the rest of you.'

'You should do what you like with your life,' Edward says. He glances at his daughter, who, oblivious to them both, is working her way methodically through the plate of biscuits in front of her. 'You should do whatever you want.'

'That's funny,' Alba says, 'I always thought it didn't matter what I wanted, all that mattered was that I lived up to the family name. Although, I suppose I'm not really an Ashby after all, am I? So perhaps I should just make up a pseudonym.'

'Woodenum.' Tilly giggles, spluttering a shower of crumbs onto her aunt's lap.

'Why a pseudonym?' Edward asks.

'Well, I've started doing a bit of writing. I'm sure nothing will come of it, but . . .' Alba shrugs, too nervous to confess the full extent of her hopes.

'Oh, okay, well that sounds great.' And because Edward is too nervous to pry, they sit in silence for a while, sipping tea and chewing biscuits. Tilly licks her lips and kicks her feet under the table.

'We're thinking of selling the house,' Edward

says. 'The upkeep is enormous, and now that mother's gone, none of us really want . . . Anyway, it'd give us all a nice little nest egg. Then you could stave off the lacklustre jobs for a while and just write, if you wanted to.' He shifts in his chair, trying to gauge his sister's reaction.

Alba wonders exactly how to frame her response. She doesn't want to offend her brother, she must temper her delight at the idea just a little. 'Well, I . . .'

Misreading her hesitation, Edward rephrases. 'It could be a fresh start,' he says. 'A new beginning. What do you think?'

Alba offers him the single biscuit remaining on the plate, the sole survivor of Tilly's culling. 'I think I'd like that very much.'

'Good.' Edward smiles and bites into it. 'So would I.'

It's three days since Alba's seen Stella, and she's getting worried. Last night, she fell asleep at the kitchen table, trying to rewrite Carmen's song, waiting up for Stella, who never appeared. But she can't worry now. She has to focus on wonderful, witty things to say. She's never been on a date before and has no idea what to say or do. Perhaps they'll just end up as friends. Though it isn't a matter of 'just', really. Alba would love a real friend, someone who isn't a character in a book or a ghost in a kitchen, someone who's set firmly in the land of the living, with whom she can visit bookshops, libraries and the like. Alba's experience with Edward has shown her that the house is careful not to be magical around strangers. Which is why, in a rash act of intimacy, she invited Zoë to visit. She's now feeling a little nervous about it, but she wants to show Zoë something of herself – all her books and, most important of all, the place that has changed her life forever.

An hour later, when Alba opens the door, her heart lifts and she smiles. For a moment they stand awkwardly together, not sure what to do next. Alba resolves the question by stepping aside. 'Come in.'

'Thank you.' Zoë smiles as she steps over the threshold. 'Gosh, this place is amazing.' She notices the pictures. 'Who are all these women?'

'They've all stayed here, over the years,' Alba explains, just as Peggy had nearly three months ago. She points out Florence Nightingale, Joan Greenwood and Emily Davies as they walk toward the kitchen. At the sink, Stella smiles, knowing she isn't needed anymore.

'The house is over two hundred years old.'

'Really? That's amazing. I can't believe I never noticed it before.'

'Yes,' Alba says. 'It's a little secretive. Do you want anything, tea, coffee, biscuits?'

'I'm fine, actually, thanks.'

'Would you like a tour of the house?'

'Yes.' Zoë grins. 'I'd love that.'

The tour, including a careful examination of

most of the rooms and nearly all the photographs, concludes in Alba's bedroom.

'Oh my goodness, this is incredible,' Zoë whispers, 'absolutely incredible. All these books! Why did you ever need to come to the library?'

'You'd be surprised by what's missing.' Alba smiles, thinking of Stella and the sneaky plan she finally realised the ghost had been plotting all along.

Zoë turns from examining a first edition of *The Old Curiosity Shop* and meets Alba's gaze. Little flashes of silver spark around Zoë's hair. It would be the easiest thing in the world to inch forward and kiss her now. And the hardest. Alba blinks and glances away.

'You have the best bedroom in the whole wide world,' Zoë says.

'Yes, I certainly do.'

And then, to their mutual amazement, some of the books float slowly down from the top shelves, brushing past their heads. The books on Alba's bed begin to rustle their pages.

'I don't believe it!' Zoë laughs. 'I don't believe it.'

Secretly thrilled that the house is showing off for her new friend, and even more delighted that Zoë is enjoying it so much, Alba reaches up for a book as it passes by.

'*Persuasion*,' she reads. 'I hate to admit it, but I've never read any Austen.'

'Seriously?' Zoë stares at her as if this revelation is even more unbelievable than the flying books.

'Never? So, it looks like we're going to have to further your education.'

'Well, I'll never say no to more reading,' Alba says. She follows as Zoë walks along the shelves, stopping to pick another book. '*Pride and Prejudice.*' She hands it to Alba. 'And *Sense and Sensibility*, of course.'

'Of course.' Alba smiles. 'But after this I'm going to take you through three years' worth of history textbooks. Maybe four, if you're very lucky.'

'I am,' Zoë says. She glances back at Alba as she walks on. 'And I look forward to it.' Then Zoë comes to a sudden stop and Alba, caught unawares, bumps into her. They move closer together, until they are only an inch apart. As Zoë reaches for her hand, hundreds of sparks of sunlight explode in the air around them. 'Oh,' Alba whispers, as she finally feels *it*.

Stella was right. Her heart has burst open, she's been knocked for six, yet feels safe, loved and more alive than she's ever felt before. And Alba knows that whatever this turns into now, whatever happens next, it has been the very best afternoon of her life.

That night, creeping down the corridor to the bathroom, Alba stops by Daphne to give her a gloriously detailed account of the day's events. When Alba finishes, the author claps. 'But you didn't kiss?'

'No, not yet.'

'Well, all in good time,' Daphne says. 'It's lovely anyway, to at last see you smile.'

'Yes,' Alba says, 'it's rather nice for me too. I'm thinking . . .'

'Yes?'

'The song, it's not,' Alba says, 'not . . .'

'Not what?'

'I don't know.' Alba shrugs. 'It's not quite true.'

'Ah.' Daphne smiles. 'Now you're discovering the great secret of great writing: one line of true feeling is worth a thousand pages of clever thinking.'

'Yes.' Alba nods. 'Exactly. I need to rewrite it, but I don't have time.'

'Why don't you give it a go?' Daphne suggests. 'You might surprise yourself.'

That night and the next, Alba stays awake, channelling her feelings of first love into her rewrite of Carmen's song. Finally, at four in the morning the day of the show, Alba thinks she might have it: something beautiful, real and true. She opens her bedroom door, listening for the muted music drifting out of the living room – she knows Carmen plays into the morning hours with the muffler pedal – and, seeing bright red notes floating down the dimly lit hall, dashes on tip-toes toward them.

'I've got it.' Alba flies into the room, holding an open notebook above her head, the pages flapping like wings. 'I've got it!'

'*O que e?*' Carmen frowns. 'You have one verse more?'

'No – a whole new song.'

319

'Really?' Carmen brightens. 'Show me.'

Alba hands her the notebook, virtually hopping up and down with excitement. Carmen quickly scans the sentences, pausing now and then to translate a word, then begins to play. And when Carmen at last falls silent, Alba's so thrilled she can't help but clap. 'Brilliant, that's absolutely brilliant!'

'*Sim*,' Carmen nods, delighted. 'This one is *perfecto*.'

'A little more to the left,' Peggy says, 'yes, that's right. Stay there.'

'Why are we doing this?' Alba asks, trying not to sound as embarrassed as she feels.

'I'd think that you, of all people, would understand the importance of documenting everyone who stays inside the house.' Peggy steps back a little further from the kitchen table. Alba sits at one end with Carmen on one side of her and Greer on the other. 'You're the one who spends so much time talking to all the women who've lived here.'

'Yes, but they're important women, great writers and . . .' Alba sighs. She hates having her photo taken. 'No one's going to want to talk to us.' She glances at Carmen and Greer, who are studiously avoiding catching each other's eye. 'Well, I mean, me anyway.'

'I wouldn't be so sure about that,' Peggy says. 'I think the next generation will be wanting to talk to you. And I think you'll have a lot to say to them.'

Alba scowls slightly, though secretly she's flattered. The other two, so intent on avoiding each other, don't hear anything their landlady is saying. Then, suddenly, Carmen turns to Greer.

'Okay, you must please forgive me,' she pleads. 'You must understand I did not know anything, I did not plan anything. I did not want to hurt you. Please believe this.'

Greer doesn't lift her eyes off the table. 'I do,' she says softly. 'I do.'

'So why you won't speak to me?' Carmen asks. 'Why you won't look at me?'

'Because I can't, not yet,' Greer says. 'Because if I do I think of him. I think of you kissing him. And I'd rather not right now. But it's not your fault, I know that. I just need a little time, okay?'

'*Sim*,' Carmen nods, knowing that time is the one thing she no longer has. 'Okay.'

'All right then, enough chitter-chat,' Peggy pipes up. 'Smile, everyone!' She clicks the camera shutter then looks up at the awkward little group sitting around her kitchen table.

'Oh, well.' She sighs. 'I suppose that will have to do.'

That night Greer leans against the wardrobe with the enormous book of dress designs in her lap. She's been studying them in the moments when she's not thinking of Edward and his little

321

girl. Having submitted all her teaching applications, she's rewarding herself with a little frivolity. And so, while trying to ignore the sound of Carmen singing – and the images of Blake the music evokes – Greer examines each pattern until, all of a sudden, she's seized with the desire to draw something of her own.

She glances up to see that a large notebook has materialised on her dressing table. Smiling, she hurries across the room. On top of the notebook is a tin of multicoloured pencils. Greer picks them up, too, walks back to her spot on the floor and sits with the notebook in her lap.

Two hours later she's surrounded by discarded drawings, hundreds of pages ripped out and thrown in every direction. As Greer sighs and puts her head back against the wardrobe, she catches sight of a new addition on her dressing table: an old-fashioned sewing machine, enamelled in black and gilded with burnished gold.

Contestant 453 steps off the stage, still hurling swearwords at the judges, pushing past Carmen. 'Good luck,' he snarls. 'They're bloody buggering idiots.' Carmen presses her hands together, palms sweating, trying to stop shaking, trying not to think of Tiago and only to remember the words of Alba's song.

Carmen had requested a piano and the eager producers had provided her with a baby grand. It sits in the middle of the stage, a black island floating on a sea of grey linoleum. She walks toward it slowly, trying to calm the rush of blood through her veins and still the thudding of her heart. After what seems like an hour, she reaches the piano and sits down.

Three judges smile, the fourth just nods. 'So, what will you sing?'

Carmen squints into the bright studio lights, wiping her sweaty hands on her lucky blue dress, searching the audience and seeing Alba waving from the centre of the third row. For a split second Carmen forgets herself, delighted. *From a caterpillar into a butterfly*, she thinks, *that is the power of music*. To Alba's left sits Peggy; to her right, Nora and Sue, wearing their opera gowns of taffeta and silk, waving gloved hands frantically above their heads and cheering with such enthusiasm it almost brings tears to Carmen's eyes. Greer isn't there, just as Carmen knew she wouldn't be, but it still makes her a little sad. She would have liked her friend to hear her, she would have liked to say goodbye.

'Okay, today, please,' the judge sighs.

'*Sim*, sorry.' Carmen collects herself. And then, at the centre of the storm within her, she remembers Peggy's advice. Faith still feels like a stretch but Carmen reaches for it. She turns back to the piano and, for the first time since her husband died, she prays. She prays she has got the song memorised, prays she will be able to do it justice, prays she won't mess up this incredible chance.

'My friend writes this special song. She tell me she write it for Zoë and the singing is to be dedicate to Stella,' Carmen says, her fingers over the keys, 'and I will sing to also honour them, and all the women of Hope Street.'

In the darkness Alba smiles and hopes that somehow, Stella is watching. She already knows that Zoë and Albert are, since she asked them to. She only hopes that Zoë doesn't hate the song or think that it's too much too soon.

'Very well.' The judge is nonplussed. 'Go ahead.'

Carmen nods, draws a deep breath, hits the first note and begins to sing.

> *I spoke without sound, before you came,*
> *But you gave sound to my heart.*
> *I lived without breath, before you came,*
> *But you gave breath to my life.*
> *I wrote without words, before you came*
> *But you gave words to my song.*
> *Now I will tell a tale of two together*
> *One forgotten and one found,*
> *Of hope that was lost forever . . .*

The sullen judge raises his hand and Carmen stops. He didn't give her a chance to finish. That can't be a good sign. The silence in the studio is the loudest she's ever heard. Even Nora and Sue are mute. The blood rushes through her head, tumbling through arteries and veins in rivers and rapids, drowning out everything else. Her heart hits her chest so hard it hurts. She feels tears welling up and prays to God not to let them fall. And then, all of a sudden the entire audience explodes into cheers and Alba and Peggy, Nora and Sue stand, clapping louder than everyone else.

'Well, well.' The sullen judge smiles as the roar finally subsides. 'I'd say that was far and away the best performance we've had today. Well done. You're through to the next round.'

The crowd erupts again, another judge dabs at her eyes. Carmen grips the piano to stop herself falling off the stool. And, for that single glorious moment nothing else matters, not her past or her future, because the house has given her back what she lost: her voice, her music, herself. And Carmen knows that, no matter what happens next, she will never lose them again.

CHAPTER 25

'A toast!' Peggy lifts her glass and waits for Alba, sipping lemonade, and Carmen, Nora and Sue, all drinking champagne, to join her. 'To a beautiful song and a beautiful singer.'

'The best we've ever heard,' Sue cheers.

'Hear! Hear! My dear.' Nora gulps down her drink, then offers her empty glass to Peggy, who tops it up again with a smile.

The two ladies stand side by side, beaming delightedly at Carmen.

'The best night of my life,' Sue says. 'Even including my wedding night.'

'Which one?' Nora nudges her. 'Second or third?'

'Oh, hush,' Sue giggles, 'you know very well Bernard had performance anxiety, but he well made up for it in other areas.'

'Yes, I remember,' Nora says, 'such gentle hands—'

'No.' Sue looks horrified. 'You promised me you didn't . . .'

'And I didn't,' Nora smiles, 'at least not in real life. But one can't control the imagination.' She lets out a satisfied sigh while Alba frowns, looking a little shocked.

Carmen watches the two women with an ache in her chest. She can't tell them she's leaving. She can't explain why or say goodbye.

'It really was beautiful,' Alba turns to Carmen. 'I, I . . . Thank you.' And even though she can't find any other words than these, Carmen smiles and nods to show she understands.

An hour later they are standing on the pavement, all rather tipsy except for Alba, ready to part. Carmen can't look directly at anyone or she knows she'll start to cry. She hugs Alba extra tight when they part and kisses Peggy, who whispers in Carmen's ear, reminding her to have faith and to simply keep walking until she finds her way.

Alba is giddy with joy. Hearing her song being sung to the nation by the most beautiful singer she's ever heard will forever be on her very short list of phenomenal experiences, second only to her first date with Zoë. She wishes her father could have witnessed it live. Albert has invited her over for a late supper after the event. They sit together on his sofa eating fish and chips out of newspapers on their laps. Alba tells Albert everything and he listens intently with absolute delight and enormous amounts of pride.

'The song was beautiful,' Albert says, for the hundredth time, 'so very beautiful.'

'Thank you,' Alba says softly.

They sit in silence while the flickering television plays repeats of Carmen's song.

'Do you like my flat?' Albert ventures, discarding a half-eaten chip.

'Sure,' Alba says, 'it's nice.'

'Not too small?'

Alba eats another chip, rather thrilled at the decadence of a TV dinner. After a childhood of suppressive suppers around a sixteenth-century oak table, sitting on the sofa eating fish and chips gives her a sense of illicit delight. 'Nope,' she says, 'seems fine to me.'

'We could sit in the kitchen.' Albert offers, embarrassed at not being able to offer his daughter the comforts he knows she grew up with.

'No, it's fine,' she says. 'I like it.'

'So.' Albert peels a strip of batter off his cod. 'So, I was thinking . . .'

'Yes?' Alba looks up.

About to ask, at the last moment Albert folds. 'Well, um . . . tell me more about this girl you want me to meet. Stella, yes? You had an aunt called Stella, you know. Your mother's sister—'

'I did?' Alba asks, confused. But both her parents were only children. She'd grown up without aunts, uncles or cousins. At least, that's what she'd always been told. 'No, I don't think so.'

'Yes, I'm sure,' Albert says. 'Her name was Stella. She was older. She died when Liz was a little girl. I remember her telling me . . .'

And then all the pieces of the puzzle suddenly fall into place.

Her mother: Elizabeth. Liz. *Beth*. Stella's sister, Beth.

Of course Ella was Stella, as a child might say the name when she is learning to talk, a nickname that stuck. How did Alba miss a clue like that? Poirot would be most disappointed.

'I can't believe it.' Alba laughs. 'I can't. She's my aunt! My aunt. Of course. I can't believe I didn't . . . They even look alike. And the things they said . . . Oh, my goodness. I can't . . . it's incredible, so incredible.'

'Wait.' Albert frowns, now slightly confused. 'If you didn't know about Stella, how do you know what she looks like? I don't understand.'

Alba shakes her head, unable to explain yet. So that was Stella's secret. She can't quite believe it, can't believe she didn't guess. She starts to laugh.

Still puzzled, Albert opens his mouth to ask why Alba's laughing but, to his shock and slight dismay, the question he's been rehearsing for the last few weeks blurts out instead.

'Alba, would you like . . . would you like to live with me?'

Alba stops laughing and smiles. 'Yes.' She says it so fast it rather takes her by surprise. 'I'd absolutely love to.'

'Really?' Albert says. 'You would?'

Alba nods, quite unable to believe her luck. Right now she can't imagine anything she'd love more. And, now that the problem of her impending homelessness has been taken care of, Alba can't wait to get back to Hope Street and interrogate Stella.

Greer is lying on her bed, unable to sleep. She's still trying to ignore the sewing machine, but it won't let her. It sits on the dressing table, gold letters glinting in the moonlight, even after she's closed the curtains and switched off the light. She's found a temporary job as a waitress along with a dingy room to live in, a roof over her head while she waits to start the teaching course and prepares applications to adoption agencies. She doesn't know how long it will take, or what she'll have to do to be successful but, as she stares at the ceiling now, Greer knows she'll do whatever it takes.

There's a sharp knock on her bedroom door and before Greer can sit up or say anything, the door opens and Peggy shuffles in with a cup of hot chocolate.

'You missed a beautiful show,' Peggy says. 'Carmen was quite breathtaking. You really should have come.'

Greer scowls. 'I was asleep.'

'No you weren't, dear,' Peggy says. 'I've brought you a drink.'

'I don't want one, thank you.' Greer knows she sounds a little rude but doesn't really care. It's ten o'clock and she could have sworn her door was locked.

'It's topped with cream and laced with liberal

amounts of rum. I've just had one myself, it was quite delicious. Anyway, I hope you don't mind the interruption, dear.' She eases herself onto the bed next to Greer. 'But I didn't imagine you were doing anything productive.'

'Well, I . . .' Greer takes the cup Peggy places in her hands.

'Exactly.' Peggy smiles. 'I know what you're up to and I've come to tell you not to do it.'

'Do what?'

'Now don't play dumb with me, young lady.' Peggy raises an eyebrow. 'The house is heaping gifts of inspiration upon you and you're stubbornly and stupidly ignoring every last one.'

'That's a little unfair.' Greer frowns. 'I'm being realistic.'

'Oh, tosh!' Peggy snaps.

'Well, hold on now.' Greer sits up straighter, abandoning the hot chocolate to her bedside table. 'That's a little harsh—'

'Not at all,' Peggy retorts. Every now and then she has to get a little tough with a particularly stubborn resident, one who won't pay attention to the more subtle signs, and in all honesty she rather relishes it. 'If it's right for you then it's possible. You're not eighty-two, you're not even forty. You've plenty of time to live the life you want, without compromising anything.'

Greer's frown deepens. 'Having a child *is* what I want, more than anything. I know I can be a wonderful mum, and it'll make me happy—'

'Yes, no doubt,' Peggy says, 'for a time, at least. But when your child needs to learn about her own heart, what will you teach her? To give up one herself, to sacrifice what she wants?'

'No, I won't, because she, or he, they won't have to. I'll tell them that.'

'But she'll have seen you do it,' Peggy says. 'And children are sharp little buggers you know. You can't simply say one thing and do another—'

'Really?' Greer leans forward to regard the old lady more closely. 'Is that true?'

'Of course.' Peggy nods, shifting a little uneasily under Greer's gaze. 'And when she grows up and leaves you altogether, what will you be left with then? A mother who's given up on herself is the worst sort of role model—'

'Really?' Greer says again. She looks into Peggy's eyes and, as her landlady glances away, Greer is greeted all of a sudden with a flash of insight. During all her days of recent self-reflection a sense of intuition has been growing more strongly inside her and now she sees something she can't back up with evidence or reason but something she knows, quite clearly, is true. 'So you, the landlady of this marvellous house, the role model to all the women who live here, the mother-figure, essentially—'

'Now, wait here,' Peggy protests, 'this is not—'

'Oh no, I rather think this is about you,' Greer interrupts. 'You, as my . . . my surrogate mother are telling *me* not to give up on *my* life because that would be setting a bad example to my child. But then isn't that exactly what you've done?'

A flicker of sorrow passes over Peggy's face. It's gone in a second but Greer sees it and now she's absolutely certain she's right. She has no idea where this sudden ability to see into people's souls has come from but she knows, unequivocally, that she can trust it.

'You're being a little hypocritical, then,' Greer says softly. 'Don't you think?'

A little drunk on celebration cocktails and euphoria, Carmen wanders through the streets of Cambridge. It's a perfect night, cloudless and full of stars. The moon is full and the air is warm; it brushes Carmen's face as though stroking her cheek. She doesn't know what she's going to do now and the terror of being adrift and alone, not allowed to return to Hope Street, is only slightly tempered by the lingering thrill of the show and the song.

She stops for a moment to gaze up at the silhouette of King's College, its turrets and towers lit by the moon, marble against the dark purple sky. *How can the world be so beautiful*, she wonders, *but so painful, all at once?* For another hour, with the ring still hot in her pocket, Carmen meanders along streets and through parks, just as she did before she found Hope Street, stopping sometimes to look at things she loves: the Bridge of Sighs, punts tied up along the river waiting for tomorrow's tourists, the golden grasshopper clock, the chapel in Clare College . . . She memorises each one, imprinting them in her mind like photographs so that she'll never forget. And just after midnight, though Carmen never knew where it was, she finds herself crossing the park in front of the police station. She stands on the pavement, looking up once more at the moon. Her cheeks are wet. Not with tears of sadness, but relief. Carmen takes a deep breath.

She releases one last, long note of song into the air, and then walks inside.

CHAPTER 26

I t's long past midnight when Alba unlocks the door. The house is so silent and still, that it's almost as if it's holding its breath. She takes off her coat and hangs it up, then slips off her shoes. The floor sinks softly under her feet, welcoming her home, the ceiling dips down and she glances up, blinking into the bright light of the chandelier that switched itself on as she walked up the garden path. On her way to the kitchen Alba is stopped by Joan Greenwood.

'We're all very proud of your progress,' she says, her husky voice sending a little shiver of delight through Alba. 'I know you've only written a lovely little song, so far. But we all have a feeling that you'll make quite a mark in literary history one day.'

'You do?' Alba asks. 'Well . . . thank you.'

'You're welcome.' Joan smiles. 'It's been a pleasure watching you.'

Alba walks into the kitchen, glancing around for her aunt Stella. *Her aunt.* She has so many questions, so much she wants to know. Of course Stella is still nowhere to be seen, but this time

Alba has decided she's going to wait at the table and not move a muscle until Stella materialises. No matter how long it takes.

Ten hours later, when Peggy shuffles into the kitchen the next morning, Alba is sitting in the same chair, gently snoring. Peggy coughs until Alba stirs. 'Oh, sorry, I was just—'

'Yes, pet,' Peggy says, 'I know who you're waiting for. But I'm afraid she's gone.'

'No.' Alba tries to contain a rush of panic. 'She can't, not now, I haven't . . .'

'I know, dear, but she has. I'm certain. I can feel it.'

'But, no, she can't . . . I thought she couldn't leave, I thought she had to stay forever.'

'She only had to stay until she was done.' Peggy flicks the kettle on.

'Done with what?'

'With you.'

'But how could she leave, just like that?' Alba protests. 'She didn't say goodbye.'

'I don't think she knew,' Peggy says, taking a teacup from the cupboard above her head. 'I don't think she had any warning.'

'But she . . . she was my aunt,' she says, the word still feeling strange on her tongue.

'I know, I'm sorry,' Peggy says softly, wishing she at least had a better explanation. She pours water into her cup then carries it to the table and sits.

'She was waiting for me,' Alba says. 'Did you know that?'

Peggy nods as she sips her tea. Alba watches as the steam curls into the air in pale blue spirals, perhaps unsurprisingly, quite a different colour from everyone else's.

'I still don't understand, though,' Alba says. 'How did she know I was coming? How did she know to wait for me?'

'The dead understand all sorts of things we couldn't possibly hope to,' Peggy explains. 'They know everything that's happened and most of what's going to happen, time is rather different for them than it is for us.' With a twinge she remembers that this will be true for her soon, and she's sorry for it. She's not scared any more, but she would have liked longer, she would have liked to say a proper goodbye to Harry. Seeing the look of longing on Alba's face, Peggy suddenly knows that a letter isn't enough. She has to go to him. She has to be with him for as long as she has left. Greer was right. To hell with the house. She's given it sixty-one years of her life, nearly as many years as Queen Victoria gave to the British Empire. Surely that's enough?

'It's more than enough!' Peggy exclaims suddenly.

'Sorry?' Alba frowns. 'What's more than enough?'

Peggy looks at Alba across the table, coming to her senses. 'Oops, my apologies, that wasn't, I was having another . . . What was I saying?'

Alba frowns, a little concerned. There is a look of fierce determination in Peggy's eyes that she's never seen before, and it's a little unnerving.

'About the dead understanding,' Alba says. 'But I don't understand how I knew to come here.'

'Oh, my dear, but didn't you realise?' Peggy says. 'It wasn't a coincidence. You didn't simply find yourself on the doorstep, you weren't beckoned by the house, like everyone else. You came because Stella called you.'

Alba is silent, because what can she say? She is loved. Really and truly loved.

Peggy is standing in front of her wardrobe, hurling clothes in the direction of a suitcase that lies open on her bed. Mog sits next to the suitcase, eyeing his mistress reproachfully.

'There's no use looking at me like that, kitty, I'm not changing my mind,' Peggy says, without turning around. 'You can come with me, if you like, but I'm not staying. I don't kn°ow how many days I have left, but I'm going to spend every single one of them with Harry.'

Mog emits a little sneeze of disgust.

'I'm not listening.' Peggy discards three skirts she hasn't worn in twenty years, dropping them on top of the pile at her feet. She thinks of Alba and Stella. She's already torn up her letter to Harry. Before rushing up to the tower, Peggy had told Alba one more thing, the last piece of family history Stella hadn't had a chance to tell her niece. Just over forty years ago Elizabeth had come to Hope Street, the only woman to arrive on the doorstep who didn't stay. Peggy had opened

338

the door before Elizabeth had a chance to knock, startling her so that she stepped back, nearly falling into the flowers.

'Nice to meet you, Beth.' Peggy had smiled, rather enjoying the woman's shock. 'She's been waiting for you. It's the door at the end of the corridor.' And with that, she disappeared up the stairs.

Elizabeth stumbled along the corridor, staring at the photographs, just as her daughter would do forty years later. The ceiling came down to have a look at her, the chandelier flickered above her head. The floor softened under her feet and the pipes gently rattled in greeting. That morning Elizabeth had been shopping at the farmers' market in Covent Garden, tasting chocolate brownies with spiced cherries, elderflower truffles and ginger biscuits. Just as she bit into a biscuit, Elizabeth had heard a song in the air, the words floating past her, the letters sparkling silver and gold – the lullaby her sister had sometimes sung to help her sleep. She had followed it. She found a train to Cambridge, walked through the city and arrived on the doorstep of the house at the end of Hope Street, without knowing what she was doing or why.

When she reached the kitchen door, Elizabeth slowly opened it and peeked inside. There, sitting in the sink, was her sister. It was several moments before Elizabeth could speak. It wasn't the shock of seeing a ghost that silenced her, since she had grown up seeing things that most people couldn't. Her sister's ghost was a different matter altogether. Elizabeth had always held out hope that one day she might meet Stella again. And here she was. Elizabeth walked slowly to the sink, wondering if perhaps her sister was a figment of her imagination, a desire so desperate it'd tricked her unpredictable mind. But when her sister smiled, she knew.

'Oh, Ella,' she sighed, 'I've missed you so much.'

'I know, sis, I've missed you too.'

'I never stopped looking for you, around every corner, in every room . . .'

'I know, my love. I'm sorry. I couldn't stay. I wanted to be with you but I couldn't risk it,' Stella said. 'Somehow I thought that seeing ghosts wouldn't have made you feel much saner.'

'Yes.' Elizabeth smiled. 'I know. But I'm on medication now. It's not perfect but it's better, I'm better, as long as I take it.' The last ten years seemed to disappear then, and she felt as though they'd never been apart. 'I can't believe you really are here, that I'm not imagining things.'

Stella floated down from the sink to the table and sat cross-legged next to her sister. 'I'm sorry, Beth, I'm so sorry I left you while I ran off round the country with—'

'It's okay, I survived.' Elizabeth smiled, though they both knew it had only been barely. 'Are you okay – like this, I mean?'

'Oh, I'm fine,' Stella said. 'Apart from anything

else, death does give you a rather beautiful perspective on life. So, tell me how on earth you ended up being engaged to that idiotic, self-centred philandering playboy known as cousin Charlie?'

'Don't say that,' Elizabeth protested. 'He's fine and I love him, at least I think – anyway, he wants to marry me, Ella, and we've . . . I wanted to wait, but Charlie said we should give it a go, so . . .'

'Oh, that's nothing, it doesn't matter.' Stella laughed. 'It doesn't mean you have to get married.'

'I know I don't *have* to,' Elizabeth said. 'I want to. Anyway, how did you know? He only asked me this morning. We haven't told anyone yet.'

'I've never left you, Beth, I've always been watching, just in case you needed me.'

'Oh? And why do I need you now?' Elizabeth frowned. 'I needed you when you died, when I was a kid, all alone in that house. Now I'm actually happy. Why have you waited until I'm happy?'

'I couldn't go to you,' Stella explained. 'I had to call you to me. I couldn't do that when you were a little girl. Goodness knows I wanted to.'

'Well, I don't need you now,' Elizabeth said. 'I'm fine.'

'Please, Beth, I know you think you love him, but you don't, not really, he isn't the love of your life—'

'Stop it, Ella,' Elizabeth snapped. 'Look, I'm really happy to see you again. But please don't tell me I don't know my own mind. I've had people doing that all my life. I thought at least you would respect me enough not to.'

'Oh, Beth, I do. I don't mean it like that. It's just, I know more than you do about—'

'You know what I want?'

'No, that's not . . .' But it was no good. Stella knew it. She'd called her sister here to stop her marrying Charlie, to save her years of heartbreak, but it was too late. The grand dames upstairs had attempted to explain what could be influenced and what couldn't, and why. But she hadn't understood it then and she didn't understand it now. She wanted to save her sister.

'You really love him?'

'Yes.' Elizabeth nodded. 'I do. I'm happy. For the first time in my life, I'm really happy. So don't worry, it'll all be okay.'

'I hope so, Beth, I really do.' Stella looked at her sister's innocent smile and only wished she could hug her, one more time. 'But just in case, I'll always be here. Until the day you die. Okay? You can talk to me, wherever you are, and I'll hear you. Don't forget, all right? Promise me that.'

'Don't be silly; don't talk about such morbid things. You should be happy for me.'

Stella nodded. 'Just promise me, please.'

'Okay, I promise,' Elizabeth said. But she knew she didn't have to worry, that nothing bad was going to happen. She would have a husband, she would have babies. Everything was going to be wonderful.

★　★　★

'I'm leaving.' Peggy stands in front of the door to the forbidden room. Mog is at his mistress's side, twitching his tail in a rare moment of support and solidarity. She won him over with thirty minutes of tummy tickling. Peggy knocks on the door again. 'I know you can hear me. I'm going to spend my last days with Harry. I gave up my life, everything I might have wanted . . . And now that I'm going to die, I'm going to do something for myself for once. So, if you want another martyr to run Hope Street, then you can find her on your own.'

She turns back to the kitchen table and sits down to her waiting cup of tea, the last she'll enjoy in her kitchen. Mog jumps up on her lap, pushing his face against her cheek – and the door finally swings open. Peggy is surprised, but her resolve is strong. The inhabitants of the forbidden room won't sway her now.

'That won't work.' Peggy sips her tea. 'It's too late, I won't change my mind. Frankly, I don't know why you'd bother, I'm not much use to you for much longer—'

'Stop sulking, you silly woman,' Virginia Woolf's voice snaps through the air. 'Before you flounce off in a huff, we've got something to tell you.'

'Well, I don't want to hear it.' Peggy scratches Mog's ears. 'All these years I've been trying so hard to help the house. Then you tell me I'm dying and you leave me entirely alone to manage it—'

'We can explain that,' George Eliot calls out.

'Well, I don't care if you can,' Peggy says. 'I'm not interested any more.'

'Please, Peg.' Beatrix Potter's gentle voice drifts into the air. 'It's important.'

But Peggy just shakes her head, sips her tea and lets Mog drool into her lap.

'Peggy Abbot, you need to listen to me.' Grace Abbot, the founder of Hope Street, finally floats out of the forbidden room and settles on a kitchen chair, transparent arms folded, powdered wig quivering slightly atop her head. 'You are not going to die.'

Alba feels like a walk. She can't be bothered to go upstairs and get dressed. When she reaches the front door she slips on a jacket over her pyjamas and a pair of shoes, glancing at the photographs around the door. Then she stops and stares, squinting to be sure she is really seeing what she thinks she's seeing.

Standing there, in a picture Alba has seen a hundred times before, is Stella. It's a group photograph of ten women standing on the lawn in front of the house. The wind has blown autumn leaves from the trees, swirling them around the women as if they are inside a leafy snow globe. Now, at the edge of the group is an eleventh woman: Stella, wearing a dress splashed with red poppies that falls to her feet, bare on the grass. Alba smiles.

'There you are.'

'Here I am,' Stella says. 'And here I'll always be.'

Alba puts her hand to the picture, her finger touching her aunt's face. 'Thank you. I . . .' She wants to say more, wants to tell Stella everything she feels, everything she hopes, everything . . .

'It's okay,' Stella says, and blows her niece a kiss. 'I know.'

'Of course you do.' Alba laughs. 'Well then, I'll see you later.' With a grin and a wave, she turns the doorknob and steps out into the garden. When Alba reaches the gate she doesn't know where to go, so she just walks down the street, following the direction her feet take. Twenty minutes later, like some sort of pyjama-clad homing pigeon, Alba finds herself at the avenue of trees leading to the library. She finds a bench and sits, ignoring people's perplexed glances in her direction as they pass her on their way to work. She retreats into her own world, thinking of her aunt. Then Zoë is standing in front of her.

Alba glances up and smiles.

Zoë hesitates, pulling her fingers through her spiky blue hair. 'Are you okay?'

'I'm fine.'

'Well . . . You're sitting on a bench at nine in the morning,' Zoë says, 'in your pyjamas.'

'Good point.' Alba nods. 'But I'm okay. I'm better than okay.'

Zoë smiles. 'I'm glad.'

'Me too.'

'Have you tried Austen yet?' Zoë sits on the bench.

'I have. And I loved them. Especially *Pride and Prejudice*.'

'You've read *all* of them?' Zoë asks.

'I'm a fast reader.'

'I'll say.' Zoë puts her hand on Alba's knee. 'You're amazing.'

Every other thought in Alba's mind evaporates then and all she can think of is Zoë's hand on her knee and how it's making her whole body tingle. She wonders if people are watching them, if they know what's going on.

'Should I not?' Zoë asks quietly.

But Alba can't answer. The warmth of Zoë's touch soaks through the thin cotton of her pyjamas, seeping into her skin, and the very last thing she wants now is for Zoë to take it away. Slowly, Alba shakes her head. She looks up at Zoë, who smiles, waiting. Little sparks of sunlight burst between them again and, not taking her eyes off Zoë's lips, Alba leans forward for her first kiss.

The four ghosts sit around a small wooden table, their bridge game momentarily on hold. The room is a parlour from the early nineteenth century, dating from the time the house was built and decorated with silk cream wallpaper stencilled with rows and rows of fleur-de-lis. Heavy deep purple velvet curtains hang from the ceiling to the floor, drawn back from long windows. The dark blue carpet is soft under Peggy's feet. She stands in the doorway, glaring at the four ghosts.

'Of course you will die eventually,' Grace admits, patting her wig into place and tickling Mog under his chin. 'But not until you're a hundred and five.'

'Why are you saying this? Why are you lying?' But, as Peggy scowls at Grace, she can see that she's not lying, not now. 'What the hell is going on? So why did you tell me I was going to die? Why did you torture me with that, what was the point?'

'We wanted to give you a gift,' George says, 'for all your years of service.'

'A gift?' Peggy cries, 'I can hardly see—'

'Yes, exactly,' Virginia explains. 'You needed to see yourself, to know yourself. We told you that so you could realise how you truly felt and what you truly wanted. Impending death always has a way of clearing the fog.'

'What?' Peggy needs to sit down. 'I don't understand.'

'Exactly,' Beatrix whispers. 'You understand everyone else so well, but you've spent years lying to yourself.'

'You love Harry,' George says, 'and you want to be with him, but you didn't fully realise it until you thought you were going to die.'

'What? I . . .' Peggy's head is heavy with confusion and shock.

'You may be magical,' Virginia says, 'but you're still human. And, like most people, you're too scared, stubborn or stupid to give yourself what you need until you're shaken awake by something.'

'Such as a near-death experience,' George says.

'So we gave you one,' Beatrix smiles.

For a full five minutes Peggy stares at the four women, replaying their words. Slowly her anger subsides and she only feels sad. 'I always thought that I didn't . . .' she whispers, half to herself, 'how could I not know, how could I not know my own heart? . . .'

'Did you think that the house would give so many women what they needed,' Beatrix asks, 'without doing the same for you?'

'But what's the point? Why did you help me to see myself now?' Peggy protests. 'If I still have to stay for another . . . however many years, and I still can't have H—'

'Oh no,' Grace interrupts. 'We're releasing you. We think you've paid your dues. You're free to be with Harry now.'

'Really?'

The four women nod.

Peggy shakes her head, not quite believing it. 'Why did you leave me a note and lock me out of the room? Why couldn't you tell me to my face?'

Beatrix smiles. 'That was my fault, I'm afraid.'

'Bea can't lie,' Virginia says with a sigh. 'She's useless at it.'

'That's true,' Beatrix admits. 'You would have guessed in a second that it was a trick.'

'But if I am leaving,' Peggy says, still not entirely able to believe it, 'then, who will . . .?'

'Well, that's simple,' Virginia says. 'The mother, of course.'

Greer stands in the bathroom, squinting into the mirror. Her new uniform is pretty revolting and clashes horribly with her hair, but there's nothing much she can do about it. She adjusts the bright orange cap, tilting it at a jaunty angle in a vain attempt to try.

'That is, without a doubt, the most disgusting outfit I've ever seen.' Peggy stands in the doorway. 'And I see you didn't listen to a word I said.'

Greer pushes the orange cap firmly onto her head. 'If love means wearing this hideous uniform, then it'll be more than worth it.'

'You'll regret—'

'Pot. Kettle.' Greer glares at Peggy. 'And what else exactly do you expect me to do?'

This is the opening Peggy has been waiting for. 'Live here.'

Greer gasps. 'Really, can I? Well, thank you. That'd be amazing, it'll certainly save me money on rent—'

'Well, not quite,' Peggy says, a little taken aback. 'That wasn't exactly what I meant.'

'No?' Greer's smile drops.

'I meant that you would inherit the house. You would take over from me. Stay forever.'

'Forever?'

'Yes. That's what I'm offering. Would you like that?'

'I don't understand,' Greer says. 'What about you?'

'I'm retiring.' Peggy grins.

'But, but . . . But I can't run this house. I can't replace you,' Greer says. 'I can't do all the things you do. The notes, the advice . . .'

'Oh, don't worry about that.' Peggy waves a hand dismissively. 'I don't write the notes, the house does. And I usually hear the advice before I say it. Anyway, with that little insight you pulled on me the other night, I rather think you're a lot sharper than you give yourself credit for.'

'Well, yes, but—'

'And you'll see and learn more, the longer you stay here.'

'Okay. But what about the rules, then? About having no husband, no family.'

'Times are changing. I've just been having a word with the women upstairs. We're evolving, modernising like the royals. So you won't have to live here like a nun. Not that I ever exactly did that.' Peggy isn't bitter about the change of protocol. She may have lost twenty years with Harry, but she gained them all back and they're still ahead of her.

'The royals?' Greer asks. 'What women upstairs?'

'I'll introduce you to them tonight, if you like,' Peggy says. 'So Edward can stay, he can even live here if you like.'

'Edward?'

'Oh, please.' Peggy shuffles over to the bathtub

and perches on its edge. 'I felt the sparks between you two all the way up in the tower.' Peggy pats the edge of the bathtub. Greer sits down and takes off her cap.

'But, still,' she says, 'you can't just *give* me this house. It's too much. It's—'

'Oh, don't worry, it has a price,' Peggy says.

Greer might have known there had to be a catch. This was simply too good to be true. 'Well then, unless it's twenty quid, I'm afraid I can't really afford it.'

'Oh, it's not money.' Peggy laughs. 'The price is that you must always do what you love. You must cultivate your own heart while caring for your surrogate children.'

Greer laughs, too, as the glorious absurdity of this price sinks in. 'Oh, is that all?'

'Yes, that's all. But it's not always easy, you know, so you must promise.'

'I promise.'

Peggy smiles. 'Good. Now, tell me, just how long are you going to wait until you call Edward?'

Alba stands on the doorstep, clutching a small bag. 'Okay, well . . .' she bites her lip and suddenly pulls Peggy into a hug, squeezing the old woman so tightly she coughs. 'Oh, gosh.' Alba lets go. 'Sorry, sorry, I'm not really used to . . . I didn't mean to hurt you.'

'No, no.' Peggy catches her breath. 'Don't be silly, it's quite the best hug I've ever had. But you don't have to go yet, you know. You can stay a little longer, your ninety-nine nights aren't up for another two weeks.'

'I know,' Alba says. 'But I'm ready.'

'Yes.' Peggy smiles. 'Yes you are.'

Feeling the familiar brush of fur along her ankles, the old lady glances down at her feet in surprise.

Alba sees a big fat orange cat winding in slow, lazy figure eights around Peggy's legs. She kneels to stroke him, and he purrs.

'Well, well. Mog's come to say goodbye. You should be honoured, he's never bothered to before,' Peggy says, a little shocked. Though she should hardly be surprised that, of all the residents she's ever had, Alba is the one who can see him. 'He likes you.'

'He's beautiful,' Alba says, and Mog starts to drool.

'I rather think he wants to go with you,' Peggy says, the admission a little tinged with regret. But since she's moving out herself she can't be possessive over Mog any more. 'Would you like to take him with you?'

'Really?' Alba's eyes light up. 'Can I?'

Peggy nods.

With a grin, Alba kisses the old woman on her papery cheek. 'Thank you for everything, for all of it. You, Stella, the house, you saved my life.'

She turns then and hurries down the garden path, tears rolling down her face. The walls of the house shudder slightly, a mournful breath blows through the pipes, the electricity momentarily short-circuits, as it watches her go. Mog pads along beside Alba, his tail high in the air. When she reaches the gate Alba wipes her eyes. A moment later she is walking along the pavement. Each step is a goodbye.

Then she stops and turns around to wave. But Peggy has gone.

The house has disappeared. And all she can see now are trees.

EPILOGUE

Two Years Later

Greer sits in the garden with Tilly in her lap, brushing her long, black hair, winding the curls gently around her fingers. 'You're so beautiful,' she says. 'Do you know how beautiful you are?' Tilly nods and Greer laughs. 'Excellent, healthy self-esteem, that's what I like to see.'

'A toast.' Edward lifts his glass. He waits as Greer and Harry pick up theirs. Peggy, who hasn't put her glass down all afternoon, already has it in the air.

'To the house.'

'The house,' they chorus.

'The horse!' Tilly shouts, then giggles.

Every year they have a picnic party to celebrate the anniversary of Greer moving into the tower. Greer supplies the crockery, Edward mixes the drinks, Harry provides the food, Peggy brings a three-tiered chocolate cake, which she's made herself, and an enormous bowl of cream.

'Perhaps we ought to get new cups and plates.' Edward lifts one to reveal the White Queen taking

Rumpelstiltskin's clothes off. 'Yesterday she was with Lancelot. We don't want Til unduly influenced by these kinky characters, they aren't exactly promoting family values.'

Harry raises his eyebrows at Peggy, who snorts with gentle derision.

'Oh, love.' Greer smiles. 'She's not even five. I think we've got a little while yet until she starts asking questions about—'

'Sex!' Tilly shouts, then giggles again.

They all look at her, astonished. Then Peggy starts shaking with laughter, spilling her cocktail. 'She's got the gift, that one, must be her godmother's influence.' From where she sits Peggy takes a little bow and raises her glass again.

'Oh dear,' Edward sighs. 'Oh dear.'

'Speaking of influence.' Harry quickly changes the subject. 'How are this year's residents coming along?'

'Oh, they're fine,' Greer says, 'but all so young, my goodness. They try to steal my clothes, they hound me to make outfits for them. It's maddening.'

'Maddening, but flattering,' Edward says. 'They all came to Alba's play last month. When they found out Greer had done the costumes, they wouldn't leave her alone.'

'We saw it.' Peggy reaches for another slice of cake. 'It was bloody brilliant.'

Edward quickly puts his hands over his daughter's ears.

'Buddy bwilliant!' Tilly exclaims, then giggles again.

The club is dusty and dark. Carmen waits in the wings, pacing. Narciso, the scruffy manager of the dingy bar, pokes his head around the door.

'Okay, it's time,' he yells. '*Vamos!*'

Carmen feels all the blood leave her body and her knees buckle under her.

'Are you having a seizure?' Narciso snaps, ''cause we ain't insured for that.'

'No, no.' Carmen shakes her head, getting a grip on her nerves. 'I'm fine.'

'Good,' Narciso says. 'Now, get out there and get on with it!' With that, he gives her a friendly shove and Carmen falls through the flimsy blue curtain and onto the stage. She stumbles toward the microphone, grabs it and clings on for dear life, as if she is drowning in the ocean and it is an obliging dolphin.

Relaxa, Carmen chants to herself, *relaxa, relaxa, relaxa* . . .

She blinks into the single bright light, desperately wanting to close her eyes, but forcing herself to squint into the crowd. *If I could cope with a courtroom,* she thinks, *then I can cope with this.* For a moment Carmen looks back at the last two years: the judge, the jury, the cell and Tiago's ghost, who sat with her every night so that she barely slept. But Peggy was right. The judge and jury were sympathetic. Tiago's violent nature was well-known and, when Carmen finally took the stand and told them Tiago would have killed her if she hadn't stopped him, they believed her. And when she walked out of court she never saw or dreamt about her husband again. She was, at last, finally and forever free.

Carmen gazes out onto the audience and her breath stops in her throat. There is something worse than thirty people staring back at her, something much, much worse: absolutely nobody at all. Carmen looks over the rows and rows of empty chairs. Now she really is floating in an ocean, a sea of endless emptiness, completely and utterly alone.

With the exception of one single soul.

A woman sits on the very edge of the back row, rapidly typing on her phone. Carmen stands absolutely still, contemplating how likely it is that, if she runs offstage right now, the woman will never realise she's been there at all. She glances back at the curtain, where Narciso is gesticulating wildly, urging her to get the hell on with it and sing something, anything. Reluctantly, Carmen turns back to the chairs, looks out at her inattentive audience of one, and takes a deep breath.

The first note rises up and Carmen begins to sing her newest song: one of hope, forgiveness, gratitude for everything expected and unexpected, wanted and unwanted, chosen and bestowed. She lets the song fill her and gives herself completely to the music, holding nothing back, feeling her spirit soar up, through the ceiling of the dingy nightclub and out into the night air.

Slowly, the music producer glances up from her phone. For a second she seems shocked, and then a smile of pure joy gradually spreads across her face. She will remember this moment for the rest of her life, for she has been waiting her whole career to hear a voice like this.

Alba sits on the sofa, her knees pulled up to her chin, with Zoë on her left and Albert on her right. They're all watching the television, rapt.

'It's not as good as the book,' Alba whispers.

'It's not as good as your play.' Zoë squeezes her hand.

'True, but hush,' Albert hisses. 'This is my favourite part.'

They watch Lucy Honeychurch step into a field of flowers to be swept off her feet and into George Emerson's arms. Albert lets out a little sigh.

'Dad, are you crying?'

'Don't be ridiculous.' Albert sniffs. 'I'm far too manly for that.'

'Of course you are, Al.' Zoë winks at Alba. 'Of course you are.'

'It's being around you two.' Albert pauses the film to blow his nose. 'You've gone and turned me soft – very soft.' He pats his belly.

Alba and Zoë giggle. On the screen Lucy and George are frozen in a sea of flowers.

'"*From her feet the ground sloped sharply into view,*"' Albert begins.

'"*. . . and violets ran down in rivulets and streams and cataracts,*"' Zoë continues.

'"*. . . irrigating the hillside with blue,*"' Alba finishes.

'Oh dear.' Albert laughs. 'What a funny little family we are.'

'"Little" being the operative word,' Zoë says, 'being that we're all under five foot two.'

'Steady on,' Albert says. 'I'm five foot seven in my socks.'

Alba laughs. 'Of course you are, Dad, of course you are.'

'All right then, enough ridiculousness,' Albert huffs. 'Back to the film. I want to see what happens next.'

'Dad, you know what happens next.' Alba laughs. 'If we turned the sound off you could quote every single line from beginning to end.'

'Hush,' Albert says, as the screen flickers to life again. They all gaze at the screen. Alba pulls Zoë's hand into her lap.

A fine mist of gold, the colour of contentment, settles over them.

And they sit together, until the credits roll.

A GUIDE TO THE WOMEN OF HOPE STREET

Upstairs Hallway

Elizabeth Garrett Anderson (1836–1917)

The first female to qualify as a doctor in England.[1] At first a nurse, she was refused admittance by every medical school to which she applied. Finally, Anderson was admitted for private study by the Society of Apothecaries. She qualified to practice medicine in 1865, but the SoA immediately amended its regulations to prevent other women from following in her footsteps. Not allowed to practice in any hospital, she set up her own practice, fighting for the medical rights of women. In 1873 she was admitted as a member of the British Medical Association, but it would be another nineteen years before other women were allowed to join her.

---

[1] Another Englishwoman, Elizabeth Blackwell, was the first woman to qualify as a doctor in the United States, in 1849. The two met in London in 1859.

Millicent Garrett Fawcett (1847–1929)

Elizabeth's younger sister Millicent was a suffragist who campaigned for British women's right to vote.[2] She believed in moderate methods, disapproving of the more militant Pankhursts. Like her sister, she fought to improve women's educational opportunities and in 1871 cofounded Newnham College, the second Cambridge college for women, after Girton College in 1869. However, while female students at Cambridge studied to degree level and took the exams (Millicent's daughter Philippa ranking highest in the Mathematical Tripos in 1890), they weren't awarded full degrees until 1947.

Daphne du Maurier (1907–1989)

A British author and playwright,[3] du Maurier's most famous novel is *Rebecca* (1938), which opens with the line 'Last night I dreamt I went to Manderley again.' This book, along with her short stories *The Birds* and *Don't Look Now*, were made into major films. The film version of *Rebecca*, directed by Alfred Hitchcock, won the Oscar for best film in 1940.

---

[2] In 1918 women over thirty were given the vote. In 1928, all women eighteen and older could vote.

[3] Daphne was a cousin of the Llewelyn Davies boys, who inspired J. M. Barrie's 1904 play *Peter Pan*. Du Maurier's other brilliant works of literature include *Jamaica Inn*, *Frenchman's Creek* and *My Cousin Rachel*.

Emmeline Pankhurst (1858–1928)

Emmeline Pankhurst was a suffragette, a radical campaigner for the rights of women. Widely criticised for her militant tactics,[4] she still, like the less militant Fawcetts, played a pivotal role in finally achieving the vote for women. In 1999, *Time* named her one of the 100 Most Important People of the Twentieth Century.

Elizabeth Taylor (1932–2011)

Taylor was born in London to American parents. She was the winner of two Academy Awards for her roles in *BUtterfield 8* (1960) and *Who's Afraid of Virginia Woolf?* (1966). She also received the Presidential Citizens Medal, the Medal of the Legion of Honour, and a Life Achievement Award from the American Film Institute, which named her seventh in their list of the 'Greatest American Screen Legends.' In 2000 she was made a Dame of the British Empire. She married eight times, twice to actor Richard Burton.

Bathroom

Sylvia Plath (1932–1963)

Born in Boston, Plath studied at two all-female colleges: Smith College, Massachusetts, and

---

[4] These included smashing windows and assaulting police officers. Pankhurst, her daughters and other members of the Women's Social & Political Union were frequently

Newnham College, Cambridge. There she met the poet Ted Hughes. They courted with poems, married in 1956, and had two children before he left her for another woman. In 1963 she committed suicide. In 1982 she became the first poet to win a Pulitzer Prize posthumously, for *The Collected Poems*. Plath's most famous work is *The Bell Jar* (1963), an auto-biographical novel about depression.

Dorothy Parker (1893–1967)

Dorothy was a poet famous for her great wit. She sold her first poem to *Vanity Fair* in 1914 and worked there and at *Vogue* for several years. At *Vanity Fair* she met Robert Benchley and Robert Sherwood and together they informally founded the Algonquin Round Table.[5] In 1925 Harold Ross founded *The New Yorker* and Parker's first piece appeared in its second issue. Her first collection of poetry, *Enough Rope* (1926), contained the famous poem 'Résumé', about suicide. She received two Academy Award nominations for screenplays and worked very successfully until she was placed on the Hollywood blacklist for her liberal politics. She married three times, twice (like Elizabeth

---

put in prison, where they staged hunger strikes to protest the dreadful conditions.

[5] A celebrated group of New York City writers, critics, actors, and wits, including Harpo Marx, Art Samuels and Charles MacArthur. They met for lunches at the Algonquin Hotel from 1919 to 1929.

Taylor) to the same man. Despite attempting suicide several times she ultimately died of a heart attack.

Living Room

Doris Lessing (1919–2013)

Lessing left school at fourteen and thereafter educated herself. Doris Lessing's most famous novels include *The Golden Notebook* (1962), a significant feminist text influential in the women's liberation movements of the 1960s, and *The Grass is Singing* (1950). In 2007 she was awarded the Nobel Prize in Literature, the eleventh woman in 106 years. In 2008 the *Times* ranked her fifth on its list of the 50 Greatest British Writers Since 1945.

Vivien Leigh (1913–1967)

Also known as Lady Olivier, from her marriage to Sir Laurence Olivier, the British actress won two Academy Awards for her roles in *A Streetcar Named Desire* (1951) and *Gone With the Wind* (1939). Leigh pursued the lead role in *Gone With the Wind* with great determination, despite being relatively unknown and British, telling a journalist long before the film was cast that she would play Scarlett O'Hara. Leigh suffered from bi-polar disorder, which gave her a reputation for being difficult to work with. She divorced from Olivier in 1960.

Vanessa Bell (1879–1961)

Born Vanessa Stephen, sister of Virginia Woolf. Bell was a painter and member of the Bloomsbury Group, an influential circle of English writers and intellectuals including Virginia Woolf, E. M. Forster and Lytton Strachey. Her significant paintings include portraits of her sister and of Aldous Huxley. Bell is considered one of the major contributors to British portrait drawing and landscape art in the twentieth century.

Agatha Christie (1890–1976)

Born Agatha Mary Clarissa Miller, Christie, according to the *Guinness Book of World Records*, is the best-selling novelist of all time.[6] Her novels have sold approximately four billion copies and have been translated into more than 100 languages. Her best-loved books are the Miss Marple and Hercule Poirot mysteries, though she also wrote short stories, and romances under a pseudonym. Her play *The Mousetrap* is the longest-running play of all time with more than 24,000 performances since 1952.

When in 1926 Christie's first husband asked for a divorce, she disappeared and, after a nationwide search, was found eleven days later. She never gave any account of her disappearance. Some speculated

---

[6] As Alba mentioned, Christie's estate places her third in the list of best-selling books of all time, after Shakespeare and the Bible.

that (like Charles Ashby) she wanted the police to think her spouse had killed her. She later married Max Mallowan, an archaeologist, and remained happy with him until her death.

Kitchen

George Eliot (1819–1880)

Mary Anne Evans took the male pseudonym to publish all of her seven novels, the most famous being *Middlemarch* (1871–72), *Silas Marner* (1861), *Daniel Deronda* (1876) and *The Mill on the Floss* (1860).

She lived with George Henry Lewes for more than twenty years, referring to him as her husband and calling herself Marian Evans Lewes, even though, because Lewes was already married, they never wed. At the end of her life, after Lewes died in 1878, she married John Cross, a man twenty years her junior. Queen Victoria was a devoted reader of Eliot's novels and admired *Adam Bede* (1859) so much that she commissioned an artist to paint scenes from the book. Virginia Woolf was also an admirer of Eliot's work, calling her 'the pride and paragon of all her sex' and writing that *Middlemarch* was a 'magnificent book which, with all its imperfections is one of the few English novels for grown-up people.'

Dora Carrington (1893–1932)

Dora de Houghton Carrington was a British painter who painted portraits of E. M. Forster,

Lytton Strachey and other well-known figures of her day. She was not a member of the Bloomsbury Group but closely connected with it through her relationship with Strachey, a homosexual writer with whom she lived, along with another man, for a time. Carrington was also bisexual. Virginia Woolf wrote of Carrington that she was 'an odd mixture of impulse and self-consciousness . . . so eager to please, conciliatory, restless and active . . . so red and solid, and at the same time inquisitive, that one can't help liking her.'

Vita Sackville-West (1892–1962)

The Honourable Victoria Mary Sackville-West, Lady Nicolson, but known as Vita. Her parents shared their surname, being cousins. Sackville-West was a writer and a poet, most famous for her novel *The Edwardians*. She and her husband Harold Nicolson had an open marriage and Sackville-West had affairs with several women, including Virginia Woolf.[7] Her greatest love affair was with Violet Trefusis (daughter of the mistress of King Edward VII), whom she met when she was twelve years old.

Mary Somerville (1780–1872)

Mary wasn't formally educated but spent her childhood reading books. When she discovered

---

[7] Virginia Woolf wrote the novel *Orlando* in tribute to Vita, whose son described it as 'the longest and most charming love-letter in literature.'

mathematics she studied so hard her parents worried for her health. Unlike her first husband, Mary's second husband encouraged her learning and love of math and science, so she began publishing papers to great acclaim. In 1835 Mary Somerville and Caroline Herschel became the first women to be elected honorary fellows of the Royal Astronomical Society. Mary was the first person to sign John Stuart Mill's petition for women's suffrage. Somerville College, Oxford, was founded in 1879 and named in her honour. It was the second college to be established solely for female students, after Lady Margaret Hall in 1878. Mary was friend and teacher to Ada Lovelace (daughter of Byron), a mathematician in her own right, whose discoveries assisted the invention of computers. Before she died Mary was awarded the Victoria Medal by the Royal Geographical Society.

Caroline Herschel (1750–1848)

Born in Hannover, Germany, Caroline lived to be ninety-seven. During her long and illustrious life she made her mark in the field of astronomy, discovering eight comets at a time when fewer than thirty were known. In 1828 the Royal Astronomical Society awarded her its gold medal, an honour it wouldn't bestow again on a woman until 1996. Together with Mary Somerville, Caroline was elected an honorary fellow of the Royal Astronomical Society in 1835, though the society wouldn't actually allow female members until 1916. Caroline worked with her brother (William Herschel, who discovered Uranus in 1781) throughout his life and continued alone after his death. Just before she died, the King of Prussia bestowed upon her the Gold Medal for Science in recognition of her great contributions to the subject.

Downstairs Hallway

Florence Nightingale (1820–1910)

Florence Nightingale was born into an upper-class British family that opposed her desire to take up nursing. But inspired, she said, by a call from God in 1837, Nightingale was determined to flout the social mores of her milieu and rejected marriage[8] to the politician and poet Baron Richard Monckton Milnes, to pursue nursing. Famous for her pioneering work during the Crimean War, she was called the Lady with the Lamp. Nightingale established her nursing school at St Thomas' Hospital in London in 1860. International Nurses Day is celebrated on the anniversary of her birth.

Joan Greenwood (1921–1987)

An actress famous for her sexy, husky voice, Greenwood's most notable roles were as

[8] Of course, there is no evidence to suggest that Nightingale was, as Peggy told Alba, 'a little too fond of sailors.' That was the author's little joke.

Gwendolen in *The Importance of Being Earnest* (1952), one of Oscar Wilde's most delightful plays, first performed on Valentine's Day, 1895, and as wicked temptress Sibella in the glorious black comedy *Kind Hearts and Coronets* (1949).

Emily Davies (1830–1921)

Emily Davies was a feminist and suffragist who, with Barbara Bodichon, founded Girton College, Cambridge, in 1869, the first university college in England to educate women. A lifelong friend of Elizabeth Garrett Anderson and Millicent Garrett Fawcett, Davies campaigned all her life for women's rights to a university education.

Davies also campaigned for the vote for women and, like Mary Somerville, supported John Stuart Mill's petition to Parliament in 1866. Refusing to surrender the cause despite widespread opposition, in 1906 she headed a delegation to Parliament. Great Britain gave all women over thirty the right to vote in 1918. In 1928 all women over eighteen could vote. The United States gave women the vote in 1920.

The Forbidden Room

Beatrix Potter (1866–1943)

Helen Beatrix Potter came from a wealthy family and was privately educated by a governess. She wrote, illustrated and self-published *The Tale of Peter Rabbit* in 1901. A year later it was published by

Frederick Warne & Co., and Potter fell in love with her editor, Norman Warne. Because Warne was a tradesman Potter's parents disapproved of the match but Warne died before they could be married.

Establishing herself as a novelist, Potter bought Hill Top Farm in the Lake District. Over the years she bought more farms in an effort to preserve the countryside and left nearly all her property to the National Trust, thus creating much of the Lake District National Park.

At forty-seven she married William Heelis and they lived happily together until her death. Potter published more than twenty beautifully illustrated books featuring animals, including *The Tailor of Gloucester* (1903), *The Tale of Mrs Tiggy-Winkle* (1905) and *The Tale of the Flopsy Bunnies* (1909).

Virginia Woolf (1882–1941)

Born Adeline Virginia Stephen, her most famous works include *Mrs Dalloway* (1925), *To the Lighthouse* (1927) and *Orlando* (1928). Her essay 'A Room of One's Own' (1929) extolled the importance of women's independence, famously noting that 'a woman must have money and a room of her own if she is to write fiction.' The daughter of Sir Leslie Stephen, Virginia was educated by her parents and raised among the Victorian literati, including Henry James. However, unlike her brothers, Virginia and her sister Vanessa were not permitted to attend Cambridge University.

The death of her mother in 1895 triggered the

first of Virginia's several nervous breakdowns, and when her father died in 1904 she was briefly institutionalised. She committed suicide at fifty-nine by filling her pockets with stones and drowning herself in the River Ouse. Although she had several love affairs, most notably with Vita Sackville-West, in her last letter to her husband, Leonard Woolf, she wrote, 'I owe all the happiness in my life to you . . . I don't think two people could have been happier than we have been.'

Other Women of Hope Street

Greer Garson (1904–1996)

Eileen Evelyn Greer Garson was Greer's namesake on account of Garson's glamour and her red hair. Greer Garson performed in a television production of *Twelfth Night* in 1937, possibly the first time a Shakespearean play was shown on television. Garson received her first Academy Award nomination for her role in *Goodbye, Mr Chips* but lost to Vivien Leigh for *Gone With the Wind.*

She was nominated by the Academy five times, winning for *Mrs Miniver* in 1942, and giving the ceremony's longest acceptance speech – five minutes and thirty seconds – after which the Academy set a time limit.

More Literature in the House

In addition to all the books written by the women of Hope Street, the works of E. M. Forster play a significant role in the story. Forster (1879–1970) wrote a great many beautiful novels, most famously: *A Room with a View*, *A Passage to India*, *Maurice* and *Howards End*. He was an honorary fellow of King's College, Cambridge (Alba's college) and lived there for much of his life. He was gay, though he didn't admit to it and his only novel about homosexual love, *Maurice*, was published after his death and he always lived a bachelor. Another significant work to feature in Hope Street is *Tractarians and the 'Condition of England'; The Social and Political Thought of the Oxford Movement* (2004) by Dr S. A. Skinner. This is the only book that Alba keeps reading after she's thrown out of King's College. This real-life Dr Skinner was the author's much admired and beloved professor of modern history while she took her degree in the subject at Balliol College, Oxford. While she borrowed his irresistible name for the character of Dr Alexandra Skinner in Hope Street, the only quality both Dr Skinners share is the brilliance and beauty of their lectures.

THE COLOURS OF ALBA'S WORLD

Bright Green – Truth and strength

Royal Blue – Sorrow

Sky Blue – Kindness and friendship

Silver – Hope

Bright Red – Lust

Violet – Joy

Magenta – Desire

Puce – Passion

Rich Orange – Insight

Bright Yellow – Inspiration, youth and the breath of trees

White – Belief

Dark Red – Obsession

Gold – The colour of ghost's words and the colour of contentment

Scarlet – Dedication

Deep Purple – Wisdom

Black – Complaints and arguments and lies

Dirt Grey – Disgust

Dark Brown – Boredom

Fire – Zoë's words when she talks about love

Radioactive Egg Yolks – Ridiculous optimism

.